# DareDreamers

**Kartik Sharma** is an alumnus of IIT Delhi (2009) and IIM Ahmedabad (2011). With experience in investment banking and strategy consulting, he now works as a public health professional. The idea of choices and where they take individuals fascinates him. He finds inspiration in optimism and hope in those who choose not to be cynical.

Website: www.kartiksharma.co.in
Facebook: www.facebook.com/Daredreamersnovel/
Twitter: https://twitter.com/sykartik
Instagram: https://www.instagram.com/sykartik/

**Ravi 'Nirmal' Sharma** is an alumnus of Delhi College of Engineering (1982). He works as a creative conceptualizer, after being a serial entrepreneur for more than two decades.

Website: www.ravinirmalsharma.com
Twitter: https://twitter.com/syravi

The father-son duo is Delhi based. They are passionate about telling stories that bring joy to the readers while being thought-provoking. Their first novel, *The Quest of the Sparrows,* received widespread critical acclaim. In this novel, they take up Kartik's investment banking experience and Ravi's entrepreneurial drive to create Rasiq, an amalgamation of Ravi and Kartik.

**Also by the authors**

*The Quest of the Sparrows*

# DareDreamers

## A Start-up of Superheroes

**Kartik Sharma** & **Ravi 'Nirmal' Sharma**

For Katie,

    I hope you enjoy this book
and share with Harper and
the baby boy some day! ☺

    Many congratulations!

Warmly,
Kartik Sharma

RUPA

Published by
Rupa Publications India Pvt. Ltd 2018
7/16, Ansari Road, Daryaganj
New Delhi 110002

*Sales centres:*
Allahabad Bengaluru Chennai
Hyderabad Jaipur Kathmandu
Kolkata Mumbai

ISBN: 978-93-5304-087-1

10 9 8 7 6 5 4 3 2 1

Printed in India by HT Media Ltd, Gr. Noida

*For Nana and Nani*
*through whose love, I understood love itself*

*Prologue:*
*The Hare, the Tortoise and the Twist*

'Dude, why are we running?' the hare asked the tortoise at the start line.

'Because you brag that you run fast,' the tortoise retorted. 'My community and friends in the jungle chose me to challenge you. I'm here to prove we are no less!'

'Running fast is one of my strengths and yes, I am proud of it. Just like a long life of three hundred-odd years is yours. I don't feel that you brag about it! It's the truth and I accept it,' the hare said. He sniffed curiously and looked at the tortoise with his big, ever curious eyes. 'Why should I run this meaningless race? It doesn't make any sense.'

'Then beat me,' the tortoise smiled. 'The old folks tell me that slow and steady can win any race. I am determined to beat you and I am sure I can do it if I work hard enough.'

'That's exactly the point. Why should you work hard and not smart? Surely you have abilities that I don't have, and I have qualities that you don't. Where does this race fit in?'

'Survival of the fittest, that's where it fits in,' declared the tortoise, puffing out his chest.

'But aren't both of us survivors? Otherwise, only one of us would have been standing here. Creation is about diversity. Besides, what happens after I win this race? Should I compete with a cheetah next and be the laughing stock that day? If at all I run, it will be for myself—my dreams and my desires. Not for you or this jungle.'

'So, what do you want to do right now? Got anything better to do than run this race?' the tortoise quipped.

'Yes,' the hare answered. 'I want to sit in the shade and relish a fresh, juicy carrot. Get lost chasing the clouds in the endless blue sky. Dig deep burrows to unearth new and exciting finds. Play with my friends, explore what lies beyond that horizon. I won't live the three hundred-odd years that you will. My life is too short to waste running mindless races.'

'That's funny,' the tortoise sneered. The gun went off and he started running. That is, he started moving as fast as he could. The hare stood in his spot and shook his head. Then, without warning, he ran, far from the madding crowd. He followed his heart.

The tortoise won the uncontested race.

∽

Two hundred and forty years later, time hung heavily over the tortoise's mundane routine of eat, swim, sleep, repeat. He was tired of hiding beneath the shadow of his shell, afraid of the vultures that dotted the skies. The hare had told him the sky was an endless blue with clouds of many shapes. Was the hare not afraid of the predators? He had dared to be a dreamer. Why was he so different?

Life is complicated, the tortoise thought as he entered the swamp for his last swim. He disappeared without a ripple. Despite living and being an intrinsic part of the jungle for almost three hundred years, not a soul missed him.

The race that had been the cornerstone of his life was made into a fable by his community.

The legend of the hare, however, remains to be told.

## Part One

.......................................

## The Start Line

# I

## Dream turns to nightmare

The alarm rang and Rasiq woke up without hitting snooze for the first time in his life. He checked the clock—6.00 a.m. Rasiq had spent a fitful night, anxious about the coming day.

*Today is the first day of the rest of my life*, he thought as he got out of bed and stretched. Still drowsy, he pulled out his toothbrush from his travel bag and headed to the bathroom. While brushing, he thought about his mother's advice: first impressions are hard to erase.

The shower he took was unusually long. He scrubbed himself obsessively, as if to cleanse himself of ages of dirt. His shave was closer than ever, thanks to the new Mach 5 razor that his father had gifted him. Next, he put on cologne, again something he had never done before. Deodorants he understood, but colognes were an enigma.

He applied a little gel on his thick, straight hair, which had been cropped short, to make sure it didn't stand up at odd angles during the course of the day.

He wore his new shirt—double-cuffed—with the cufflinks that his girlfriend, Ruchika, had gifted him. His new Van Heusen suit had cost him a bomb considering he had not earned a rupee in his life yet. Finally, he wore his new Aldo shoes. He didn't know anyone who wore shoes that cost 10,000 rupees, but then he didn't know any investment bankers either.

He checked himself in the full-length mirror and was satisfied with what he saw.

At five feet and eleven inches he just missed the 'tall' benchmark, but his lean frame made him seem taller. A dusky complexion, sharp features and a square jaw added up satisfactorily enough, but it was the intensity in his eyes that made him, according to Ruchika, hard to ignore in a roomful of people.

He stepped closer to the mirror to wear contact lenses for the first time in his life.

'You have beautiful eyelashes,' Ruchika had told him when they were shopping at the mall a week ago. 'You shouldn't hide them behind your thick spectacles.'

'Yuck,' Rasiq had reacted. 'Who puts a foreign object in their eyes? That's so ridiculous!'

'You know I love your lashes. Why can't you do even this much for me?' she had pleaded with her index finger dangerously close to her thumb, the gesture suggesting that the favour asked was insignificant. He ought to carry it out with grace.

Rasiq had acceded to her request. What choice did he really have in the matter?

His bloodshot eyes spilt a small waterfall by the time he overcame his struggle with the lenses. He took out his silk handkerchief and mopped his eyes and face.

He checked himself in the mirror a final time and nodded in appreciation of his new avatar.

*The first day of the rest of my life.*

He went down to the lobby of the hotel; the Trident, Nariman Point, was his transitory home courtesy of his employers. He had a week to find an apartment in Mumbai.

'Good morning, sir,' the woman at the reception greeted him.

*Sir?* Rasiq thought. *Wow. I'm only twenty-three! Was she the*

*one who checked me in yesterday? She wasn't that courteous when
I was in my worn jeans and T-shirt!*

His office was a short walk from the hotel. It was 7.30 a.m.
He had been asked to report at nine. Plenty of time.

He crossed the road and walked to the waterfront. *Pristine!*
Rasiq inhaled the fresh morning air—a small luxury that Mumbai
afforded its residents. He caught the rare sight of the morning
sun, its orange hue reflecting radiantly off the sea. The streets
were mostly empty. He had an hour to gaze at the shore which
was waking up, but he couldn't sit on the low boundary wall
along the promenade, as he had done the evening before with
Ruchika. He couldn't afford to ruin his new suit. He stood
looking at the horizon, dreaming about a future that was about
to unfold.

'Chai, boss?' came a shout from behind him.

'Cutting,' Rasiq responded like a Mumbaikar. He had heard
people order tea that way the day before, an oddity unique to
Mumbai.

The man served him super hot tea in a plastic cup of dubious
quality. *This can't be hygienic,* Rasiq thought. The thought
was immediately followed by the realization that he had never
bothered about the quality of cups before. His transformation
had begun from the moment he had worn his suit.

'First time in Mumbai?' the tea guy asked him in a thick
Mumbai accent.

'Yes,' Rasiq acceded. 'In fact, it's my first day here. I arrived
last evening. How did you know?'

'It's obvious, boss!'

Rasiq smiled. 'Can you give me a Classic Milds too?'

The man took one out from a pack and gave it to Rasiq.
He lit the cigarette for Rasiq.

Rasiq pulled deeply on his cigarette and asked, 'How much?'

'Arrey boss,' the man said, 'today is your first day in town. I can't take money from you.'

'No, no,' Rasiq insisted. He put his cup down on the promenade boundary wall and pulled out his wallet. 'I have to pay you.'

'No, boss,' the man said, as he started walking away. 'Pay me tomorrow onwards. I cannot forget my first day in Mumbai. I was penniless and managed some food that day thanks to a kind man. I am just repaying the debt I owe to the city.'

The man rushed to serve other people.

'At least tell me your name,' Rasiq shouted after him. The man turned around, grinning. He walked back to Rasiq and extended his hand, 'I am Gopi.'

Rasiq felt slightly odd at the formality of shaking the man's hand, but he didn't want to be rude. 'Rasiq,' he said. 'Thank you for the chai and the cigarette.'

The man grinned again, all thirty-two teeth on display, and walked away.

Rasiq turned to face the sea. He picked up his tea and smoked his cigarette in silence, waiting for the rest of his life to begin.

∞

'You have been cornered,' Samar, a second-year associate, four years senior to Rasiq and his assigned mentor, declared with a smirk on his face.

'What?' Rasiq asked. He was confused.

'The corner office is calling you,' Samar replied.

'What?' Rasiq was even more bewildered.

'*Abey dhakkan*,' the associate snapped, 'the head of the investment banking division has summoned you to his office. It's the one on the corner of the floor.'

Rasiq felt like an idiot but wondered why. Was he supposed to have come prepared with the lingo these guys used?

As he reached the corner office, he saw an older man talking animatedly on the phone. His short hair was peppered with grey. Rasiq waited outside patiently, observing the man. He was dressed in a pinstriped suit that looked much more expensive than his own.

After waiting for about fifteen minutes in complete silence, Rasiq started sweating in anticipation. *Moving, in any direction whatsoever, keeps the mind occupied*, Rasiq thought. *It is only in moments of silent contemplation that the mind grows agitated.*

The man slapped down the receiver of the landline phone. His action communicated anger, but his face was expressionless. *Classic poker face. Or banker's face? Wait! Is that why bankers are good at poker? All of them as lively as walls.*

When the man paid no heed to him waiting at the door, Rasiq knocked. The man glanced up before returning his gaze to his computer screen. He gestured with one finger for Rasiq to enter.

'Yes?' he enquired without looking up. Rasiq could sense that his uneasiness gave the man a strange sense of control.

'You called me, sir?' Rasiq managed with a quiver in his voice. The man and his office intimidated him. Rasiq noticed the office had two glass walls overlooking Marine Drive and the Arabian Sea. The view was breathtaking, especially from the twenty-first floor.

Finally, the man looked up. 'Who are you?'

'Rasiq, sir,' he replied. 'First-year analyst,' he added, when the man made a strange face on hearing his name. 'I joined today.'

'Oh,' he said. 'I'm Raghav. Listen, boss, I want to tell you a couple of things before you start here.'

*Boss? Who talks like that?* Rasiq thought. *I understand Gopi, but this guy?*

'Do you think this is your dream job?' Raghav asked, not bothering to ask Rasiq to sit.

Rasiq nodded, uncertainly. His wobbly voice stumbled on the way and never made it out of his throat.

'Wrong,' the man continued, clearly satisfied with the effect he had on Rasiq, 'it is your nightmare.'

Rasiq wondered if he was expected to agree.

'We don't have room for dreamers and we are going to ensure we nip the problem in the bud. You are going to slog the whole of next year. Not much time to sleep, so there won't be any dreams.'

Rasiq stared at the man, not knowing how to react. He swallowed hard and was afraid that it was audible. He imagined Raghav laughing like a possessed monster from a Tim Burton movie. *I would have wet my pants if he had done that*, Rasiq thought. Ironically, the humorous thought calmed him.

'Tell your family and girlfriend, if you have one, not to visit you here in Mumbai: it would be a waste of a trip. Let's be clear about that, boss.'

Rasiq was too intimidated to say anything. The man smiled out of the corner of his mouth and extended his hand, 'Welcome to investment banking!'

Rasiq managed to thank him before leaving his office.

∽

'That was quite something,' Rasiq said when he reached Samar's desk.

'Not interested. Who are you?' Samar dismissed his observation with a question and rose from his chair. He was a good half-foot shorter than Rasiq and wore his thin, wavy hair long, probably to hide the balding that had started at his temples. His gold cufflinks competed for attention with the four gem-laden rings on his fingers. The shiny, pointed leather shoes were from Armani, much more expensive than Rasiq's, of course. He started walking without saying anything to Rasiq.

Confused by the question, Rasiq resigned himself to following him. 'Rasiq,' he answered feebly as they walked, aware that it wasn't the answer expected.

'That's your name,' Samar said dismissively, louder than was necessary considering how close Rasiq was to him. 'Who are you?' he asked again.

Rasiq could feel everyone in the office looking at them as they walked by the array of cubicles. 'First-year analyst?' Rasiq enquired.

'Wrong again. That's the designation on your card,' Samar corrected him, 'not your identity. Who are you?'

Rasiq was annoyed with the unnecessary third-degree. 'Do you have the answer?' he finally gathered an iota of courage to ask. 'Why don't you tell me?'

'You are a whore!' Samar burst out laughing, pleased with his joke.

Rasiq stood aghast. He opened his mouth to say something, but nothing emerged. He could hear laughter from the audience of the theatre of the most embarrassing moment of his life.

'That's right!' Samar continued relentlessly. 'You are everybody's bitch.'

*I'm sorry, I think you have me confused with your wife*, Rasiq thought. That's what he should have said. 'What do you mean?' he asked politely instead, his ears burning with embarrassment.

'One team picks up an analyst from the second year onwards. But in the first year, you have to work with all the directors so they can decide whether they want you on their team. Which means anyone can and will ask you to work on anything they want. Ergo, you are everyone's bitch.'

Colour drained from Rasiq's face. He had no idea how to respond to such talk.

'You thought you were fortunate to be the only guy on campus to get an offer from us?'

'Yes,' Rasiq replied sincerely, despite the situation. Jobs were difficult to get during the recession, but he had received his placement an hour into Day Z: a bastardization of Day Zero, which was actually the first day of the campus placement season.

'Well, you're probably the unluckiest guy in the world,' he declared. 'The firsties have to do the grunt work on all the deals. We typically hire four or five. This year, you are the only one, which means your life is going to be four or five times harder than that of any other first-year analyst. And boy, what a shitty life they have!'

Rasiq could hear muffled laughter from the other associates and vice presidents in the office.

'Here's your only real friend,' Samar pointed to the coffee machine. 'You'll need litres of it, so feel free to walk in anytime. We have an unlimited supply to keep you alive, alert and awake. I'll show you your desk now.'

*What have I gotten myself into?* Rasiq thought, feeling every bit like a lamb destined for the slaughterhouse.

He followed Samar quietly, his ears still burning and his face an embarrassing crimson. This level of humiliation was a first for him. And to make matters worse, he had never felt so handicapped in giving a fitting response.

'This is it,' Samar said, when they reached a cubicle furnished with an extended desk and four chairs. A single desktop rested on it. 'Normally, four first-year analysts sit here for a year before earning a proper cubicle in the team they join.'

'I guess I am lucky then,' Rasiq tried to smile, but couldn't pull it off. It had sounded funny in his head but came out as desperate and meek.

Samar ignored his reaction. 'You can set up your office account and email. Familiarize yourself with the system. I'll send you the presentation for the deal I'm working on in a couple of hours and we can discuss the sections you need to work on.'

'Umm,' Rasiq said. 'I have an onboarding session starting in an hour, which will be for the rest of the day.'

'Rest of the day?' Samar asked.

'Yes,' Rasiq said taking out the agenda for the session and handing it to Samar.

'It's till six,' Samar looked at him. 'That's not even half a workday. We'll start at six then.'

# 2

# *A first day that refuses to end*

$T$he mind-numbing presentations on the organizational structure of the bank and the role of every division drained Rasiq. He had never thought that expressions like 'need to know basis only' and 'client names codified for confidentiality' could sound so boring coming from a Human Resources guy in a conference room, instead of from Liam Neeson in an action movie. He called Ruchika during his forty-five-minute lunch break, but there was no response. He was eager to know about her first day on the job. He hoped it was going much better than his.

Post lunch, the HR representative droned on about organizational strategy, ethics, values and code of conduct in a soporific, singsong monotone. Rasiq lost interest after the representative said: 'Respecting our colleagues is integral to our success.'

He returned to the twenty-first floor at 6.15 p.m.

'Come,' Samar caught him when he stepped into the investment banking bay. 'Grab a cup of coffee and come to the meeting room. We have a truckload of work.'

They sat in a small meeting room, discussing the context of the presentation. Rasiq had to work on an extensive section on benchmarking and valuation for a sell-side pitch to a prospective client.

'Basically, I've done everything for you. Now you have to just create the presentation.'

'Sure,' Rasiq said, ignoring the fallacy in the statement. The research required to prepare the presentation would be humongous. 'When do you need this?'

'Tomorrow morning, daybreak,' Samar spelled out the deadline and stood up. 'Come, I'll log in to Bloomberg on your terminal with my password. You'll get yours tomorrow.'

Rasiq's eyes widened in surprise. Maybe it was the coffee that triggered it, but he felt a rush of anxiety.

'Samar, I don't know anything about this sector,' he protested. 'I don't think I'll be able to even finish the reading by tonight. I am sure there must be a million analyst reports that I will have to go through before I can even begin to put my thoughts on the slides. We need a compelling story if we are to convince anyone to partially divest their business!'

'Sure,' Samar said, scratching his chin. 'I'm sorry,' he said after a long pause. 'I guess I forgot that you will be working on this alone. It would have been manageable had there been four of you, isn't it?' He pointed at the empty seats next to Rasiq's.

Rasiq breathed easy, 'Exactly!'

'Did you check your salary in your contract?'

'Yes,' Rasiq failed to understand the intent behind the question.

'And of course, we know this year's average on-campus salary.'

Rasiq was beginning to comprehend where this was going.

'Four times,' Samar's fingers spelled out the number close to his face. 'That's what you get paid. Never forget that. We didn't hire four people but one to do the job of four.'

Rasiq's head hung low.

'Stop complaining or stop surviving,' Samar said as he left for his desk.

Rasiq took off his jacket and pulled out his cufflinks. He threw them in his jacket pocket and rolled up his sleeves as he started his reading.

*Great start, Rasiq.*

∾

Samar walked to Rasiq's desk, his brown leather bag slung across his chest, at 8.30 p.m. He carried an expensive-looking umbrella, his shield against the unpredictable rains in Mumbai. 'I am heading home now,' he said. 'Call me if you need anything. And you can order dinner for up to 1,500 rupees and get it reimbursed.'

'Alright,' Rasiq said with a single wave of his hand. 'See you tomorrow.'

'9.30 a.m.,' Samar repeated and left without waiting for a response.

Rasiq picked up his phone. There were three missed calls from Ruchika. He waited for Samar to step into the lift, then went into the lobby and pressed the button to call the lift. Once downstairs, he walked to Marine Drive and stood on the promenade, again. He dialled Ruchika. She answered after a single ring this time.

'I have been trying to reach you for so long now,' she complained.

'I was in a meeting—' Rasiq said. His brain did a somersault. *What a lame thing to say. So clichéd.*

'Oh,' Ruchika said, 'my busy man! Are you at the hotel now? How about dinner together?'

'I can't,' Rasiq said. He was sitting on the boundary wall of the promenade, and no longer cared about his expensive suit getting spoilt. 'I have an unholy pile of work. Don't think I'll be able to sleep at all.'

'What?' Ruchika uttered. 'You're kidding me!'

'I wish I were,' Rasiq said. He buried his forehead in his palm.

'Are you alright? Everyone told us about the crazy work,' Ruchika said, 'but this is madness! On the first day!'

'I swear to God,' Rasiq felt his emotions boil within, 'if I had met this asshole of an associate outside work, I would have punched him in the face till his teeth fell out.'

'He's your boss? What's his name?'

'Samar,' Rasiq said. 'He's my mentor. And everyone in the company is my boss, Ruchika. I am supposed to work on anything anyone asks me to.'

'Sounds horrible,' Ruchika said. 'This guy sounds more like a tormentor rather than a mentor! Hopefully the others will be better.'

'Always the one looking for the silver lining,' Rasiq smiled, for the first time that day. 'How did it go for you?'

'Oh! I had the best day!' Ruchika gushed. Her boss had taken her and the other new recruits out for an extended lunch. This had been followed by their onboarding session, which had lasted only a couple of hours. Then they had met a few senior colleagues who had briefed them about the work culture at the office and the functioning of their team. At 5.00 p.m. they had gone out for an icebreaking session over drinks.

'But I had only one glass of wine,' Ruchika said, 'because I thought I would come and meet you.'

Rasiq listened silently, too numb to feel anything. Was he upset because she was insensitive to his misery or was he envious of her happiness? Maybe it was neither, maybe he was just missing her.

'Your job sounds way more fun than mine,' he said. 'I wish I could work there.'

'You can join us at the speed of light, Rasiq,' Ruchika said. 'You know you'll be a catch for them. But your job pays way more than mine, which makes it a fair trade-off. Wait till you receive your first salary.'

Rasiq hung up after exchanging declarations of love. He put his phone down and buried his face in both his palms.

'Chai, boss?' Gopi had appeared again, grinning.

Rasiq half smiled. 'You are working late too?'

Gopi laughed while pouring him a cup and took out a Classic Milds cigarette for him.

'Thanks,' Rasiq said. Gopi had put out the matchstick. Rasiq took a drag and reached for his wallet.

'I told you I can't take payment from you today,' Gopi reminded him. 'Pay me tomorrow.'

Rasiq smiled at the man's kindness and slowly walked back to his office.

A first day that refused to end.

## 3

## *Endless work*

'Started early?' Shilpa said, when she arrived at 8.30 a.m. She was the head of the administrative staff.

Rasiq nearly jumped out of his seat, startled. He had worked through the quiet of the night and the human voice seemed alien to his caffeine and adrenaline-enhanced senses.

'No,' he said, gathering himself. His voice was grainy from lack of use.

'Oh! Poor kid,' Shilpa empathized. She returned with a small kit and handed it to Rasiq. 'Take this and freshen up.'

Rasiq took the kit and looked inside: a toothbrush, paste, razor and a small shaving cream.

'Thank you!' Rasiq said. He was touched by her kindness. 'You are a lifesaver, Shilpa!'

In the washroom, he looked at his creased shirt and dishevelled hair and tried to control the damage. However hard he tried, he couldn't manage the fresh look he was hoping for. He went down at close to 8.45 a.m. and saw Gopi selling his tea and cigarettes on the promenade. He smiled widely as he saw Rasiq approaching him.

'You look different,' Gopi remarked.

'A lot has happened since yesterday,' Rasiq sighed.

'I knew this city changed people, but this is quite a transformation. No coat, no smile, no enthusiasm!' He poured him a cup of tea and handed him a cigarette. 'And I think you have something in your eye.'

Rasiq rubbed his eyes, 'What is it?'

'A dying dream,' Gopi replied, philosophically.

Rasiq laughed and took out his wallet. Gopi smiled and took the money, 'Doesn't seem as if it's your second day, though.'

'No,' Rasiq said. 'A first day that refuses to end.'

'But I will define a new day with the sunrise,' Gopi smiled. 'Or you might single-handedly bankrupt me!'

At 9.15 a.m. Rasiq hurried to The Coffee Bean & Tea Leaf and bought five cups of coffee before returning to the office.

People started coming in from 9.30 onwards. 'I have coffee here,' Rasiq offered to the associates.

A few of them smiled, walked to his desk and exchanged greetings. They took their coffee and walked back to their desks.

*No time for small talk*, Rasiq thought.

'Thanks for the coffee,' Samar said. 'But I hope it's not a bribe to get out of a yelling.'

'Yelling?' Rasiq asked, naively.

'Have you completed the work?'

'Oh,' Rasiq said. 'I sent it to you two minutes ago.'

Samar smiled, nodding. 'I'll call you to discuss my comments.'

'Sure.'

In the two hours that Samar took to review Rasiq's work, he got several new work requests. Rasiq didn't know whether it was a good or bad sign that no one noticed he was wearing the same clothes as the day before and hadn't slept a wink.

He inhaled deeply and started working on the new requests.

∽

'This is good work for your first day,' Samar said. He placed a set of printouts on Rasiq's desk. 'I have marked the minor changes you have to make. It shouldn't take you too long, so let's review this at lunch.'

'Sonali has given me some work,' Rasiq informed him. 'Shouldn't I complete that first?'

'No,' Samar insisted. 'This takes priority.' With that, he walked back to his desk.

Rasiq stood and went to Sonali. 'Would it be okay if I complete your work after lunch?'

'Why?' she asked, irritated.

'I received comments from Samar on the Konkan deck and he wants me to prioritize that,' he said.

'Why is my work not done yet?' she asked, looking at her watch. 'It's 11.30 and it shouldn't have taken two hours!'

'I'm sorry. It'll take me another thirty minutes to complete it, tops!' Rasiq said. 'I had to do some research and there were a few more things…'

'What did they teach you at IIM Ahmedabad?' Sonali shouted. Her nostrils flared in anger. 'This is basic finance! I didn't know they were breeding morons on that campus, or I would have fought harder to recruit from IIM Calcutta!'

Rasiq felt a growing anger in his chest. Although not the biggest fan of his institute, he still felt a need to respond to the scathing, personal attack on what was a big part of his past. Today was not the best day though, and maybe there never would be a good day for that.

'Samar,' she shouted across the floor. 'Give him thirty minutes before he starts on your deck. He hasn't completed the small task I gave him this morning.'

'Cool,' Samar acceded.

'Thanks,' Rasiq blurted. He didn't know why he was thanking them. He walked back to his desk, wondering what had happened.

He worked quickly on Sonali's request, sent that out on time and started working on the deck for Samar.

At 1.30 p.m., Samar came to Rasiq's desk with his tiffin.

Rasiq smiled, clearing some papers from his desk to make room for the lunch box, thinking they would be eating together.

'Will you finish the deck in the next thirty minutes?' Samar asked, ignoring Rasiq's actions.

'Yeah, sure,' Rasiq said. He hoped the grumbling in his stomach wasn't audible. Samar nodded as he turned to leave and join the other associates for lunch.

He left the office close to 2.00 a.m. and crashed on his bed as soon as he entered his hotel room. He woke up at 7.30 a.m., without an alarm.

Repeat.

∽

His circumstances remained unchanged for the rest of the week. On Friday morning, before he left the hotel, the staff reminded him that his check-out time was noon the next day.

*Shit!* His complimentary stay was over and he couldn't afford to continue staying at the Trident since he didn't have any money. He had borrowed close to a lakh from his dad, but he would need that to pay the deposit and brokerage for the apartment he would be renting.

He called Ruchika.

'Hey,' she said in her most charming voice, brightening the day for Rasiq. 'Such an early call! Are you missing me already?'

'Yes,' Rasiq said. He was not lying. 'It's been only four days, but it seems like a month.'

'You've probably done a month's worth of work already,' Ruchika remarked.

'Ruchi, I need your help in looking for an apartment today.'

'What? You haven't looked?'

'You know I haven't had any time for that,' he said. 'Did you look for yours?'

'Yes. I'm moving in with Shweta, my friend from undergrad. Her roommate is planning to leave at the end of the month and we'll manage until then.'

'Wow! You are lucky! But can you please help me out?'

'Rasiq, I was planning to go clubbing tonight. It's Friday, not a dry day.'

Rasiq's shoulders slumped. 'Cool,' he said. He wondered when he had picked up that habit from Samar. 'I'll think of something.'

'Sorr...'

Rasiq cut the call. He was too busy to talk more.

∞

Back at the office, Rasiq sent out the piece of work he had completed. He knew he had about fifteen minutes to himself before the next assignment came his way. He had timed that over the past week. He took out his notebook and turned to the last page.

Balance Sleep, he wrote at the top of the page, almost in a trance.

3 April, Sunday: Hardly

4 April, Monday: 0

5 April, Tuesday: 5 hours

6 April, Wednesday: 2 hours

7 April, Thursday: 3 hours

Ten hours over five nights. He was sure his brain cells had started dying by the millions. He should not be able to even sit right now. He should crash. He was defying all logic.

*Yes*, Rasiq thought. *I am defying all logic. Logic applies to mere mortals. Not me. Because I am not an ordinary person. I am superhuman.*

∽

'Hey,' Ruchika called Rasiq at nine that night. 'We are leaving for the club now.'

'Did you get late at work?'

'No. I went to the parlour at six and it took a while to get ready.'

'Oh!' Rasiq said. 'Send me a pic, please?'

'You got it, naughty boy! Why don't you join us after you finish work?'

'Ha ha. That's funny! Even if that turns out to be a possibility, I would prefer to crash, like a logical person.'

*But I am superhuman, am I not?*

'Maybe I'll pop in for a bit,' he changed his mind. 'Where will you guys be?'

'Hawaiian Shack in Bandra.'

Another Mumbai altogether. It would take him an hour to reach there in a cab. Thirty minutes after midnight though.

'Cool,' he murmured. He couldn't ask her to come to Colaba because he might not even be able to meet her.

∽

At 1.30 a.m., as he was leaving his office, Rasiq got a call from Ruchika.

'What's up?' she sounded excited.

Rasiq pulled the phone away from his ear. He could hear the loud music that Ruchika was shouting over.

'I finished just now,' Rasiq said. His voice betrayed his tiredness.

'Come na,' she said. She was slurring a little. 'We're still here and not planning to go anywhere till they throw us out!'

'What time will that happen?'

'What?'

Rasiq rolled his eyes. 'When does the club close?'

'Nevaaa!' she shouted.

Rasiq laughed. 'I'll be there in thirty minutes.' He was missing her like crazy.

# 4

## Get the drift of her drift

$R$asiq reached the club at around 2.00 a.m. He saw Ruchika dancing with her friends. Spellbinding. He took a minute to absorb her presence. The short, dark blue dress accentuated her figure. It ran halfway down her thighs and her beautiful, shapely legs moved with grace despite her drunken state. Her parlour-fashioned hair bounced over her shoulders as she danced. *Breathtaking!*

He walked up to her and smiled, not even trying to say anything over the deafening music. Ruchika let out a whoop of joy, and hugged him tightly. Rasiq hugged her back and realized just how much he had missed her. He found her lips and they kissed briefly. She broke free from him, embarrassed, and gestured for him to dance with her.

A group of people surrounded them, none of whom Rasiq recognized from IIM. Her work colleagues, presumably. Rasiq ordered a large rum and Coke and joined the gang. They danced to the beats of the DJ, losing all sense of gravity and time until the club staff pushed them out at 4.00 a.m.

Rasiq hadn't had too much to drink but his sleep deprivation worsened the impact of the little alcohol in his bloodstream.

A guy, who Rasiq didn't know, put his arm around Ruchika's waist as they stepped outside. Ruchika didn't object and Rasiq couldn't understand how to react. Or whether to react at all.

*Should I be angry and tell the guy off? Or is this the new normal of our working lives that I am expected to adjust to?*

'Hi,' he said to the group. 'I am Rasiq.'

'Oh,' a short girl in the group exclaimed. 'Finally, I get to meet you!' She walked toward Rasiq with quick little steps in her high heels and gave him a sideward hug. Rasiq reciprocated. 'Ruchi has told me so much about you, Mr Big Shot Banker!'

'What?' Rasiq said.

'You work in investment banking, no?'

'Yup,' he said. He was observing Ruchika with the guy, who was still holding her at the waist, both lost in deep conversation. He shrugged. 'How about you? Do you work with Ruchika?' he asked.

'Oh no!' she said. 'I work with Ogilvy in digital marketing.'

'And how do you know Ruchi?'

'We're childhood friends. Hasn't she told you about me?'

Rasiq raised his eyebrows and shrugged. Even if she had, it would have been difficult for Rasiq to recall.

'I'm Priyanka,' she said, extending her hand. 'I am going to kill Ruchi for not telling you about me!'

'I am sure she must have told me,' Rasiq shook her hand. The formality of the gesture seemed weird after the hug. 'I've barely slept in a week and I have lost control over critical parts of my brain.'

Priyanka laughed, but Rasiq was reminded of how tired he was. The week's fatigue hit him at that moment and he longed to snuggle under the sheets in his hotel room.

'You and I should catch up sometime,' Priyanka offered. She did not let go of his hand. 'Especially if Ruchi hasn't told you anything about me, we have a lot of ground to cover!'

'Sure,' Rasiq said, more as instinctive small talk than anything else, slipping his hand out of her grip.

'Cool. I'll call you to schedule something?'

'Yeah,' he said. His gaze searched for Ruchika who was lost among the revellers. 'You can get my number from Ruchi.' He yawned. 'I'm sorry, but I need to leave. I'm exhausted and should probably catch up on my sleep.'

'Hey,' the guy with Ruchika called out. He seemed to have walked up to Rasiq from nowhere and startled him. Ruchika was following closely behind him. 'I am Abhishek.'

'Rasiq,' he responded awkwardly, shaking his hand.

'So,' Abhishek started with a slur, 'do they have you bring coffee for them every day already?'

Rasiq looked at him with bloodshot eyes. 'I'm sorry?' he said. He had taken a step towards Abhishek, the anger rising in him, ready to erupt.

'No, no,' Abhishek stepped back. 'I have friends in investment banking who do that, that's all.'

'So?' Rasiq asked. His eyes darted towards Ruchika who was still standing behind Abhishek and smiling self-consciously.

'So, it seems like we have finally arrived at the price of a man's self-respect!' Abhishek laughed.

Rasiq realized that none of the associates had asked him to bring coffee for them. It was something he did of his own volition. *Why?* He wondered. *It took me all of a day to become subservient in a hostile environment to appease my bosses.*

Rasiq looked at Ruchika who was laughing with Abhishek.

He shook his head and left. He was disgusted, more with himself than with them.

# 5

## An apartment that meant ripping apart

*T*he next morning, the doorbell rang incessantly. When Rasiq could no longer ignore it, he rose sluggishly.

'Sir, it's after noon,' said the hotel employee. 'You need to check out now.'

'Oh shit!' Rasiq remembered the deadline. 'Can you at least give me an hour to get ready and pack?'

'No sir, we have guests coming in at two and we need to prepare the room before that.'

'But...' Rasiq said. The man shut his eyes in frustration and Rasiq dropped the negotiation. 'I'll be down in five.' He shut the door on the man's face and began dressing quickly, throwing his stuff in his bag. In less than ten minutes he had checked out.

Saturday. Nowhere to go. He called Ruchika but she didn't pick up.

He looked online for brokers in Colaba and started calling them. After a few unanswered calls, someone finally answered. He went to see a property with him and took the apartment. He immediately paid for the brokerage and deposit by cheque.

Rasiq dumped his bags, locked his apartment and rushed back to office. 3.00 p.m. He had a crazy backlog of work to finish if he were to avoid a night at the office.

Ruchika called him around 4.00 p.m.

'Hey baby,' she said. Her voice was raspy, the first sound of someone who just woke up.

'Still sleeping?' he asked.

'Yeah. I have a bad hangover.'

'Too many Long Islands?'

'Yeah, and some shots too...'

'Jesus!' Rasiq said. 'Be happy you're alive.'

'Ha ha!' she laughed. 'I saw your missed call. Is everything alright?'

'Yes. Now it is. The hotel practically threw me out, but I managed to find an apartment and moved in.'

'Oh. So quick? Where is it?'

'Right here, in Colaba.'

'Wow!' Ruchika exclaimed. 'That's so cool! You are a hotshot now, aren't you! Most of us can't afford to live there!'

'I can't afford to live elsewhere if I am to catch even a moment of sleep!'

'True, that. I'll come over in a couple of hours to look at it. Send me the address.'

'I'm at work, Ruchi. Come around by nine? We can have dinner together!'

'Oh, poor baby. Working even on weekends! Okay, I'll go back to sleep then.'

'Drink plenty of water!'

∞

Ruchika came over to his office around half past nine and they left together for his new apartment.

'What the fuck is this?' was her first reaction once they stepped inside.

Rasiq closed the door hurriedly. He did not want his new neighbours to hear profanity from a girl in his apartment.

'What?' he asked, when they were out of earshot.

'No windows! And just this one room?'

'So? It's Colaba, baby!' Rasiq tried, with an accent.

'How much is the rent?'

'Forty thousand a month.'

'What? Seriously? For this hole? You'll die without any ventilation!'

'There's a bed, a fridge and an AC,' Rasiq said. 'I don't need anything else. I'll be sleeping rarely and this is good enough for that.'

'You are moving out of this shithole, now!' She began to pack whatever little of his stuff was out of his bags.

'I already paid for the deposit and brokerage by cheque. That was the lakh that I borrowed from my parents, Ruchi. I have nothing else.'

'Cancel the payment on the cheque!' Ruchika was yelling now. 'Can't you see? You CANNOT stay here!'

'Why? What's the harm? And where will I go now? Can I stay with you for a few days till I find a better place?'

'No,' she said. 'I wish, but we have no room with the three of us there. Plus, the other girls might feel weird. Go back to the hotel. You can afford it for a few days.'

'I have no money and I can't afford to stay in a hotel. I have a loan to pay back, Ruchi.'

'Fuck you,' she shouted. 'I'm leaving. You do whatever you want with your life, okay?' She stormed out of the apartment. Rasiq hit the bed, breathing heavily. He ordered Chinese food for one.

# 6

## Lot of pain, lot of gain

*T*owards the end of his first month, Rasiq received an SMS while he was still at work. His first salary credit! A smile escaped his lips when he saw the amount. He knew how much he was making, but the physical evidence of the money in his account was something to savour.

Thirty days of suffering. Less than five hours of sleep a day. Inhuman and insane working hours. Abuse. It all started seeming a little bearable. He rose from his seat, instinctively, unable to control his excitement.

'You look happy, Rasiq. No analyst has that right. What happened?' Sonali asked, trying to be funny in her typical doomsayer's way.

'I got paid,' Rasiq said. He wouldn't let even a dementor take his joy away right now.

'Oh!' She rolled her eyes. 'That makes sense. I still remember when I got my first salary. Nothing had ever made me as happy as that moment.'

*Is that true for me too?* Rasiq sat back at his desk, reflecting. *No, he remembered, I know when I was the happiest. At IIT, waiting for the most important result of my life.*

His thoughts travelled back to the past to relish that beautiful moment, yet again.

'Shhhittt!' the eighteen-year-old Rasiq cursed when he finally woke up at 8.15 a.m. in his hotel room at IIT Delhi. He knew he should've stayed up and not slept at all after watching movies till 6.30 a.m.

He jumped out of bed, toothbrush in hand.

8.20 a.m. He sprinted down the stairs, two at a time. He ran past the nearly empty mess, the smell of sambhar and dosa flooding his nostrils. His stomach grumbled. *Relax dude*, he rubbed his belly. *No time to indulge in luxuries when dealing with an existential crisis.*

An unnerving, ten-minute run to the institute building ensued. The malevolent sun stretched that one-kilometre dash to a sweaty marathon. A few other late starters joined the rush. A large majority, however, were still sleeping and would miss their classes. The few sincere ants were already in their classes.

8.32 a.m. Rasiq skidded to a stop outside the lecture theatre. The teaching assistant was just about to shut the door, outlawing the latecomers. She saw him. Like a chameleon, he acquired a look that was a healthy mix of shame and fear. She gestured for him to step into the class and then locked the door behind him. *Mission accomplished!*

The professor glared as Rasiq and the teaching assistant took their seats but fortunately did not throw him out of the class. Rasiq fell into his seat and crouched to avoid the professor's attention.

*Phew, that was close!* But it wasn't all luck. He had worked hard after barely managing to pass in the first semester. Over the next two semesters, his grades had defied the black holes of sadistic professors and he had topped the batch. He had earned that little bit of leniency extended to him today.

The lack of sleep made him drowsy. Despite the muscles they had built by remaining open most nights, his eyelids seemed to be failing. He buried his head in his hands and drifted off...

'The list is out!' A shout disturbed Rasiq's classroom siesta.

9.30 a.m. The undergraduate section must have put up the day's important announcements on the notice board. Among them was the one that he had been keenly waiting for. Rasiq's heart beat uncontrollably. The professor droned about mass transfer phenomenon. When he finally let the class go, Rasiq jumped to his feet. He started running but was arrested by a worry. What if he hadn't made it? There were just eight seats for his batch of six hundred students. He calmed himself—it didn't matter if he got there early or late. The list was already out.

A sea of students had engulfed the notice board by the time he got there. Most of them had come with friends to see the final list. An enviable few had come with their romantic interests. If India had an overall poor sex ratio, his college gave the impression that the fairer sex was on the verge of extinction.

He inched towards the notice board cautiously.

There! His name was on the short list. He was one of eight students selected from his entire batch to represent his college in the prestigious and much sought-after semester-long exchange programme to France!

'I am going to France,' he whispered, to no one in particular. 'YES!' He leapt high and punched the air.

∾

'What puttar!' Rasiq's father had found it hard to believe when Rasiq called him to share the news. 'Are you sure?'

'Ye...' Rasiq was unable to complete the mono syllable word.

'Are you one hundred per cent sure?'

'Yes, pops! I am sure!'

'Great! I am going to tell your mother. She is going to be on cloud number one hundred.'

'It's cloud nine, pops!'

'Oye, why would she be hanging on such a low cloud? She'll be so happy she will be on hundred, na!'

'Dad,' Rasiq said. 'It doesn't work like that.'

'Oye you don't tell your father how things work. I am a mechanical engineer. I make the bloody things work.'

'Sure,' Rasiq gave up.

'Well done, son,' Rasiq's dad said, turning serious. 'You did well. I am proud of you. Everything that you have done so far has added up to this moment. Be happy about the choices and decisions you have made.'

'I am happy, pops!'

'Don't take this lightly, puttar. If even a leaf had fallen another way or a drop of rain that fell on you had not, you wouldn't be where you are.'

'That's a little extreme.' Rasiq laughed.

'The present is a function of each moment, each incident in your life until now. Change anything, even an iota, and you will move into an alternate, parallel universe different from this reality.'

Rasiq was quiet, assimilating what his father was telling him.

'It's profound, puttar. You should now say that I am awesome!'

'I am awesome,' Rasiq joked. 'I gotta go now, pops. I'll see you over the weekend.'

༺༻

Rasiq snapped out of his reverie, but his smile lingered as he logged in to his net banking portal and transferred most of his salary to his loan account, keeping only the bare minimum he needed for his monthly expenses. He was living in post-graduation poverty. Money did not make him happy; not yet, at least.

## 7

### *Livid with live-in*

$S_{ix}$ months went by and nothing much changed. Rasiq sometimes worried about his relationship with Ruchika, but he felt that it was her responsibility to ensure its survival. He had no time for it even on the weekends. He stole time when he could, to go out with her, but she was always accompanied by her friends. It annoyed Rasiq that she did not even try to ensure that the little time they had together was at least quality time. They were both letting the fire in their relationship die slowly—he simply didn't have the bandwidth to fix things and she didn't seem to want to.

∽

When Rasiq got his salary on a Friday, he logged in again to his net banking account to transfer the payment towards his student loan. He was overjoyed to see that there was just over a lakh of it left. He assassinated his debt with a click of his mouse.

*End of one tormentor. Plus, a huge surplus!*

This was truly the first penny he had made for himself.

He stepped out of his office and called his dad. 'I am done,' he announced, when his father answered.

'Hi, Done. I am Gun. One day you should meet my son.'

'What?'

'What what? If I am Gun, who's my son?'

Rasiq rolled his eyes, 'Son-of-a-Gun,' he replied. 'But what do you mean by that?'

'Not everything has to have a meaning,' his father declared. 'What did you mean when you said you are Done? I remember having named you Rasiq.'

'Dad,' Rasiq laughed, 'I am done with my loan!'

'Oye! Already?'

'Yup,' Rasiq said. 'I just paid the last instalment!'

'Wow! Didn't I tell you that you worry too much about it? You are now free to live your life as you want.'

'Yeah, for the first time in my life, I have money that I don't know what to do with. Should I send it to you?'

'No, no, we have enough and more for us, puttar. What will we do with the excess cash? Didn't Ruchika want you to get out of the hole you are living in?'

'Yeah,' Rasiq said. 'You think I should find a better place?'

'No puttar,' his father whispered. 'I meant you should make a fixed deposit. Always do the opposite of what a woman tells you. You'll go far in life.'

'Is mom not around? You can only say such things when she is away,' Rasiq laughed.

'Oye! Why are you LOLing at your own joke? Only losers do that. If you are a man, then try to make me laugh.'

Both started laughing.

'Dad, I'm going to call a few brokers now.'

'Go ahead, puttar. God bless you. You are a crazy diamond. Keep shining!' his father said. He seemed to have a lump in his throat.

Rasiq never understood how his father could change gears so quickly—from cracking bad jokes to saying something so sentimental that it brought him to the verge of tears. *He misses me*, Rasiq thought. *And I miss him too.*

∽

Rasiq looked at several properties over the weekend and opted for one in Parel. A swanky apartment on the fifteenth floor with a great view of the city. It had a sprawling balcony—by Mumbai standards, overlooking the sea in the distance.

He moved a month later and called Ruchika.

'Hey,' he said. 'Do you want to meet tonight?'

'Sure,' Ruchika said. 'Where?'

*Flat voice. No excitement. Busy or disinterested? No way of knowing. No time either.*

'Can you come to Parel? I found this romantic place to eat.'

'Cool. I'll bring some of my friends too. We were already making plans...'

'Umm,' Rasiq hesitated. 'Can it be just the two of us this evening? I want to talk to you about something personal over dinner.'

Ruchika was silent for a bit. 'All right. I'll cancel with the guys.'

'Awesome!' Rasiq said. 'I'll meet you at the KEM Hospital and we can go together from there. See you at eight?'

'Sure.'

'There's a dress code. It's a posh place and you should wear the dress I gifted you last week.'

'All right!' Ruchika said, now sounding excited.

∽

'Hey, you look stunning,' Rasiq complimented when Ruchika got out of the cab. She was wearing the dress he had asked her to. He himself was dressed in his most expensive suit.

Ruchika hugged him.

'Hi handsome, where is this place? You got me curious.'

'That's a surprise. Care to walk with me, my lady?' He extended his arm to Ruchika.

'Yes, my dear,' Ruchika mimicked Rasiq's British accent and wrapped her arm around his.

They walked for five minutes and Ruchika had started to slow down because of her heels. 'Almost there,' he said, sensing her discomfort.

'Here?' Ruchika said. 'Isn't this a residential area? I don't think there's a restaurant here.'

'I don't think I ever said that we are going to a restaurant. I was careful about that.'

Rasiq smiled as they entered his apartment building. 'After you,' he offered, when the lift opened.

He pressed fifteen and Ruchika looked at him, grinning. 'What did you do?'

'Nothing. Why do you ask?'

'You moved, didn't you?' She hugged him, unable to contain her excitement. Rasiq hugged her back and smiled. The lift stopped and he held her arm in his and escorted her to the door of his apartment. He opened it and gestured for her to walk in.

'Oh my god!' Ruchika exclaimed. She looked around the apartment, taking in its splendour. 'This is marvellous!'

'No, just a version upgrade. Hi,' he smiled, extending his hand—the dramatic flamboyance annoyed him in others, but now he revelled in it, 'I am Rasiq Two Point O.'

'Hi, Mr Two Point O,' Ruchika said. 'Who are you and what did you do to my boyfriend?'

Rasiq took her in his arms and kissed her on the lips for a good minute.

'Please accompany me,' he offered. 'I shall lead you to your dinner.'

They walked, arm in arm, to the balcony where Rasiq had

laid out the dinner and a bottle of wine. He pulled out a chair for Ruchika and tucked her into the table. He sat across her with a happy smile. With a lighter from his pocket, he lit the two candles he had set on the table.

'Bon appétit! Exactly two years of being together,' he said. He opened the wine bottle and poured a glass each.

There was a momentary pause; an awkward silence.

'Gosh! How could I forget? I am really embarrassed,' she blushed

'*Aucun problème*, madame. No issues,' Rasiq smiled.

'For once your French doesn't annoy me!' She took the glass from Rasiq.

'Cheers,' he said. They raised their glasses and looked into each other's eyes when their glasses clinked. 'To us!'

Ruchika picked up her fork and tasted the pasta. 'You didn't make this, did you?'

'Nopes,' Rasiq said. 'If only I had the luxury of time.'

'And talent,' she laughed.

'That too. I can't cook to save my life. Sorry if the food is cold. I wanted to surprise you.'

'Don't worry about it,' she said. 'It's totally worth it. But what was it that you wanted to talk about?'

'Straight to business, then?' he said. He paused momentarily before he spoke. 'I guess this is as good a time as any.'

'Trust me when I say that it is the best time in months,' Ruchika smiled.

Rasiq rose from his chair and walked next to Ruchika. He got down on one knee and Ruchika shrieked in surprise, covering her mouth with both her hands.

'Ruchi,' Rasiq said, 'I have been with you for just a couple of years, yet it feels as if I know you as much as I know myself. I think you are the coolest, hottest girl I will ever meet. So,' he paused and took a key out of his pocket, 'I would like you to move in with me.'

Ruchika rose from her seat in shock. 'For a moment there, I thought you were proposing an engagement!'

Rasiq laughed, nervously. *What made her think so? I'm only twenty-four, for Christ's sake!*

'But I guess this is the next best thing,' she said with an expressionless face.

'Exactly,' Rasiq said. He was still down on one knee, the key held in his extended hand. 'You can save on rent and we will get to know each other so much better like this. The little free time that I have, I would like to spend with you.'

'I know,' Ruchika said. 'I understand.'

Rasiq smiled.

'Like this, you can fuck me as much as you like without a commitment!' she said, shoving her plate aside and walking back inside the apartment.

*What the hell happened?* Rasiq thought, getting up.

'This is a commitment, Ruchi,' he said. 'A way to take our relationship forward.'

'I am not that kind of girl.'

'Just the kind that lets random guys hold her at the waist,' Rasiq retorted, unable to control his anger.

'What?'

Rasiq stared at her, not dignifying her question with a response. She must know what he was talking about, however drunk she was that night. 'Nothing,' he said under his breath.

'And what's with the lighter in your pocket!' she yelled. 'Have you started smoking now?'

'I've been smoking since before we met! What do you mean, "have I started now"?'

'Yeah, but you never carried cigarettes and a lighter! You

smoked occasionally. Now you're carrying these around?' She threw a pack of cigarettes, which she had found lying on the coffee table, at Rasiq.

Rasiq let the pack hit him and it bounced off his chest.

'Don't you ever throw anything at me ever again.'

'Or what?' Ruchika snapped.

'I didn't say "or what".'

'No,' she screamed. 'But you implied it, ever so subtly. You want to hit me now? Is that what you have become?'

Rasiq sank down on the couch, burying his head in his hands. Ruchika kept yelling at him, but in his sleep-deprived, stressed-out state, he was beyond caring. He wondered how he had ever felt lucky to be with Ruchika when they had starting dating on campus.

He wasn't aware when she left. The slam of the door shook him. He was alone in his massive apartment, the spare key still in his hand.

# 8

## *Be a Bond to bond*

'Do you want to check the valuation model for Violet?' Rasiq asked Samar.

'Sure,' Samar said. 'Let's take the small meeting room and you can project the model on the big screen and take me through it.'

'Cool,' Rasiq said. 'I'll see you there in five?'

'You got it.'

In the meeting room, Rasiq explained the model, based on direct cash flow that he had developed for a prospective client's IPO. They were working on a competitive presentation for a deal the bank would be pitching for the following week. Rasiq's job involved making a valuation model for the company so that they could pitch a price point during their presentation.

'Good,' Samar said at the end of the walkthrough of the model. 'The broad structure is in place, but I want you to change the way you have calculated the WACC because they might—'

'They might claim that they have a lower cost of capital,' Rasiq said. 'I have built the sensitivity around the WACC assumption. Here,' he pointed to the section of the model that had different valuations according to the varying weighted average cost of capital for their client. 'Besides, it's currently built using the industry benchmarks, which are all in the references.'

'Wow,' Samar said. 'Excellent. You can start working on the bull and bear case for the model.'

'I've done that too. This is not my first model, Samar. Here are the scenarios for more and less aggressive growth estimates and I am planning to include all the ranges in the presentation deck.' Rasiq clicked on the radio buttons that changed the assumptions dynamically and updated the model.

'Rasiq,' Samar said. He faked a lump-in-the-throat voice, 'I have nothing left to teach you, my padawan.'

'Padawan? Are you a *Star Wars* fan?'

'Do you think I'm a geek?' Samar asked.

Rasiq thought about it. 'Yes?'

'Then of course I'm a *Star Wars* fan, bro!' Samar shouted.

'Whoa!' Rasiq exclaimed. 'I didn't know this about you!'

'There's a lot about me you don't know, Rasiq,' Samar said. He paused for a few seconds then added, 'What say you and I go out for some drinks today?'

'Sure, Samar. I would love that.'

'How long have you been here?'

'Almost ten months,' Rasiq replied.

'We should have done this sooner, no?'

Rasiq nodded.

'Go and make the deck.' Samar rose from his seat. 'If you don't finish by nine, you can go for the drinks alone. Unlike you, I have a wife to get back to.'

*I should probably go and hang out with Ruchika*, Rasiq thought. *We haven't been spending much time together and the one evening that I can leave work early, I'm making drinking plans with Samar.*

After they had fought—it had been a few months since then—Ruchika had called Rasiq a week later as if nothing had happened. Like before, they continued to meet together with her friends whenever Rasiq could find time from work, which was much rarer than before. He never asked her to move in again and Ruchika didn't bring up the topic of engagement.

∾

'Samar,' Rasiq said later that evening as they were having drinks at Geoffrey's, a bar in Nariman Point that had always seemed too expensive to Rasiq, 'why do you work here?'

'What do you mean? Why does anyone work here?'

'I mean you've been here for like what, five years now? You must have a huge corpus already.'

'Of course I do,' Samar replied. 'But what will I do if not this?'

'I don't know. But did you always want to be an investment banker, since you were a kid? Did you always want to slog for more hours than is possible?'

'Sure,' Samar sighed. 'I had dreams. Everyone has.'

*He isn't disclosing them for sure!*

'But you know, it's not easy for me,' Samar continued, getting serious. 'My dad runs a business and earns more than I ever will.'

'Why don't you join your father's business then? Why work for someone else?'

'Love,' Samar's face lit up.

'Sorry?'

'My wife likes a certain lifestyle, a great degree of independence. She won't survive more than a month if we were to live with my parents.'

'I am sure you can work around that,' Rasiq said. 'What if you lived in a separate house and just went to work for your dad, for example?'

'Are you fucking kidding me? They'll never tolerate that! The only reason they let us live here, away from the family business and themselves is because they respect my ability to make more money than any salaried person they know.'

'Fuck,' Rasiq said. His voice slurred a little. 'Are you serious?'

'Life's a bitch, dude.'

'What do you mean?'

'It's simple. I have to stick in this job because I love my wife. But because I have to do this job, I can't spend any time with her. Ergo, life's a bitch.'

'You're screwed, man!'

'I'll drink to that.' Samar took a big sip from his beer mug. 'What about you though? How do you feel with everyone fucking you simultaneously? Do you like it?'

Rasiq was used to the vulgarity by now. 'I have been thinking of quitting, honestly speaking.'

'Ha ha. Everyone thinks about it. No one quits.'

'What do you mean, "no one quits"?'

'I mean no one quits. There hasn't been a single voluntary exit in the past several years. People get fired, but no one has ever had the guts to quit. The money is not just good, it's almost obscene.'

'Lucky bastards then, huh?' Rasiq said, thinking. 'Those who get fired, I mean.'

'Maybe, but you don't have to worry about that.'

'What? Why?' Rasiq enquired. His heartbeat had spiked.

'You're good, Rasiq. Too good for your own good.'

Rasiq smiled. 'That's the first time you've said that to me. Thank you.'

'Don't start flying too high,' Samar warned. 'Don't forget it's also because there is no one in the year immediately above you and you are the only one in your batch.'

'Ah,' Rasiq said. 'Headroom to be promoted?'

Samar nodded. 'Not just headroom, my friend, vacuum. Don't get me wrong, if you fuck up even a little, you're out.

We can deal with vacuum, but not with mistakes.'

They were silent for a time, drinking their beers and thinking about their lives.

'What do you do with all the money?'

'I don't know, man. It's lying somewhere in my bank accounts.'

'What should I do?' Rasiq enquired. 'I am done with my loan and for the past few months my salary has been accumulating in my account. I've done nothing with it—apart from paying the rent and living expenses.'

'How old are you, fucker?'

'Twenty-four. Why?'

'Go, live your life, man! You have no worries in the world—splurge, do whatever the hell your heart tells you to. Waste the fucking money, who cares? Book a flight to Europe that you'll never use. Go and buy new suits, shoes. Get the most fucking ridiculously expensive haircut ever and think about what the difference is between that and the one you can get for fifty bucks in a small shop,' Samar laughed.

'That's solid advice,' Rasiq said, raising his pint. Samar raised his too.

∞

On the way back to his apartment, Rasiq wondered about what Samar had said. *Was his story about being wedged between a rock and a hard place really true? Or has he ingeniously built an inescapable argument to stick to investment banking? It does seem ironic that his wife would let him do this to himself if she loves him.*

*But Samar was right about one thing. I ought to live a little. It isn't like I will be able to do whatever suits my fancy all my life. Soon some EMI and a mundane routine will start slowing me down. Doesn't everyone have more and more constraints as they grow up?*

The cab stopped at a red light near Pedder Road. A kid tapped on the window of his cab, asking for money. *A life mired in constraints*, Rasiq thought.

Behind the kid, Rasiq saw a Harley Davidson showroom. Ten thirty at night and it was still open.

'I'll get down here,' Rasiq announced impulsively.

'What?' his cab driver turned around to look at him, surprised.

'How much do I owe you?'

The cabbie looked at his meter, 'Fifty.'

Rasiq took out his wallet and paid the driver fifty bucks.

'Sir,' the driver protested. 'You hired me for Parel! This is not even halfway there.'

'Sorry,' Rasiq said, 'I changed my mind.'

'That's not how it works, boss,' the cabbie objected.

'Oh,' Rasiq said. 'Then how does it work?'

The cabbie shook his head and exhaled deeply.

'No,' Rasiq insisted. 'Tell me how it works? Would you have refused to bring me here from Nariman Point? I don't need to ask your permission to get down here—that's the law.'

'The law is by the rich for the rich, boss,' the cabbie said. 'I will have to go back without a ride and that's a waste of my time.'

'Waste of your time?' Rasiq was incredulous. 'You don't have even an inkling of how precious time is!'

He took out another hundred bucks from his wallet and threw it on the passenger seat. 'Take that,' he snapped, 'and don't bug me. That's more than the fare you would have made till Parel.'

He stepped out, not listening to the driver cursing him.

∽

'Good evening, sir,' the salesman at the showroom greeted Rasiq.

*Good evening? Isn't it late night?* Rasiq looked down at himself. He was wearing his suit and his shoes still shone. *Still got it*, he thought.

'Do you wish to take a test drive?' the salesman asked.

'No,' Rasiq said. 'I am here to buy.'

'Oh, have you already taken a test drive?'

'It's Harley Davidson,' Rasiq said. 'I'm sure I won't change my mind after a test drive. But if you feel I might, please arrange a bike for a test drive.'

The salesman flushed. 'No sir, I just wanted to make sure you knew how good...'

'Save it,' Rasiq said. 'You're embarrassing yourself.'

The salesman stiffened, his silence conveying his impotence. His manner betrayed his violent thoughts towards Rasiq.

*This is power*, Rasiq thought. *I have it, and I can say anything to a man bigger and older than me. He could beat me to a pulp outside this context in which we are both playing a role—I am a buyer and he has targets. I am his salvation.*

'I want that one,' Rasiq pointed towards a bike that was on display. He had no idea about the different models.

'Fat Boy?'

'Yeah,' Rasiq walked towards the bike and ran his hands on its plush seat. 'Sure.'

'This one costs fifteen lakh plus change,' the salesman said, still sulking.

'Sounds good,' Rasiq said. 'What do you need to complete the sale?'

The salesman excused himself and returned with an older man, his superior.

'Good evening, sir,' the senior salesman greeted him.

Rasiq nodded.

'You want to buy the Fat Boy?'

'Yes please,' Rasiq said. 'If you are willing to sell it.'

Both the salesmen laughed nervously. They gave him a list of documents they needed and Rasiq asked if he could log in to their computer. They allowed him and he printed the relevant documents from his Google Drive.

The junior salesman checked all the documents and made out the sales invoice in Rasiq's name.

'How much advance would you like to pay, sir? We'll arrange the best financing options for the rest.'

'Can I pay the full amount now and take the bike with me?'

'Oh!' the senior salesman looked surprised. 'Have you brought cash?'

'No,' Rasiq said, 'but I can transfer it via net banking.'

∽

A few hours later, close to 2.00 a.m., Rasiq left the showroom with his bike. He could feel the power of the 1,690-cc engine humming under him. He was glad the roads were empty. He drove slowly to Marine Drive and did a tour of it twice.

He pulled over next to the promenade in front of his office.

'Wow, Rasiq!' Gopi shouted as Rasiq got off his bike. 'When did you buy this?'

'Just now,' Rasiq said. 'What are you doing here at this hour? When do you sleep?'

'I am a free bird! I work when I want to or have to. But where are the sweets?' Gopi asked, pulling out a cigarette for Rasiq.

Rasiq gave him a five hundred-rupee note and lit his cigarette. 'You keep this,' Rasiq said, 'to buy those sweets.'

Gopi pocketed the money without objecting. 'You have become a big shot, Rasiq,' he said. 'I pray for your success and hope that you keep growing like this.'

Rasiq sat on the promenade boundary, facing away from the sea and looking at his bike. Its new metallic paint glistened under the yellow street light. It looked majestic and Rasiq smiled with pride. He had never done anything this impulsive before, he thought.

*No*, he reflected. *That's not true. Today seems different only because of the ticket size. Didn't I buy skates just as impulsively in France when I went there on the exchange programme?*

∞

Rasiq had gone to a flea market in Nantes, France over a weekend during his exchange programme. It was still early in the morning and people were setting up their stalls. He was lazing with a book at a coffee shop when he saw an old man across the street lay out a pair of inline skates in his stall. Rasiq's heart skipped a beat. He crossed the street immediately, as if pulled by the skates.

'How much are these?' he asked the man in French.

'Fifteen euros,' the man said. 'Try them.'

'That's too much. How about I pay ten?' Rasiq bargained. He had taken off his shoes and was putting one skate on. Perfect fit!

'Ten?' the man said, scratching the back of his head. 'Okay, I'll give you one for ten.'

'One?'

'Yes. Ten for one and fifteen for both. Take the left one or the right one. Your choice.'

From what Rasiq could tell, the man was serious.

'What will you do with the other?' Rasiq asked, confused. 'Aren't they a pair?'

'Aah,' the old man said. 'Good point. You buy one for ten, then the other one becomes useless, so I give it to you free.'

The man was clearly high.

'Okay,' Rasiq said taking out a ten-euro bill and handing it over to the guy. He wore the other skate as well and zipped out of the flea market, his shoes in his hand.

∽

A shrill car horn shattered the smile on his face and brought him back to the present. *Did I really negotiate for five euros?* He thought, looking at the fifteen-lakh beast gleaming under the street light.

He wondered if he was thinking more and more about his exchange programme days because the present was unliveable and mechanical. He wasn't generating any aha moments or memories he would look back upon and savour. Just cash. The present was rich in the physical sense, but the past was richer in the metaphysical one.

∽

'What the fuck did you do?' Samar said as Rasiq dragged him downstairs the next morning.

'I did what you told me to,' Rasiq said.

'For a change!'

Rasiq pointed towards a bike, waiting for Samar's reaction.

'Harley fucking Davidson!'

'Yeah baby!' Rasiq shrieked.

'You bought this last night?'

'Yup,' he said. 'I was returning home in a cab thinking that it's so lame to be commuting in this kaali peeli every day. Then, a Harley showroom appeared! It was as if the universe was listening to my thoughts.'

'Sure,' Samar said. 'That showroom has been around for several months now.'

'You're missing the point,' Rasiq said. 'I didn't know it was there—I pass it every single day and I never noticed it before last night. I saw it when I was searching for what my heart wanted.'

'And you just went in and bought this?'

'Of course,' Rasiq said. 'Just like you told me to. Wasted the fucking money!'

'That's bitching!' He high-fived Rasiq. 'My man! This is Miss Glory herself, reincarnated.'

They laughed.

# 9

## A disaster waiting to happen

$O$n a Saturday evening a few months later, Rasiq rode his bike to Worli Sea Face from the office. He heard the sounds of people partying, music blaring loudly, and drove in that direction. It was the Four Seasons hotel and the sound of music was coming from the rooftop. He parked his bike in the hotel's parking lot and took the lift up to the open-air lounge and bar called Aer.

From high up, Rasiq saw the skyline of Mumbai. He ordered a drink and smoked a cigarette standing next to the railing, savouring the magic of the moment. The setting sun reminded him of another sunset in a not so distant past that he had enjoyed with his best friends.

*

They were lazing on the beach in Nice, in the south of France, drinking beer. A two-week mid-semester break had triggered their wanderlust.

'This is how life ought to be lived, man,' Kshitij said.

'Yeah bro,' Mihir said. 'It's better than any vacation.'

'We should make every effort to come back here after we finish IIT,' Rasiq suggested.

The October afternoon sun was descending into the evening. The breeze was pleasant and the sea calm.

'Did you read that they are planning to reduce the working

hours to thirty-five a week here?' Rasiq informed when the other two didn't show much enthusiasm for his suggestion.

'What? Seven hours a day?' Mihir said.

'Even our parents work ten hours a day, man! This is surreal!' Kshitij chuckled.

'Look at the people here,' Rasiq said. 'They do what they want to do. If they don't know what they want to do, they take a break to think about it. They live every moment of their lives. Because it's their time and therefore, damn important. They live to experience life.'

'Exactly,' Mihir said. 'We seem to be mindlessly walking down a predestined path. I don't even know if I wanted to be an engineer. I never got a chance to evaluate any options.'

'Same here, man! I know that I would have loved to be a pilot,' Kshitij said.

'Me, probably a teacher,' Mihir said.

Rasiq smiled. He had no idea what he wanted to be. And France had taught him that was okay. 'I would love to do nothing,' he said after a long pause. 'For a while, at least. Just sit amid nature, breathe and think.'

'Yeah, man,' Kshitij said. 'Doing something is so overrated. Why does it always have to be about becoming something, doing something? Seems a little obsessive, if you ask me.'

'Are we drunk?'

'You mean on beers or on France?'

'Both, I guess!'

They laughed and lay down on the beach, watching the sun go down.

'You know,' Mihir said, 'if you stand up right now you can see the sunset again.'

'Yeah,' Kshitij said. 'We know. We too prepared for JEE.'

'Do you want to see?' Mihir asked.

'No,' Rasiq said. 'It's nice where I am. Experiencing life.'

∞

'Hi, hotshot,' a familiar voice brought him back to the present.

He turned around to see a short girl wearing a shorter dress that also revealed her cleavage. Priyanka looked absolutely stunning in the orange hue of the setting sun.

'Hey!' Rasiq said. He stubbed out his cigarette in an ashtray and walked towards her. He gave her a bear hug, not his usual sideways hug. Alcohol had lowered his inhibitions. He felt her hands on his back and they sent a warm feeling up his spine.

'Are you here alone?' she asked.

'Yeah,' Rasiq said, 'I was driving by and I heard music coming from up here. Decided to check it out. Got arrested by beauty of two kinds. Nature and...' he let his voice trail away as he looked into Priyanka's eyes with a coy smile.

'Is this your first time at Aer?' she smiled, blushing.

'Yeah,' Rasiq admitted, 'I didn't even know about this place.'

'That's a pity. It's the place to hang out in Mumbai!'

'I can see that now.'

'But where's Ruchi?'

'I think she already had plans with her friends. It's getting harder to catch her.'

'She says the same about you; that you're always working. Someone stole the time for life from you. Life's passing you by, man.'

'Not stole,' he corrected. 'Rented.'

'And they are paying a good price for it,' Priyanka said. 'Why don't you join us?' She pointed to her group of friends.

'Sure,' Rasiq said as he picked up his drink and looking at the now sunless sky longingly, cursing his luck. He was finally relaxing a little after a really long week. *Didn't anyone want to be alone anymore?*

Rasiq chatted with Priyanka's friends about everything under the sun—politics, environment, Delhi versus Mumbai. After an evening of entertaining conversation and a crazy amount of alcohol and cigarettes, they called for the cheque.

The digits on the bill shocked him. More than 7,000 rupees per person. Rasiq was pulling out his card when one of the guys in the group stopped him. 'I got this, brother,' he volunteered. He didn't listen to the protests from the group.

'I got a new car, guys,' he announced. 'It's my treat tonight.'

'Again?' Priyanka said. 'Which one?'

'Audi Q4,' he beamed with pride. 'I'll drop you home tonight so you can ride in it. It's unbelievably awesome.'

'Cool,' Priyanka gestured a hi-five. 'And congratulations!'

They went down in the lift to the parking area. Everyone gathered around the new car. Rasiq glanced at his watch. 'I'll carry on from here. I had a great time hanging out with you guys.'

'Wait! How are you going home?' Priyanka asked.

'I have a bike,' he replied.

'Bike?' Priyanka said. 'Did you buy a bike?'

'Yup,' Rasiq said, feeling a little shitty about his purchase compared to the big car they were standing around.

'Which one did you buy, bro?' one of the friends asked, his eyes scanning the parking lot.

'That!' Rasiq pointed to his bike.

Priyanka gasped, 'Harley Davidson!'

'Yup,' Rasiq said. His confidence was returning. 'The Fat Boy.'

'Oh my god!' she shrieked. 'I'm definitely riding that one tonight!'

Rasiq was a little surprised, 'Sure,' he said. 'I can drop you home if you like.'

They said their goodbyes to the group and saw them off before walking up to Rasiq's bike. Rasiq started the bike and Priyanka sat behind him.

'This doesn't have a sissy bar.'

'What's that?'

'The grip at the back to hold,' Priyanka said. 'I'll have to hold you, I guess.'

She wrapped her arms around him and Rasiq felt a now familiar warmth surge through his body.

'Hold tight,' he said. They rode out of the hotel parking lot to the Worli Sea Face.

'Where do you stay?' he asked once they hit the road.

'Where do you stay?' she countered.

'Pretty close by. Parel.'

'Oh,' Priyanka said, 'but I live really far away from here. Why didn't you say something before?'

'I don't mind,' Rasiq said. 'I would love the drive anyway!'

'No,' she insisted, 'you'll be drinking and driving. It's not safe.'

'Umm,' Rasiq said. 'Do you want to crash at my place tonight?'

She seemed to hesitate. 'I don't know...' Priyanka said.

'Don't worry. I live alone and there's a spare room you can use.'

'All right,' she said. 'If you're sure it won't be any trouble.'

Rasiq smiled and rode home.

Priyanka was impressed by the elegant and spacious pad. 'This is beautiful, Rasiq!'

'Thanks,' Rasiq smiled, 'I built it myself.'

'Shut up!' She slapped him on the arm. 'Let's go to the

balcony—I feel like smoking just looking at it.'

They smoked in silence on the balcony, gazing at the big boxes of light that the towers looked like at night.

'Who were those guys at Aer? Friends from work?'

'No silly,' Priyanka said. 'They were my school friends. All rich and spoilt kids of big businessmen.'

'They didn't seem spoilt.'

'Ask their parents! But why do you ask?'

'Owning premium cars at such a young age and picking up that massive bill. That surprised me,' Rasiq said. 'I thought I was doing well before tonight. But I feel kind of poor now.'

'You move up the ladder to find another ladder,' Priyanka shrugged. 'But the ladder you are on is beyond the wildest dreams of most people. Be proud of yourself.'

Rasiq nodded slowly as he leant forward, resting his arms on the balcony railing, looking at the city. He was vaguely unsettled. He had been living in a bubble that had just been burst. He was thrown off-balance.

*What is this new race that I have to run? Haven't I already beaten everyone? Do I need to keep running? To what end?*

Priyanka stubbed out her cigarette and took a step towards Rasiq. She put her hand on his back, stroking him. 'You're so tense all the time, Rasiq.'

'Yeah,' Rasiq said. 'It's the job. It is taxing.'

'Poor boy,' she said. Her tone was childish. 'Come here, let me give you a hug.'

Rasiq did not protest, and she pressed herself against him. He felt his blood rush to his head. Then, without letting go of him, Priyanka looked up into his eyes and moved her face dangerously close to his. Rasiq could feel her breath on his neck and dipped his head closer to hers. She stood up on her toes and reached his lips with hers and they kissed, passionately.

Rasiq could feel his hands sliding down to her hips, and Priyanka started undoing the buttons of his shirt even as they were kissing. They moved back into the apartment and Priyanka pushed him on to the couch. She began undressing.

'Wait,' Rasiq said. 'We're drunk.'

'So?'

'We shouldn't be doing this!'

'Come on Rasiq,' Priyanka said. 'This, right here, is the moment. Let's seize it. Don't be a prude.'

Rasiq looked at her standing in front of him in her undergarments. He pulled her to the couch and made love to her.

∽

6.00 a.m. He had woken up automatically and had stepped out to the balcony to smoke, leaving Priyanka sleeping. He shook his head and held it in his hands, controlling the urge to shout. He had behaved like an idiot. What was he doing with his life? He had never thought that he would be the one to cheat in a relationship.

He stood thinking for a long time. He wondered if Ruchika had cheated on him too. What was happening between her and that guy from her office she seemed so close to? But he knew that line of thought was flawed—that his infidelity wouldn't matter if she was doing it too.

He thought of how she had been avoiding him over the past several months. Her neglect had landed him in the arms of another girl. But no, that was at best another lame argument.

He had cheated on Ruchika with her best friend. Period.

*Should I confess and break up with her? It'll devastate her, but it's inevitable. If you stick around in this relationship, she'll be even more devastated. Do I even love her? What the hell is love, anyway?*

Rasiq put on his running shoes and slipped out. He drove

to the Worli Sea Face where he parked his bike and broke into a run.

He had deferred these questions for a long time and now he needed answers. He needed to think through the turmoil his life was in.

His life was officially a mess.

7.30 a.m. Priyanka was still asleep when he returned home.

He showered quickly and prepared breakfast for two before waking her up.

'You seem upset,' she said.

Rasiq didn't respond.

'Ruchika?' she looked up from her breakfast plate.

'Is it that obvious?' He didn't know why he was venting his anger on Priyanka.

'You do know your relationship is over, right?' Priyanka ignored his sarcasm.

'What?'

'Ruchika has moved on, Rasiq,' Priyanka said. 'That's why she didn't move in with you. She's been with this other guy from work for a while now.'

'Did she tell you this?'

'Not in as many words, but I have known her for several years. I know that she is in love with this other guy. It won't surprise me if she is sleeping with him.'

Rasiq didn't know how to react, but he could feel anger surging inside him. Nonetheless, he couldn't trust Priyanka's word for it. And he too had cheated. Still, how could Ruchika treat him like a pushover?

His mind was a muddle of guilt and anger.

'She has been spending weekends at his place, Rasiq,' Priyanka said.

'Can I drop you somewhere? I need to head to work.'

# 10

## *Am I who I think I am?*

*B*ack in office after the weekend, Rasiq faced the worst Monday morning blues since he had moved to Mumbai. *Where is Ruchika?* He stared out of the glass walls of his office when he should have been concentrating on the assignment on hand. He looked at the sea of people below. Mumbai seemed to have swallowed her.

Weeks had passed. He had heard nothing from Ruchika. Or from Priyanka. He didn't have the courage to reach out to Ruchika, so he drowned himself in work. He was avoiding the questions that troubled him. He was floating through life like a zombie, getting barely a wink of sleep. Earlier, the fatigue after a long day at work had been enough to knock him out as soon as he hit the bed. Now, despite the ten-kilometre morning jogs, sleep eluded him.

He had joined a 24x7 gym near his house and worked out every day to work up a sweat so that he could sleep, but to no avail. He had started smoking more as his brain needed the nicotine to perform the functions required by his job.

A part of him hoped Priyanka had told Ruchika, so he wouldn't have to have the difficult conversation with her.

*What the hell have I become?*

∞

As Rasiq was parking his bike outside the office one morning, a middle-aged man came running towards him.

'Boss, you can't park your bike here,' he said with what Rasiq felt was unwarranted rudeness.

'Excuse me?' Rasiq said. 'I have been parking my bike here for the past several months. What's new today?'

'You might have been doing that, boss, but I am telling you that you can't do it anymore, okay? Now move the bloody bike,' the man shouted.

Rasiq could no longer control his anger. 'Who are you, fucker?' he demanded, getting off his bike and walking towards the man.

'Should I tell you who I am?' the man said. He stared at him malevolently as he walked the remaining distance between himself and Rasiq menacingly.

Rasiq was slightly intimidated and took a step back. That instinctive move, however, hurt his ego.

With his mind reeling with frenzy, Rasiq gritted his teeth and shoved the man in the chest. 'Yes!' he shouted. 'Tell me who you are, bastard!'

The man stumbled a few steps back but recovered quickly. He made a fist and swung, connecting with Rasiq's face before he could dodge the blow.

Rasiq's lip was bleeding now. He shook his head and looked up with a maniacal smile. He charged towards the man as the past few weeks of his gym training kicked in. He punched the man in the neck with his right hand, moving with surprising speed and agility. Before the man could recover, he smacked his left fist in his face.

The man charged towards him and grabbed Rasiq's hands. He then smashed his head into Rasiq's face.

Rasiq kneed the man in his groin and freed his hands by twisting violently. As the man doubled up, barely able to stand, Rasiq grabbed his hair with both hands and threw him on the ground, face first.

A large crowd had gathered around them by then, but Rasiq noticed it only now. Nobody had tried to stop the fight, probably enjoying their daily dose of drama. Rasiq walked back to his bike, started it and realized he was shaking all over. He turned the engine off and decided to wheel it out of the parking lot.

'Isn't he the parking attendant?' he could hear people talking.

'Yeah,' someone replied. 'This town sucks the life out of the poor.'

'No,' the first man replied. 'It's these rich kids who do that. Must be feeling like a real hero after beating up a man twice his age.'

Rasiq hung his head low in shame and walked away with his bike.

∞

11.30 p.m. Rasiq's stomach was growling with hunger and anxiety when his phone rang. Ruchika. Was it the call he dreaded?

'Hello?'

Ruchika was crying at the other end. *This is it*, Rasiq thought. *Fuck, I am not mentally prepared for this.*

'Hi Ruchika, what happened?'

'Mom passed away.'

'What?'

'She passed away.' He could hear her sob.

'Why…what happened?'

'Dad said she had a heart attack in her sleep. I have no clue what to do. I can't think straight.'

'Don't wo…' *What does one say to someone who has lost a loved one?* 'Don't worry' seemed so inappropriate. 'I am com…'

Before he could finish, Ruchika hung up.

Rasiq sank into his chair. His heart raced and he felt dizzy. He pushed his monitor aside on an impulse and as he lay down on the extended desk, Rasiq realized that his desk measured exactly six feet by two feet. A perfect resting place for the moment, and the perfect resting place for him in his afterlife too.

'This will be my coffin,' he thought aloud to no one. 'Or is it already?'

*What if death sneaks up on me as quietly as it did for Ruchika's mom? No warning signs, no alarms. Tomorrow. Just now? In that moment of passing, what will I feel about my life?*

*I made good money*, he thought. *That ought to be something. I have been more successful than many twenty-four-year-olds in the world. I have achieved a lot.*

*Yeah, but have I created any value? I have become a douchebag and that's because of the money. I let my success go to my head and ruin me. I have become the guy I detested as a kid. Smoking, drinking, obsessed with my career. What's more, I cheated on my girlfriend. I don't have any empathy for anyone let alone those less fortunate than myself. And where is all this arrogance coming from? I behave as though it is an occupational perk that investment banking affords me.*

Rasiq's phone rang again. He didn't answer it; he continued to simmer in self-loathing.

A minute later the phone rang again. Rasiq reached for it and looked at the screen. An unknown international number.

'Hello?'

'Hi Risky!' The warm, familiar voice at the other end was an excited shout. Only one person called him by that name.

'Kshitij?'

'I thought you'd never recognize me,' he said.

'What's up, bro? Where are you?'

'I'm at the top of the Alps, man. You won't believe how beautiful it is from up here. It reminded me of you and our awesome conversations. What are you up to?'

'I am at the top of a tower in Mumbai, man,' Rasiq said. 'Instead of a valley, I see people below me in the pyramid of supremacy. You won't believe how pathetic the view from here is.'

'Yuck!' Kshitij said. 'At least your sarcasm survived the treacherous climb to the top. Are you still at work?'

'Yeah man. I mean, I was. Right now, I'm playing dead. Thinking about my passing and how full of regrets it's going to be.'

'Aren't you dead honest!' Kshitij laughed.

Rasiq chuckled.

'But you'll have to find another day to die,' Kshitij said. 'Today is the day to live, bro! Happy birthday! Congratulations my friend. You are a quarter of a century old today. Two and a half decades. Quite some turns for the hands of the clock, man.'

Rasiq jumped up from his desk and checked the date on his computer.

'Damn! I forgot! Must be getting old in the head!'

'And Ruchika forgot too?'

*Ruchika!*

'Her mother passed away. I just got the news.'

'What the...!' Kshitij blurted. 'And you are still at work? You should be by her side!'

'You're right, I should be leaving now.'

'All right man,' Kshitij said. 'Take care of yourself and her. I'll see you when I'm in India next. Stay awesome. Stay true to who you are, who you always were.'

# 11

# Mid-air break-up

*R*asiq accompanied Ruchika to her hometown and stayed by her side throughout the last rites for her mother. He couldn't help but wonder if her mother had been happy when she was alive. But this was not the right time to be asking such questions.

On their flight back to Mumbai, Rasiq brought up what he had been thinking.

'The news of your mother's passing shook me. It forced me to think of the short time we have on earth and how temporary everything is.'

He paused, but Ruchika simply stared at him impassively.

'I am planning to quit my job,' he continued when there was no response from her.

'What? Why?' she asked. 'You're kidding, right?'

'I don't think I want to be an investment banker all my life,' Rasiq said. 'I have been running a race for sometime now. I thought this was what I wanted. Now, however, it feels like I am living a life dictated by society. My life in this urban jungle feels like that hare in the race with the tortoise. I thought I wanted appreciation and accolades. It wasn't until now that I realized that's not what I want.'

'What about the money?' Ruchika asked. She ignored his explanation.

'I'll make money doing what I love as well,' Rasiq reasoned.

'It's not as if I am going to sit idle at home.'

'And what is it that you love?'

'I don't know yet.'

'All right,' Ruchika said. 'You should try to figure out what you want to do while you're working.'

'No,' Rasiq said. 'I can't work at the investment bank anymore. My mind doesn't work like that. I am either in or out. I can't do justice to the job or myself if my heart is not in it.'

'Yes, I do understand. I know you very well, Rasiq.'

'What?'

'That you are either in or out,' she said. 'How did it feel when you were in Priyanka?'

Rasiq's eyes widened with surprise. *So, she knew all along.*

'Don't worry,' Ruchika said. 'I don't mind one bit. Tell me if you are in this relationship or out?'

'I am not the only one who needs to decide, Ruchi. You have been avoiding me for a long time too. I've wanted to ask you the same question.'

'Yeah,' Ruchika said. Her voice rose. 'It's my fault. I pushed you into Priyanka's vagina.'

'Please don't shout, Ruchi,' Rasiq whispered, trying to calm her.

Passengers in the flight were staring at them.

'Don't call me Ruchi. It's over.'

It was Rasiq's turn to be angry now.

'Were you waiting for me to tell you that I was quitting before bringing this up?'

'What? Are you accusing me of being in this relationship for your money?' Ruchika looked at him wide-eyed.

'You tell me,' Rasiq hissed. 'You were hanging out with that fucker from your office who holds you as if you are his girlfriend, not mine. That too in front of me! You have no time for us anymore since you always hang out with him. Priyanka told me you have been spending weekends at his house after telling me you didn't want to move in with me because you are not "that kind of girl"!'

'Fuck you, Rasiq,' Ruchika said, the tears flowing freely now.

'Fuck you too, bitch,' Rasiq said through his teeth. He had never cursed at Ruchika before, even when she had abused him. This time, however, a plane full of passengers staring at them notwithstanding, Rasiq could not control his temper at her hypocrisy.

'What's the matter here?' The flight attendant had come up to their seats. 'Is this man bothering you, ma'am?'

Ruchika nodded, covering her mouth to subdue her sobs.

'Please come with me,' the flight attendant said. 'I'll find you another seat.'

Ruchika left with the flight attendant. She was seated in business class. As she turned to sit, Rasiq could swear he saw her smile.

He stared through the window for the rest of the flight, avoiding eye contact with the other passengers.

*Why does love have to be so complicated? Am I bad at this stuff?* Rasiq wondered. *No, it's not always this hard. It's not supposed to be. In the moments when I needed help and support, she was never there. That's not love.*

*Then how is it supposed to be?*

The uncomfortable present, with its unresolved questions, took him back to an uncomplicated evening when life was simpler.

∞

He was skating inside the campus of his exchange college on a Saturday when a girl waved at him, signalling him to stop. He braked and stopped close to her. Sandra was from his Advanced Statistics class.

'Hi,' she said.

'Hi,' Rasiq said, hoping his blush was not noticeable.

'I didn't know you skated,' she said. 'Where are you going?'

'Nowhere in particular. I just bought these and thought I'd skate around the town.'

'Can you wait for me? I'll get my skates and we can go together. I know the town and can show you around.'

'Sure,' Rasiq said, even though he had been in Nantes for close to three months and knew the town well. 'I would like that.'

They skated together that afternoon and she showed him places tucked into the corners of the city. In the late afternoon, they sat outside a small, green painted café shaded by a slanting awning made of coarse yellow cloth.

'Didn't I tell you they make the best pain au chocolat in town?' Sandra asked, pushing her blonde hair back. She untied her skates and Rasiq did the same. Her forehead had beads of sweat from the skating.

'Thank you,' Rasiq said.

'Oh, what for?'

'For coming with me. I saw a side of the city I hadn't seen before.'

'I enjoyed it too. You're a good skater. You didn't have to struggle to keep up with me.'

'Keep up with you?' Rasiq raised an eyebrow. 'I had to keep braking so I wouldn't leave you behind.'

'You want to race back?' she challenged him.

'Maybe not immediately after I've stuffed myself with coffee and pastry.'

'Good excuse,' Sandra was laughing now.

'Back home,' Rasiq said, 'no one would have taken out time

for a stranger like this. We are always busy. Your spontaneity surprised me.'

Sandra nodded. 'Sometimes I wonder if that's something about us French. Are we laid-back compared to others? I see you and the exchange students from China, pushing so hard and accomplishing so much more than us.'

'But I have seen you in class. You work hard!'

Sandra blushed. 'You've been observing me in class?'

'Come on,' Rasiq said. 'You know I didn't mean it that way!'

'I'm just pulling your leg! What I meant was that we do only as much as we think is important. Beyond that we chill and party.'

'Aww! You do have a horrible life.'

Sandra laughed. 'Stop it!'

'But yeah,' Rasiq said, 'I know what you mean. And that's what I envy. In India, we have to work hard at everything. Nothing is enough. More than 200,000 students apply for fewer than 2,000 seats in my college every year. Then these 2,000 students have to compete for the twenty good jobs. So, we are all into sports, dramatics, debates, quizzes, organizing events and contesting elections. Merely to stand out from the crowd. Too much pressure, too much competition.'

'Yeah,' Sandra said. They were sipping their hot chocolate. 'That sounds like a hectic life.'

'Tell me about it,' Rasiq said.

'Come, I'll take you to my favourite place.'

They put on their skates and zipped to Centreville, the city centre of Nantes, where most of the bars, pubs, restaurants, places to shop and supermarkets were located. Rasiq had been there several times.

'Who could have guessed that this is your favourite part of town?' he teased.

'Aren't you just nonstop! We are not there yet, mister.'

They took a turn and then he saw where she was leading him. Before them stood a majestic cathedral of imposing height. Rasiq stopped beside her, awed.

'Have you ever been inside a church?' she asked.

Rasiq shook his head.

'Just follow my lead.'

She took off her skates and began to walk.

Inside, he kept close to Sandra as she showed him the murals on the walls and the painted glass windows, describing the themes they depicted in a quiet whisper. They were beautiful.

She sat on one of the benches and motioned for Rasiq to join her. They sat for several minutes in silence. Rasiq felt a calm come over him as he meditated on the moment. When they rose to leave, it was late evening.

Once outside, they put their skates back on in companionable tranquil.

'Did you like it?' Sandra asked after a few minutes.

'It was so peaceful inside. I felt serene.'

'If you let the energy in the cathedral talk to you, it can be very powerful.'

'It felt as if my batteries were charging,' he said.

'I know what you mean. I am not particularly religious, but I enjoy the quiet in there. It allows me to free my mind of all the thoughts and worries that creep in as we grow up. It lets me be a kid again.'

Rasiq smiled. 'Thank you for sharing this experience with me.'

They shared a moment of silence, looking into each other's eyes.

'Ahem…It's going to be dark soon,' Rasiq said.

'Yes, perfect time for our race back to the hostel.'

And she started speeding away.

Rasiq started slowly behind her, admiring how graceful she was on the skates. He turned to look at the cathedral again before dashing after her.

Back at the hostel, as they said goodbyes to each other, Sandra sensed his awkwardness.

'What?' she asked.

'What?' he returned.

'You seem uncomfortable.'

'I was wondering if I could host you for dinner someday. I had a great time.'

'Me too,' Sandra said. 'What are your plans for tonight?'

'I don't know. Probably going to heat a frozen pizza.'

'That sounds like fun,' Sandra said. 'Can you heat two instead?'

Rasiq laughed. 'Sure thing. What time?'

'I'll be there by nine.'

Rasiq zipped back to his room.

He took a quick shower and hurriedly cleared the clutter that had accumulated over several weeks of neglect. In the now presentable room, he opened a bottle of wine and popped the pizzas into the microwave in the common area of the hostel.

Sandra arrived at 9.00 p.m. sharp.

'Another trait that amazes me about the French,' Rasiq said, 'is how punctual they are. In India, people are always—'

Sandra closed the door behind her and kissed Rasiq on the lips. She withdrew quickly. 'Is that also different from how Indians greet each other?'

Her blonde hair was still damp from her bath.

'Yeah,' Rasiq said. 'But I don't think you did it the French way, did you?'

'No,' Sandra said. She took a step closer to Rasiq.

Rasiq's hands trembled as he held her at her waist. 'I think it's important that I learn the French way since I am on a cultural exchange programme.' He lowered his lips to meet hers.

∽

*What am I doing? It's going to hurt like crazy when I leave for India.* Rasiq was in turmoil. He was sitting next to Sandra who was concentrating on trying to solve the Travelling Salesman problem.

*So what? Do we deny ourselves the happiness of the now thinking about the pain in the future? Who could ever be happy by that logic?*

'Don't worry,' Sandra whispered, reading his mind. 'I am struggling with the same thoughts.'

'What thoughts?'

'If we are idiots doing this, knowing well that it's going to last only a couple of months,' she said

'And? Have you found the answer?'

'No. Between the two of us, you are the smart one.' She pointed to his notebook where he had already solved the problem. 'You will eventually figure out the answer to this problem as well.'

'Honestly,' Rasiq said, 'I don't want to think about this as a problem. I just want to be in the moment. Enjoy this sliver of happiness given to me.'

'That's as good a solution as any,' Sandra agreed.

∽

Now, in the flight, he wondered if he could have made it work with Sandra. Should he have gone back to France after completing his studies? He felt a pang in his chest. *What if I had true love? Why didn't I fight for it?*

In a parallel universe, he must have made that choice. In that universe, Rasiq imagined he was happy. With Kshitij, Mihir and

Sandra—his life was beautiful. Full of fun, without angst and misery. But that's the catch with choices. In moments of pain and misery, they become the source of everything gone wrong.

Rasiq didn't see Ruchika after they landed. Business class passengers debarked before the economy class. By the time Rasiq reached the luggage belt, Ruchika had already left the airport.

He went home and dumped his bag in his bedroom. Without resting for a moment, he changed into his running gear and picked up his bike keys. He was processing his thoughts, thinking about what he would do tomorrow. While riding, the cool wind from the sea dried the beads of perspiration that had started flowing down his forehead.

Rasiq stopped at the end of the Marine Drive and parked his bike. It was late on a Wednesday night and very few people were out strolling. He started his run.

*Soon I won't have any of the things that I have grown used to over the past few years—a relationship or a job. The two constants around which my life has revolved in the recent past will both be gone.*

He started feeling unsettled, confused, but then as he was about to complete the first kilometre of his run, his mind had to go to war with his body. As it marshalled every cell to execute the mission of running, his worries began to take a back seat. Three kilometres in, his legs ached and his mind was working hard to coax his muscles and his oxygen-starved lungs to continue. At five kilometres, as Rasiq turned to run back, he realized that his body was in a steady state. His muscles were used to the pain and stress. His breathing had become regular. He ran back the same distance much more easily than he had when he had started.

As he sat down on the promenade boundary and looked out at the sea, he could feel his worries grow and his heart felt like it was drowning in a dark cesspool. As dark as the night sea in front of him.

*Moving, in any direction whatsoever, keeps the mind occupied,* Rasiq remembered. *It is only in moments of silent contemplation that the mind starts growing agitated. I can't keep running forever though. It's time to sit, think and sort out my life.*

# 12

## *Indignation over resignation*

Subject: Letter of resignation

Dear Raghav,

In the *Matrix Revolutions*, the Oracle tells Neo that everything that has a beginning has an end. If you haven't seen the movie, please check out the Matrix trilogy—it's awesome.

I digress, however.

In my parting note, I want to say that I have learnt a lot during my stint here. Besides creating great presentations and being quick at building complex models on Excel, I learnt 'what not to do at a workplace'. For that and everything else, I want to thank you and the team sincerely.

I know there is a lot left to learn and sticking around here will ensure that I learn much more than any of my peers. But I think that learning will come at a heavy price. You see, I love to sleep and love to dream. But it's my ability to dream while I am awake is what I cherish the most. I tried to give it up—as you advised me to on my first day—but I think the addiction has me by the balls.

Since this is my first job, I'm clueless about the protocol

for resigning. Maybe that can be one of the last things I learn here. Lemme know.

Cheers,
Rasiq

Rasiq read the draft once and contemplated sending it to his father first. He knew he would have to deal with his father's fury later. He hit send quickly, without further thought. He was wary of the analysis-paralysis trap that could jam his will. He had to go with his instinct.

A couple of hours later, around 11.00 a.m., Rasiq was treated to the vision he was anticipating. Everyone on the floor was staring at him. Despite being mentally prepared, Rasiq felt like the circus clown facing an audience waiting to be appeased.

His desk line rang.

'Hi, Rasiq. This is Mandakni. Can you please come to my office?'

'Hi. Where's your office?'

'You don't know where the HR director's office is?'

'No,' Rasiq said without emotion. 'Do you know where my cubicle is?'

ॐ

'Mandakni?' Rasiq said uncertainly. He had opened the door to her office after knocking. 'I'm Rasiq.'

'Come in,' she said. She looked at him curiously. Samar was already there. 'Please have a seat.'

'What was that about, Rasiq?' Samar asked the moment he saw him. 'I had just started believing there was hope for you. You were doing well...'

Rasiq looked at Samar, his lips pursed. 'I thought you, at least, might understand.'

'What should I understand? That you got high and wrote this email?'

'No!' Rasiq was surprised. *Does he not remember our conversation at the bar a few months back?* 'My decision is final.'

'Do you want to negotiate salary?' Mandakni asked.

'No. I didn't know you could possibly pay me more than you already do.'

'Well,' Mandakni said, 'normally, we couldn't. But considering this is a special case, we would be willing to discuss the issue.'

*The vacuum*, Rasiq remembered Samar's words.

'No, but thanks,' he said.

'All right,' Mandakni said. 'If you don't mind my asking, is everything okay on the personal front?'

'What do you mean?' Rasiq said.

'Your parents, siblings...Is everything alright with them?'

'Yes,' Rasiq said. 'Thank you for the intrusive concern!'

Mandakni rolled her eyes.

'What about Ruchika?' Samar said.

'She's good too,' Rasiq said.

'You know,' Mandakni said, 'we offer free sessions with the best psychiatrist in town if you need to talk to someone.'

'That's good to know. I might have needed it if I had stuck around here a little longer.'

'Rasiq,' Mandakni said. Her voice was soft and reassuring, 'Can you please tell us why you are quitting this job?'

'For several reasons...' Rasiq began. 'Do you want me to get into it?'

'Yes, please; if you don't mind.'

'All right then. Right from the word go, I never understood why people would work this way,' Rasiq said. 'Why would they slowly kill themselves? I mean, I understand slavery, but voluntarily staying a slave is beyond my comprehension. Have you heard of Stockholm Syndrome? Where one falls in love with one's captor? It's kind of twisted, isn't it?'

'That's an exaggeration, Rasiq,' Mandakni said. 'No one is a captor here.'

'Oh, your innocence!' Rasiq said.

'Be civil, Rasiq, please,' Samar said.

Rasiq looked at him with knitted eyebrows and raised his shoulders. 'I am trying to.' He took in a deep breath and turned to Mandakni, 'Money is the captor here. We are all trapped in the prison of money. It forces us to make moral compromises. And the sheer quantity of work that we do! We know that it comes at a heavy price—the price of freedom. It cuts us away from whatever we love—friends, sleep and hobbies. Turns us into zombies. I yearn to be free.'

'Okay,' Mandakni said. She was making notes. 'What else?'

'I thought that would be good enough,' Rasiq said. 'No? Okay then. How about the lack of respect for colleagues?'

'What do you mean by that?'

'I don't want to get into the details, but talent needs to be nurtured with love and care not beaten into shape with a bludgeon. The bosses here are bosses because they have survived this shit for longer than the analysts. They are not leaders. Nothing in their behaviour makes me want to follow them, or look up to them. In fact, I am afraid that I will become like them if I stay here any longer.'

Rasiq took another deep breath. He had never liked a rant. 'Anything else?'

Rasiq shook his head.

'Are you planning to join a competing bank? Do you have an offer from any of them?'

'Have you even been listening?' Rasiq chuckled, more out of shock than amusement. He shook his head.

'We need to be sure,' Mandakni said.

'No,' Rasiq said. 'Can I go now?'

'What are you going to do next?'

'I have been thinking of doing something on my own. I have a vision of a business where everyone likes and respects one another. People help, not play games. They are united by a common mission and passion. They are driven by the desire to make something bigger than each of them. If I am going to be working for 70 to 80 per cent of my waking life, I'd rather create something beautiful.'

'Rasiq, that's not really what you can call a vision. It's barely even a thought. You don't have any idea of what to do next. But what you do have is forty-eight hours to retract your resignation. Post that it will be final,' Mandakni warned.

Rasiq pushed his chair back and stormed out of her cabin, feeling frustrated. Samar followed him.

'People hear only what they want to hear,' Samar said. 'You thought you would pour your heart out, speak with passion and change her mind about the bank?'

Rasiq exhaled deeply.

'It's not that simple,' Samar continued. 'She doesn't get paid to do that.'

'I wonder how I can incentivize her to listen,' Rasiq said. He pulled his hand from his pocket, his fingers making the shape of a gun.

'You didn't lie in your resignation note, buddy. You are a dreamer.' Samar patted Rasiq on the back. 'Come on, let's go get some coffee.'

# 13

# Some endings, thankfully, have a beginning

'What's wrong puttar?' Rasiq's father asked when Rasiq called him.

'Why does something have to be wrong?'

'It's 4.00 p.m. When, in the last two years, have you ever called me at this hour?'

'That's perceptive of you, pops,' Rasiq said.

Silence.

'Are you going to tell me, or do we pay STD charges for being characters in a silent movie?'

'I quit today, dad,' Rasiq blurted.

'Good for you. I've told you thousands of times that it's bad for your health.'

Rasiq had been expecting a massive yelling, but his father was, strangely, being supportive. 'Exactly,' he said. 'I am glad you agree with me!'

'What do you mean I agree? I have been the one telling you to quit,' his father said. 'Don't steal credit away from me by making this your decision.'

'What?' Rasiq said.

'What what? They say it on TV all the time. Smoking is injurious to health. Smoking causes cancer. It makes me worry about you, puttar.'

Rasiq exhaled. It wasn't over. 'I haven't quit smoking, dad.

I quit my job.'

'Oh my god! You quit your job and you are still smoking? How will you pay for the cigarettes now?'

'Dad,' Rasiq said. 'Will you please focus?'

'Puttar, first you focus. What the hell have you done? What made you take such a radical step?'

'I'll be home next month. I'll tell you everything then.'

'Don't come home till you have thought about what you want to do next,' his father raised his voice.

'I can't afford to pay rent here, dad. I need to come home. And I need to do some thinking before deciding what I want to do next.'

'Can't you get a job in the next few days? Just walk into the next office with your degrees, puttar...'

'That's not how it works...' Rasiq said.

'I am a mechanical engineer. I make the bloody things work...' his voice trailed off as he repeated his pet phrase.

He could now hear his mom shouting at his father as she snatched the phone from him. 'Rasiq?' she asked, 'are you alright son?'

'I'm okay, mom.'

'You can come home whenever you want. Don't worry about your father.'

'Thanks, mom. I'll tell you everything once I am home.'

∞

Time moved slowly over the thirty-day notice period and Rasiq started acknowledging the little things that he had been ignoring over the past two years. He left office at 6.00 p.m. every evening and saw the bustling rush of humanity leaving their offices to go home to be with their friends and families. Rasiq couldn't help but wonder if they were also done with only half a workday and would have to don another mask when they got home to tend to other responsibilities—kids' homework, buying groceries, doing repair work on the car or at home. Nobody was ever truly free. But he was. For now. And he was cherishing every minute of it.

But time also stretched infinitely compared to before, and for the first time in a very long time, he did not know what to do with the excess. The uncertain and neglected future looked at him accusingly, but he ignored the package of guilt it was trying to pass him. His generous savings kept the army of worry marching towards his consciousness in check. He knew he would have to confront the demons soon, but now was not the time.

∞

On his last day in Mumbai, after leaving the office for the last time, he sat on the promenade boundary, alone, as he had done on his first day in the city. *Tomorrow will be the first day of the rest of my life, he thought. I will have another chance. Another shot at making something of my life.*

He watched as the sun set. The scene looked almost as beautiful as the dawn of that first day in Mumbai.

'What's up Rasiq?'

He turned to see Gopi, smiling his huge smile with all thirty-two teeth on display.

'It's my last day today, in this city,' Rasiq said.

'You are leaving Mumbai?' Gopi was surprised. He poured him a cutting chai and lit a cigarette for him.

'Yes,' he said. 'Leaving for Delhi tomorrow.'

Gopi nodded. 'People come and go,' he said. 'But Gopi is always here. I love this city too much.'

Rasiq smiled. 'Do you also give free chai and a cigarette to people on their last day?'

'No way, I should charge double, in fact. The penalty for leaving this city of dreams.'

'That's logical,' Rasiq said. He took out his wallet and paid Gopi the money. 'Thank you for these last two years. You were probably the only one who kept me sane in this nightmarish city.'

Gopi took the money and wagged a finger at him. 'Don't say nightmare city,' he said.

'Okay,' Rasiq conceded.

Gopi smiled and extended his hand. With exaggerated emotion, he said, 'I know you are an emotional person at heart, Rasiq, but don't you cry today. We'll meet again for sure. Our story is not over.' He burst out laughing.

Rasiq shook his hand, not feeling awkward about it just this once.

# 14

## The labrarian

*B*ack in Delhi, Rasiq was caught in the whirlwind of his father's disappointment at his seeming abandonment of his race coupled with his apparent aimlessness. The loudest cheerleader of Rasiq's race had become an irritable commentator. He was constantly rooting for his return to the track and not giving up.

Despite having to deal with the incessant pressure from his father, Rasiq was able to get some normalcy back in his life. He caught up with several friends, most of whom he hadn't met in a long time. A week into socializing, he met with a batchmate from IIT Delhi—Nick, aka Sriniketh. Nick believed he was Nikola Tesla in his previous birth. Anyone who thought he was joking and dared to challenge his 'Tesla memories' was given an AC shock from his sharp tongue.

Nick hadn't changed a bit from his college days. He was short and extremely thin. His wiry hair stood on end, giving him what he believed was a nerdy look, but what his friends thought was the result of a severe shock he had received during his experiments in one of his Tesla moments.

Nick had quit his job in the Gulf about a year ago and had moved into a spacious apartment in Vasant Kunj. When Rasiq met him there, he saw books strewn all over the massive hall. Nick gave Rasiq a tour of the other rooms too which had all sorts of equipment—test tubes, beakers, oscilloscopes and some electronic equipment.

'Wow! This is impressive.'

'You think so? My parents feel I never grew beyond school projects.'

'But you're an engineer!'

'Yeah, but since they learnt that I quit my job, they fear I will settle for this labrary of mine permanently.'

'Labrary?'

'I coined the word. It's a combination of laboratory and library,' Nick said.

'Why not a liboratory?' Rasiq smiled.

'I don't know, man. Why not Shafiq?'

'Good point,' Rasiq said.

Nick smiled. 'I read everything I can lay my hands on and the Internet has made my life so much easier. But I still need to read books that elaborate on what's available online. Some things also need practising and experimentation, so I created this lab.'

'Like making bombs?' Rasiq had recognized a few ingredients for homemade bombs in the house.

'Shh,' Nick whispered. 'This is a respectable neighbourhood. They'll throw me out if they find out.'

'How do they not know already?'

'I detonate them in that controlled detonation chamber,' Nick explained. He pointed towards an egg-shaped piece of equipment in a corner of one of the bedrooms. 'I use them for explosive forming of tough metals for my gadgets. That way I get to shape them the way I want, without the use of huge punches or presses and at a fraction of the cost.'

He showed Rasiq some amazingly complex shapes he had created for his gadgets.

'And that's soundproof too?'

'Not entirely,' Nick said with a mischievous smile. 'I play

Nirvana on full blast on my 6.1 speakers to drown out the sound. There's just one constraint. I can conduct my blasts only on Friday and Saturday nights, when a little bit of party noise is tolerated by the residents.'

Rasiq laughed, 'You seem very passionate about your setup. Why don't you do this full-time now? Why are you looking for a job if you love this so much?'

'I wish man. I need cash to keep this set-up going and hence the obnoxious need to slog in silly chemical plants, whoring my chemical engineering degree.'

'Hmm,' Rasiq said. 'Seems like people have to make compromises all the time. I fear that I will have to start making a few soon too.'

'I don't think I have a choice in the matter, man. Anyway, do you want a beer?' Nick had taken a couple of beers out from the fridge and offered one to Rasiq.

'Sure,' Rasiq said. He took the bottle from Nick. 'Got an opener?'

'Yeah,' Nick said. He pulled out his key chain and placed one end on the neck of the bottle and pressed a button. The crown flew off.

'What was that?'

'I made this when I was in Dubai,' Nick said. 'It analyses and identifies the material it touches. Then it sends a shockwave of a calculated frequency to shake off anything sticking to it, without breaking it. I use this to clean my clothes and utensils too.'

'How do you do all this? This is remarkable stuff, Nick!' Rasiq was impressed. They were of the same age, had been to the same college and studied the same courses. Who could say that now? 'You're a mad genius!'

'You mean like Tesla?' Nick grinned.

Rasiq laughed.

'Look, man, I want to absorb all the knowledge I can. The Internet is the most beautiful invention of mankind, I think. I can live the rest of my life on Google and die a happy man,' Nick chuckled. They were a couple of bottles down. 'If it were possible, I would love to be buried in my Dropbox.'

'Yeah, it figures. But how did your job stop you from doing what you love? You could have kept doing these things on the side, right?'

'Yeah, that's what I ended up doing. But I felt like I was living only on the weekends. Working on designing refineries, distillers and plant layouts for ten hours a day, five days a week is a drain,' Nick said. He paused, before asking, 'Anyway, enough about me. You tell me, how have you been? How was IIMA?'

Rasiq told him stories of his time at the IIM and in investment banking.

'Dude,' Nick said. 'You've been a misfit ever since you got back from that exchange programme. Do you remember that incident with Professor Pichhupaani?'

'Which incident?' Rasiq asked.

'Advanced Fluid Mechanics in the third year,' Nick reminded him.

∞

'What are you doing?' Professor Pichhupaani asked Rasiq in his Advanced Fluid Mechanics class. Rasiq had long hair and a variety of bands on his wrists—souvenirs from friends in France.

'I am taking notes, sir,' Rasiq replied. His heart was racing as the professor had singled him out in the class of eighty students.

'No,' the professor declared. 'You are writing poetry.'

'What?' Rasiq was shocked at the arbitrary judgement that had been passed. 'No, I am taking notes,' he repeated earnestly.

'Get out,' the professor thundered.

He rose from his seat, his nostrils flaring. He refused to plead twice. That was his motto in life. That, and to never cower before unreasonable men with unaccountable power.

He strode towards the door of the lecture theatre. On his way, he tore the pages on which he had been writing the day's notes from his notebook and threw them on the ground in front of the professor. 'Check them when you find reason,' he said, as he marched out.

∞

'Hmm,' Rasiq said. 'I'm not sure what was wrong with me back then. But that trend has continued; it's pretty much why I quit my banking job too.'

'I think it's a good thing. It's refreshing to see people speak their minds for a change. Most people just suck up to their professors and bosses for grades and promotions. If you don't speak up against what you know is unjust, unwarranted crap then you continue unhappily and nothing changes. Where's the fun in that? I'd rather not half-ass something, when I can full-ass something else.'

*In or out. Never in-between.*

## 15

## *Immobility fosters serendipity*

'Thirty days and you still do not have a job. Everyone is asking me and I am running out of excuses.'

His dad vented his pent-up frustration at Rasiq's laziness one day by shaking him rudely awake.

Rasiq's cheeks burnt. *Am I supposed to deliver a miracle in thirty days? Why doesn't he let me be? What's his problem? I have done enough work for five years in the past two.*

His mother stormed into the room, 'O ji, you can say anything to those people. Don't trouble him, na! He is already stressed.'

'Stressed? He's been sitting idle! How stressful can that be? Haven't you heard, an idle mind is the devil's playground?'

'That's a misleading cliché, pops,' Rasiq said. 'An idle mind is an ideal workshop. Once all the clutter is gone, it will start working…'

'If you don't even have the desire to get a job, then how will you get one? It won't come as a nut from the blue,' his dad said, cutting him off.

'It's bolt, pops,' Rasiq replied wearily.

'Well you are a nut then. You are not even trying to get a job. I have seen all those classmates of yours. They…they look like rickshaw drivers compared to you. And look where they are. And you rot in your bed. Update your CV and start mailing it out. You'll have a job like this,' he snapped his fingers.

'How does it matter what my classmates look like?'

'You are not listening to me. As you sow, so shall you reap. Start sowing, or you'll starve when winter comes.'

Rasiq rose from his bed and threw his phone against the wall. 'I have had enough of your platitudes,' he shouted. 'Stop irritating me! I'll do what I think is right, when I think it's the right time.'

Furious, he picked up his bike keys, stormed out of the house and drove away.

'I told you not to keep pushing him all the time,' his mother said. 'What if something happens to him? Look at how rashly he's driving!'

They watched Rasiq take a turn at a dangerous speed.

∽

Rasiq drove like a mad man through the streets of Delhi. He had expected his father to understand his state of mind, but it had been more than a month of constant nagging and pressure. His father had refused to keep an open mind, turning a deaf ear to Rasiq's thousands of attempts at explaining his decision. Angry tears started flowing from his eyes, impairing his vision.

Rasiq saw a puppy make a dash across the road right in front of his bike. He swerved to avoid a collision, lost control of the bike and skidded into the pavement at great speed. Rasiq flew off the bike and crashed into the windshield of a car coming down the opposite side. He felt a sudden rush of adrenalin. *Is it from the fear of death? Or the excitement from the stunt?* He blacked out before he could decide.

∽

Rasiq couldn't think much over the next few days as he was in a drug-induced sleep at the hospital. He would wake up every once in a while, only to lose his fight against sleep.

When his painkillers were finally stopped, he gradually began to think clearly. He still couldn't move much of his plaster-encased body, and replays of the accident kept flashing through his mind. He closed his eyes, wishing them away.

*Oh god, what a mess I have made! I have been mummified while still alive.*

*What was I thinking? Why did I behave so rashly? Dad will no doubt be taking this very hard. Why did I fight with him? I have been too lazy for too long now. I have to get my life back on track...*

After a long time, he felt his brain shifting gears. It was no longer idling. It was a strange sensation—definitely a happy one. Had he finally destressed?

*Some idiots need to be literally jolted back into action!*

∽

As they completed the discharge formalities at the hospital, Rasiq sat up in his bed with some difficulty. His father's insurance had covered a part of the expenses. The remaining expenses, however, had put a considerable dent in his savings.

'Nothing happens without a reason,' he said. 'There's always an opportunity, even in a calamity.'

'Spoken like the son we know,' his father said. He gave him a hug. 'Dare to be an optimist because anyone can be a pessimist.'

Rasiq and his mom rolled their eyes. 'We can go on like this for days, pops—speaking in clichés!'

His father laughed. 'But now we know what to do when you are feeling low the next time.'

'What is that?' Rasiq asked.

'We are going to have to literally throw you under the bus,' he said.

Rasiq's eyes welled up. His father smiled. An unsaid apology was exchanged between the two of them.

'Let's get out of this hole-spit-all now,' his father joked to suppress his tears.

∽

'How did I get to the hospital?' Rasiq asked on their way home.

'Some stranger called the ambulance,' his mother recalled. 'God bless him!' She joined her hands in a silent prayer.

'No way of knowing how long you lay unconscious,' his father relived the ordeal of that day.

Rasiq pressed his head to the car's window and watched the road.

'What about the bike, pops?' Rasiq remembered on seeing one. 'Is it alright?'

'Don't worry about it. It's still in the workshop. The insurance will cover most of the repairs, so it shouldn't cost you much. But I'll sell it as soon as we get it back.'

'Why? I won't drive like that again, pops. I'll be careful.'

'It's not entirely your fault, puttar,' his father said. 'These two-wheeled motorized cycles are not safe at all. It's surprising that they are even allowed to be built. They go super fast and there is not much one can do to save the people riding them if there's an accident.'

'I promise to be careful, pops. I won't drive fast or recklessly ever again. Please don't sell it!'

His mother nudged his father. 'Don't start arguing with him again, please.'

'All right,' his father relented. 'But remember, your safety is your responsibility. It's nobody else's business.'

'Wait!' Rasiq said. 'What?'

'What what?'

'The business of safety,' Rasiq said.

'No,' his father said. 'That's not what I said.'

'I know,' Rasiq's voice held a hint of mischief. 'But I think it would be cool to make a business of safety.'

'Definitely no business in safety,' his father said. 'You can't sell safety to Indians. They break all the traffic laws meant to keep them safe. If you try that you'll end up selling softy!' he started laughing.

'That doesn't make sense,' Rasiq said.

'It does to me,' his father continued laughing.

Rasiq just shook his head. *There's something here*, he thought. *Is there a business opportunity?*

# Part Two

........................................

## Beyond the Horizon

## 16

## *One year later...*

*R*asiq sat staring out of the window of the van in which he was travelling with a group of people he had painstakingly handpicked for his start-up. He had a satisfied smile on his face as he recalled the hardships of the past year. *It doesn't seem like hardship though*, Rasiq thought. *It was a labour of love.* He felt a sense of fulfilment for having put an exceptionally talented team together. As they travelled for their first client pitch, he was filled with a hope that the idea for their start-up would create a paradigm shift.

*That's not nothing*, he thought. *It's already more than what I accomplished while working at the bank.* He wondered how many good ideas die in the minds of brilliant people because they are too scared to let go of what they are holding on to.

He also felt fortunate to have this group of people believe in his idea. He had promised each member of the team an equal partnership if the start-up took off. He had resisted the temptation of raising funds from angel investors and venture capitalists who need quick value creation through rapid scale-up for a return on their investment. He wanted to ensure control over the operations and the pace of expansion.

Rasiq had taken the help of one of his professors at IIM Ahmedabad to schedule a meeting with the founder of Ashutosh Industries, a medium-sized conglomerate. The company's office was on the outskirts of Gurgaon and his dad had got them a second-hand minivan for local commute through his contacts.

Rasiq's attention turned to the conversation in the van.

'What are you thinking?' Natasha, one of his team members, asked another. She had been Rasiq's senior in school and was an avid sportswoman. She had reigned supreme at the state junior level in athletics and gymnastics. The daredevil who loved adventure had become an acclaimed stuntwoman in Bollywood. She was as tall as Rasiq, but slightly more muscular in build. Despite her standing in the industry, she nursed a hurt, not from the many injuries she had sustained while executing stunts for Bollywood heroines, but an emotional one. The grave, personal risks she took to add thrill to films as a body double had doubled the fame of the heroines but had done little to bring her out of the shadows.

'I was wondering if we would get enough business,' said Arjun, the sharpshooter in the team. He was tall at six feet, and lean in build, just like the streamlined arrows he shot. Rasiq had hired him on Natasha's recommendation. The sportsman hailed from Chakrata near Dehradun, where he made a living as a tour guide. Arjun was an ace at archery and shooting. Initially, Rasiq wasn't sure if they needed a sharpshooter since they were a rescue team, not an attack team. But Natasha had explained a few accident scenarios to Rasiq where having a sharpshooter would be an asset. When they had approached Arjun, his sole ambition had been to use his skill to win international competitions and medals for his country. He had relented when Rasiq was able to convince him that the work he would be involved in would be no less prestigious and worthy.

'Of course, we will have enough business. What are you talking about?' Halka, who was driving the van, said to Arjun, looking at him in the rear-view mirror. Halka was a bodyguard by training. He had been fired from his job for falling in love with the daughter of the owner of his security company. His employer was vicious, powerful and influential and had ensured that Halka became an outcast in the high-paying profession. Halka had been relegated to doing odd jobs and was a drifter when Rasiq had met him at the workshop where his bike was being repaired after his accident. He was freakishly strong and Rasiq had seen him lift a car with his bare hands to rescue a fellow mechanic stuck under it at the workshop.

'I mean,' Arjun wondered, 'do that many accidents happen in the country?'

'I know for a fact that plenty of accidents happen on a daily basis,' MD Vyom, who was sitting in the front seat of the van next to Halka, turned and said. 'Very few of them result in deaths, but rescue would be needed in a lot of these cases.'

The oldest member of the group, MD Vyom was beginning to bald from worry on account of his failed medical practice. Despite being able to simply read the symptoms of his patients to arrive at the perfect diagnosis without elaborate tests, or maybe because of it, MD Vyom found the scepticism of his patients bewildering. He would be irritated when they insisted on complicated tests and elaborate prescriptions because his conscience didn't allow him to over-treat them. The patients for their part, however, seemed to equate caring with a doctor fussing about them. His abrasive behaviour coupled with his quirky methods, put off his patients and his practice dwindled.

Rasiq with his keen observation didn't miss how quick, accurate and confident the doctor was. MD Vyom had overruled Rasiq's dad's worry that he might have appendicitis, purely based on his symptoms. He was sure it was a bout of gas, despite the severity of the pain. Rasiq's father had called him a freak, convinced that he was a bad doctor. He had checked into a super-specialty hospital where, after spending a lot of money on an ultrasound and an MRI, MD Vyom's diagnosis had been proved correct. To Rasiq, MD Vyom's skill seemed almost like a supernatural gift.

MD Vyom insisted on everyone addressing him with the prefix 'MD'. He did this to remind himself of the dead weight of his doctor's degree, which hadn't gotten him anything apart from misery.

'Let's work out a quick estimate,' Rasiq said. 'Assuming everyone has just one accident in their lives and given the average life expectancy of sixty-six years, 1.32 billion people will have 1.32 billion accidents in sixty-six years. That's...' Rasiq paused briefly, 'approximately twenty million accidents each year in this country.'

The number met with a collective gasp.

'That's about 55,000 accidents every day. And 2,300 accidents every hour. That's close to forty accidents every minute.'

'Sounds about right,' Nick said. 'I just pulled this stat from Google, which says there are four deaths due to road accidents alone every minute.'

'Forty accidents every minute!' Natasha whistled.

'But that's for the entire country,' Halka said. 'Will our operations be pan-India?'

'I hope so,' Rasiq said. 'Eventually. But we will start with Delhi and NCR.'

'A population of eighteen million means more than one accident every two minutes,' Nick spoke quickly to beat Rasiq to the math.

'That's a lot of work,' Natasha said.

# 17

## *Showtime!*

'What do you want?' the executive assistant to the managing director of Ashutosh Industries asked. *The rude question that every salesman dreads*, Rasiq thought, feeling a little hurt even though he was half expecting it when they walked in.

Rasiq told him about the team's meeting with the managing director, and the assistant gave him a 'do I have to suffer you' look as he checked the calendar. He gestured them to follow him and took them to their meeting.

As they were seated in a big conference room, Rasiq quietly observed Ashutosh Rana, the managing director of Ashutosh Industries. The plump, forty-something man with ruddy cheeks was busy with a sumptuous meal laid out in front of him in the conference room. He ate alone, noisily and with relish, seemingly oblivious to their presence.

Despite his professor's contacts, this was one of the very few companies that had agreed to meet them. *And here I was thinking that I would never have to worry about being treated like shit. How naive of me!*

After about five minutes, Rasiq felt like leaving. The memory of how he had behaved with the salesmen at the Harley Davidson showroom when he had bought his bike came back to him. It helped sober his rising anger. *He wields the power today, and I am the salesman trying to sell a brand that doesn't even have any perceived value; at least not yet.*

'Aren't you going to speak?' Ashutosh finally broke the long silence. 'You have only twenty minutes left now.'

'Oh,' Rasiq said. 'I didn't realize...'

'What?'

'Nothing,' Rasiq said. 'We wanted to talk about safety solutions for you and your employees.'

'We already have safety consultants. What's their name, Gupta ji?'

'G-Force, sir,' the executive assistant said.

Halka stirred in his seat, visibly discomfited at the mention of the name.

'We are offering something different, Mr Ashutosh,' Rasiq said.

'How is it different?' Ashutosh enquired, looking up. He didn't stop feasting on the food.

'Let's start with the demo, Nick,' Rasiq said.

Nick quickly set up his laptop for the presentation; a basic-looking console titled 'ARA' flashed on the projection screen.

'What's ARA?' Ashutosh asked.

'Accident Rescue Alert,' Nick said. He then took out a remote-controlled car from his bag and placed it on the conference table. The car had a small black box mounted on its roof. 'This is the ARA device that we've developed in-house.'

Rasiq cleared his throat loudly to hurry Nick along.

'To the magic now,' Nick said. He picked up a remote. The car began to move forward to the edge of the table where it tipped and crashed to the floor.

A shrill alarm went off for a couple of seconds from the car and then stopped. A second later, an alarm went off on Nick's laptop. On the screen, Ashutosh could see an alert notification with the GPS coordinates of the car. A window had also opened up in which a video was playing. They could now see inside the remote-controlled car.

'This ARA device enables us to automatically detect any accident your company's vehicles might meet. Our 24×7 rescue team will then respond immediately, even before any ambulance can,' Nick said.

'You will also have an emergency helpline number and an app with an SOS button that will activate the alarm in our office. The SOS button or post-accident automatic activation of the ARA device will turn on our cameras. The live relay will enable us to mount a quick and efficient rescue operation,' Rasiq added.

'That's quite impressive, guys. Great job with the technology. Now, can you tell me how this helps me? We already have fire alarms and a safety and security consultant,' Ashutosh informed.

Rasiq pulled up an impressive-looking graph. 'The majority of deaths happen because the ambulance reaches the accident site too late,' Rasiq said. 'The first hour is critical to survival. It is called the golden hour. The victims lose their chance of survival or speedy recovery if they reach the hospital beyond this critical hour. Even if they are not fatal, unattended injuries can result in complications that might need expensive treatment. You can save more than 50 per cent of lives and drastic complications by using our services.'

'I still don't see how this will help me,' Ashutosh wondered.

'You'll save a lot of money on the accident allowance that your company has to pay to your employees,' Nick intervened. He understood that the man did not care about the lives of his employees. But it was clear he cared about money. 'Besides, man-hours lost translate into production losses and hence monetary losses.'

'Rasiq,' Nick said, 'can you pull up slide seventeen of the deck?'

Rasiq did and Nick demonstrated that Ashutosh Industries had paid out close to three crore to their employees and their families due to casualties, deaths and injuries over the past three years.

Ashutosh stopped eating and began listening intently.

'And this does not include the efficiency losses to your business from the longer than necessary recovery time of the victims. Like hiring a replacement, training them, et cetera. We are here to help you crunch the time from the accident to the hospital to recovery. If we promptly rescue your employees from the accidents, the casualties could be averted or at least be less severe,' Rasiq said. 'If you can save even a third of that payout, you'll recover our fees.'

'And trust us,' Natasha pitched in, 'we'll help you save much more than a third.'

'All right,' Ashutosh conceded. 'It seems like a sound investment. Do you have any clients yet? What is the scale of your operations?'

Everyone smiled. They were making headway!

'Not yet,' Rasiq said. 'But we were hoping to start operations soon. In fact, as soon as we are able to sign up clients.'

'In that case you should come to me when you have a business infrastructure ready.'

'But we can roll out the service in a matter of days, Mr Ashutosh. All you need to do is tell us how many company-owned and personal vehicles you need the device for, and we will manufacture the required number,' Rasiq said.

'See Mr Rasiq,' Ashutosh said, 'I have a big company to manage. You'll understand that I can't give a guarantee, much less sign a contract, without evaluating your service competency. And you haven't even started yet. I can't let you use Ashutosh Industries as a proof of concept. So generate that proof elsewhere.

While you do that, we are not going anywhere. We can discuss your engagement with Ashutosh Industries then.'

Rasiq was crestfallen. Although they hadn't expected to sign up Ashutosh Industries on the first visit, this was a clear dead end.

'Now if you'll excuse me...' Ashutosh continued.

'Just a few more minutes, Mr Ashutosh,' Rasiq interjected. He looked at his watch. They did have five more minutes. 'There's a little more to what we can do.'

His team members stared at him. They knew Rasiq was going to try and wing something because they were at the end of the pitch that they had rehearsed.

'We have a specialized team and each member possesses a unique talent,' Rasiq continued. 'We are far more capable than an ambulance service.'

'Why do I need that?' Ashutosh shrugged.

'We can carry out rescue missions that wouldn't be ordinarily possible. We will offer the standard doctors and ambulances, firefighters and fire engines, et cetera. But with us you also get this core team of best in class rescuers—a brilliant doctor, a daredevil, a sharpshooter, a weightlifter and an inventor,' Rasiq said.

'Don't forget a strategist for planning the operations,' Natasha chimed in, for Rasiq.

'Can you give me an example?' Ashutosh looked intrigued.

Rasiq swallowed hard, trying to mask his nervousness. His next words could either hook this glutton or end the meeting.

'In Los Angeles, two brothers decided to remove a beehive from a shed on their property with the aid of a small detonator. They ignited the fuse and retreated to watch from inside their home, behind a window, some ten feet away from the nest. The explosion blew the nest but it also shattered the window and the younger brother was seriously lacerated by the flying shards of glass. The elder brother took him outside to rush him to a hospital. But while walking towards the car, he was stung by the surviving bees. He was allergic to bee venom and died on the way to the hospital while the younger brother, bleeding profusely, couldn't help him.'

'Did that actually happen or did you just dream that up?' Ashutosh asked, sounding sceptical.

'It's a real incident,' Rasiq assured him. 'There are many freak accidents where a mission-oriented force of specialized operatives could have saved the day. That's what we offer.'

'That is freaky,' Ashutosh relented. 'I have to give you that. But what would you have done to help?'

'If they had registered for our services, our sensors would have been installed in their house,' Rasiq said. 'The explosion would have triggered our alarm. If not, they could have used the SOS switch to intimate us.'

'A simple anti-allergen, which most ambulances carry, could have saved the elder brother's life,' MD Vyom added.

'Mr Ashutosh, this is MD Vyom. He can diagnose any ailment without the aid of complex tests. He would have known exactly what was wrong with the elder brother just by looking at the video feed even if the younger one was in no position to narrate the incident.'

'You are making the doctor sound freakier than the accident, Rasiq,' Ashutosh chuckled. 'But if this is true, can you tell me what disease I have, doctor?'

MD Vyom panicked. He did not like being put on the spot like that. He stared at Rasiq in stunned silence.

'Go on. Substantiate your claim,' Ashutosh goaded him.

Rasiq nodded encouragingly at MD Vyom. *You can do this*, he thought with his heart racing.

The doctor stood up slowly and walked up to Ashutosh. 'May I?'

'Of course.'

He examined Ashutosh's hands, checked his pulse, then his hands moved to his chest and stomach and lastly his back.

'You have a thyroid problem, a fatty liver and mild onset of hypertension and diabetes.'

Ashutosh raised his eyebrows. 'Diabetes? You got that one wrong doctor. But the rest is correct. That was impressive. How did you do that?'

'The skin of your hands is dry and cracked. Your nails are brittle. Your hands are cold and your body temperature is below 98.5 degrees. That indicates hypothyroidism,' MD Vyom was speaking fast because of the adrenalin rush. Or maybe it was because of the little boost that his confidence had received. 'It was also easy to confirm because there's a minor inflammation in your neck.'

Ashutosh pursed his lips and nodded. 'Go on.'

'The veins under the skin of your hands are enlarged,' MD Vyom continued, 'and your palms are bright red. And sorry about this last one, but those things together with your man breasts imply a fatty liver.'

Ashutosh blushed slightly but nodded. 'Too much drinking. What else?'

'Hypertension is typically symptomless, but given your higher than normal pulse rate, the cigarette stains on your middle and index fingers, and the fatty liver coupled with the obesity, it was quite likely that you suffer from it.'

'What are you? The Sherlock Holmes of medical diagnosis?' Ashutosh remarked after a long pause. He seemed genuinely surprised.

MD Vyom merely shrugged before continuing, 'Do you need to pee very frequently, Mr Ashutosh?'

'Yes,' Ashutosh conceded, 'It started only a few days back. Why?'

'Your body is trying to get rid of the excess, unabsorbed glucose from your bloodstream. The way you have been eating since we entered this room and the amount of water you have had clearly indicates diabetes, Mr Ashutosh. I would suggest getting your sugar levels tested ASAP and starting medication.'

Ashutosh was taken aback. He gestured to his secretary to make a note and remind him later. He cleared his throat. 'That's good work, doctor. I'll get tested for sure. Thank you.'

'Mr Ashutosh, we are offering our services only in Delhi and NCR for now…' Rasiq started, but was prevented from completing the sentence.

A man burst into the conference room and ran up to Ashutosh. He whispered something in his ear. Ashutosh's eyes widened in horror.

'I don't believe this… Are you sure?'

The man nodded.

Ashutosh turned to face Rasiq and his team. 'It seems we have a situation for you,' he said. 'Our COO, Vinay, has to present a proposal to a multinational corporate in the next few minutes. Trouble is that he is in the restroom with his thing stuck in his zip.' Ashutosh pointed towards his groin.

Halka grimaced at the thought.

'Is that freakish enough for you?' Ashutosh continued, a look of worry on his face.

'Can't we postpone the presentation, or ask someone else to do it?' the employee asked Ashutosh.

'No. These clients have flown in from Europe and they are here just for today. No presentation means no business,' Ashutosh emphasized. 'But, it seems we have a team of specialists with us. This is critical for me,' he added. Then he turned to face

Rasiq. 'And for you!'

They ran towards the men's room. Natasha waited outside, on standby.

A tense-looking man ran up to Ashutosh. 'The doctor is advising surgery. Should I call the ambulance?'

'Give these guys a chance,' Ashutosh said. He gestured for the team to step in and handle the situation.

Vinay was doubled over, sobbing in pain.

'Can you please bring the first aid kit?' MD Vyom asked a young employee.

'My call, MD Vyom!' Nick jumped ahead of the doctor.

He bent to inspect Vinay's open fly and began to work on the zip with a Swiss Army knife lookalike that had far more attachments than the original.

'Just hold on.... This is easy.... There you go...'

There was the sound of a click.

Nick turned triumphantly to face the crowd that had gathered in the large restroom. He held up the slider of the zipper.

'How did you do that?' Ashutosh asked. 'I thought a medical procedure was the only option.'

'The doctors approach the problem like, well, doctors,' Nick said. His tone was cocky. 'No offence, MD Vyom, but sometimes the solution lies outside the box—in looking at problems like an engineer.'

The first aid kit had arrived and MD Vyom examined Vinay's injury. He treated the bruise quickly.

'Just a minor abrasion. This antiseptic and painkiller will see you through the presentation but you should go to a hospital after. How are you feeling Vinay?'

'Much better,' Vinay said. 'Thank you, doctor. And thank you, engineer! I gotta go. The client must be waiting for the presentation.'

'That was brilliant. I think I understand what you meant when you said you had a skilled team,' Ashutosh said. They were back in the conference room. 'You showcased a freak doctor and a freak engineer on the same day. You know what? I want to write you a cheque!'

Their faces brightened with hope.

'Ahem…' Rasiq interjected, 'If you are satisfied enough to pay for what we did, I would like you to consider us for a retainer. It will work out much cheaper in the long run.'

'You are right, I guess. That was a good demonstration of what you guys can do,' Ashutosh said. He was amazed at what had happened. 'Schedule a meeting with my operations team. I will ask Vinay to personally have a discussion with you.'

'That would be perfect,' Rasiq said. 'We can come back in a day or two, whenever he has a few hours to spare.'

'Now, now,' Ashutosh said. 'Why are you young people always in such a hurry? Have patience. These things take time. Let's see when… ummm...' he looked at his calendar. 'Next month, same date. You may contact Vinay directly.'

'Sure, Mr Ashutosh. We look forward to meeting your team next month.' Rasiq rose to leave, followed by the rest of the team.

Ashutosh went back to eating his meal after they left.

# 18

## Dream run

*T*hey did not get any breaks in the weeks that followed. Very few corporates agreed to meet them and most of them told them politely that they would think about their proposal. They either had tie-ups with local hospitals or turned out to be clients of G-Force.

'Are you sure we have something worthwhile to offer here? Or does it look good only in our heads because it is our idea?' Natasha asked the uncomfortable question as they drove home silently after yet another fruitless meeting. The idleness of the past few weeks was fuelling their fears and insecurities.

'All entrepreneurs face these dry spells, Natasha. We will need to have a stronger spine than one that begins to hurt in the first month of being on the road with our start-up,' Rasiq's expression was grim.

'Irrespective of people's opinion, just for a moment forget today and the difficulties we are facing. What does your heart say? Do you think we have a good idea or do you feel we got carried away with it?' Nick asked.

'I feel it in my fingers, I feel it in my toes,' Halka sang the lyrics of the song.

Rasiq smiled.

'If you have faith and you know it, clap your hands and show it!' Nick joined.

They all clapped in a show of enthusiasm.

'Watch out Halka! You're driving. We don't want us to be our first case!' Arjun warned.

The laughter dissipated their tension. Even if it was only slightly. And even if it was only temporarily.

∽

On the appointed day, the team was back at the office of Ashutosh Industries.

'I have a feeling that they are just playing with us. He was not serious about it,' Halka voiced his doubts as they were walking towards Vinay's office.

'Save the doomsday prediction. We will know one way or the other in the next hour,' Nick said.

They were made to wait for over two hours at the reception before Vinay met them.

'I am extremely sorry, but I have to go. It's a very busy day and I regret cancelling the appointment at the last minute. Can you come back a few days later? Say two weeks from now?'

'So, the tenth of next month?' Rasiq asked, looking at the calendar on his phone.

'Yes, suits me,' Vinay said.

'How did your meeting with that foreign client go?' Natasha asked. She braved a smile despite Vinay's delaying tactic.

'Oh, didn't Mr Rana tell you? We won the contract. Thanks to you! And now will you excuse me?'

They left the office in silence.

∽

More than four months had passed since the incident with the zipper and they were visiting Ashutosh Industries for the seventh time. Although they did not want to make yet another pointless trek out to the company's offices, Ashutosh Industries was the only client that was giving them appointments, even if they kept cancelling and postponing.

'He's toying with us,' Arjun punched the air in frustration as they were once again made to wait at the reception.

'We know that. But do we have anything better to do? Our appointment diary is empty,' Rasiq smiled wanly as he banged the back of his head on the wall behind the bench in the reception area. He looked at the now familiar ceiling without much hope.

'It's shameful, the way they are treating us. Especially after what we did for them. At least he could have paid for that single instance if he doesn't want to employ our services,' MD Vyom said.

'He is trying to wear us out. Testing our patience. He wants us to give up so he can sleep with a clear conscience. Convince himself that he was fair,' Halka said.

'Guys, let's be realistic about the number of trips we are willing to make here. I mean, we can't become like the furniture of this office. We should search for business elsewhere or think of a new strategy. And if nothing works, we need to take the tough call of closing down this business and going back to whatever we were doing before. I bet anything would be better than this humiliation we are facing,' Natasha rose in anger.

'Not true,' Halka said.

'I agree,' Arjun echoed his thought.

'We are doing all we can. Talking to friends, visiting their companies. Networking for contacts. But nothing is happening. We are not getting the break we so desperately need,' Rasiq grumbled. 'But you are right. Three more visits and we will give up chasing this guy. Let's lock that.'

'I'm hungry. Let's eat at the canteen. At least their food is decent, even if they themselves are not,' MD Vyom suggested, more to get his mind off the topic. He could not bear to go back to his gloomy clinic.

They went through the charade of informing the receptionist that they were going to the canteen. 'If Mr Vinay returns from his visit to the plant, please call us. We will be back here within five minutes,' Rasiq said. He gave her his card and left.

The receptionist nodded as she picked up her phone, which had begun to ring.

'As if she is ever going to call you!' Nick said. 'I bet that call is from Vinay asking her if we have left. I suspect he is inside and waiting for us to leave, like always.'

'Don't spoil my appetite,' Halka growled.

They were halfway through their half-hearted lunch—with the exception of Halka who was gorging on the food—when Rasiq's phone buzzed.

'Hello?'

'Please come to the reception immediately. It's urgent!'

They left their lunch and broke into a run. In less than forty-five seconds they were at the reception. The receptionist was pacing, waiting for them.

'Follow me!' She led them in through the doors that had always seemed closed to them.

∽

They were shocked when they entered Mr Rana's office. In front of the glutton was spread a huge buffet, exactly like the last time they had met him. On his plate was an unfinished fish. And Ashutosh Rana was gesticulating wildly, unable to breathe, his face blood red and his eyes bulging. He reached for his throat with his hands and gripped it as he struggled for breath. He was squirming restlessly in his chair. He tried to say something to them, but all that emerged was a whistle. No words.

'He is choking,' MD Vyom said.

'I have called emerg…' Vinay barged into the room. He stopped when he saw them. Their suspicion was right. He had been at the office all this time but had been avoiding the meeting. However, this was not the time to think about how the company was treating them; Ashutosh would certainly choke to death if they did not intervene.

'Halka, can you please turn him upside down?' MD Vyom said.

'With pleasure,' Halka said. He grabbed Ashutosh by his ankles and raised him up in the air, upside down, as nonchalantly as if he were holding a grocery bag.

'Give him a smack on his back,' MD Vyom said.

Halka was barely able to conceal his grin as he struck Ashutosh's back. The fish bone stuck in his throat flew out in a parabolic trajectory and landed on his desk. Halka set him back down in his chair.

'What the… freak!' Ashutosh exclaimed once he had caught his breath. His face was red and he massaged his throat as he stared at Halka in awe. Ashutosh was no small man—given his appetite, he had swelled to 110 kilogramme and Halka had picked him up as if he was an iPad mini.

A crowd had gathered when they had heard the panicked receptionist's cry for help. They started clapping.

Ashutosh withdrew a cheque book from his drawer and quietly wrote a cheque. 'I don't care when you roll out your services officially. Consider this an advance. Please send me the contract when you draw it up. And fill in your name and the amount in words on this cheque yourself. I need to rest.'

Dazed by the sudden and unexpected developments, Rasiq took the cheque from Ashutosh and looked at it in disbelief.

He counted the zeroes twice to be sure. *One crore!*

'Is this the fairy tale turning point we have heard of so many times?' Arjun asked once they were in their van.

'I don't know about fairy tales,' Rasiq said, 'but it did seem like we needed six runs to win on the last ball of the last over and the opposition bowled a half-volley. Of course, we were going to hit a six!'

'But rather than the end of the match, this is the beginning of our innings. Getting off the mark is the hardest thing to do—ask any batsman—and we have managed that. Now we need to play cautiously, rotate the strike and wait for the loose deliveries to hit our shots,' Natasha added.

'That was miraculous, though. Two one-in-a-million incidents happened one after the other at the same company, just when we were beginning to lose hope. What is the probability of such a thing?' MD Vyom asked.

'I don't know, but I am sure Ashutosh would say that it's "freakishly low",' Nick mimicked Ashutosh.

'Yeah,' Arjun said, 'I don't like that he keeps calling us freaks. Ever since Rasiq mentioned that freak accident with the bees, it's as if he looks at us and the word "freak" flashes in his head.'

'Maybe we should call ourselves the Freak Accident Rescue Team. You know what? That's FART!' Arjun burst out into an uncontrollable laughter.

Halka started laughing too, just looking at Arjun doubling over and added, 'FART: we come before shit happens!'

Natasha, MD Vyom and Rasiq too joined them. They were delirious with the happiness of their first big win.

'Guys,' Nick said, not amused, 'if we are done with the toilet humour, can you seriously tell me what name you want on this cheque before it expires? I also need to register the company and these things take time.'

'Okay, okay,' Rasiq said, pulling himself together. 'How about DareDreamers?'

'Why?' MD Vyom was intrigued.

'I have been told time and again that I am an idealist and a dreamer. And since I am a waking dreamer, I've been accused of being a daydreamer too. But I don't daydream. I dare to dream. That makes me a DareDreamer. And just think about it, how did your individual talent come about? Because you all dared to dream bigger than most. That's what makes each of you special.'

'DareDreamers Private Limited,' Nick said, out loud. 'I like the sound of that.'

'It's settled then,' Natasha said. 'DareDreamers it is.'

'I am a DareDreamer!' Halka said, thumping his chest.

'I am a DareDreamer!' the others said in unison.

∞

Backed by the Ashutosh Industries contract, the DareDreamers began setting up their operations. This included finding a suitable office space to lease, setting up their rescue teams and identifying a company to mass manufacture their Accident Rescue Alert device prototype.

They bought two life-support ambulances and a fire engine. MD Vyom fitted the ambulances with all the life-saving equipment he thought was necessary for advanced rescue operations. They hired three nurses and three drivers for each ambulance to work in eight-hour shifts each. The fire engine had a driver and four ace firefighters for every shift. In parallel, Nick completed the development of their website and started doing social media-based marketing for DareDreamers. Rasiq called in a favour from a batchmate from IIM Ahmedabad who had his own telemarketing start-up and they got a good deal to run their promotions for a couple of months.

They also placed advertisements in newspapers for the request for proposals to manufacture the accident alert device. Several manufacturers responded to the bid. Nick met with them all to explain the prototype, now patented by DareDreamers. They finally inked a deal with VisionIT, a company set up by bright youngsters like them.

'Why don't we go with the more established brands? We have the resources to do so,' Natasha wondered when they were shortlisting the company.

'Because other start-ups need an opportunity to prove themselves too, Natasha,' MD Vyom said. 'Much like we did. Ashutosh Industries could have ignored us too because we weren't an established name.'

'They almost did,' Halka grunted. 'We earned it, didn't we?'

'It's not just that,' Rasiq intervened. 'Ours is the first big contract for these guys. They'll be dedicated because they are hungry for business. Their attention and focus can make a huge difference for us.'

Halka nodded.

When it came to finalizing an office space, however, they hadn't found anything that they all liked and so they continued to operate out of Nick's apartment in Vasant Kunj. While their search for a home for DareDreamers continued, they had an operational start-up—a firm that they could call their home away from home.

# 19

## One's gain, another's pain

*R*akeysh Aurora was not in the best state of mind when he got out of his Jaguar that day. Normally, he would savour the effect that his car, his diamond-studded watch, his gold-plated phone and his custom-made Armani suit had on people, but not today. For a change, there was something else on his mind, not his usual unadulterated and unapologetic self-congratulatory thoughts.

As the Chairman and CEO of G-Force, he had run a successful business in providing safety and security solutions to business houses and corporates all over the country. His company was the biggest name in the space and had grown steadily over the twenty-five years since he had set it up. For a sixty-year-old, he was very active and in remarkably good health.

As he entered the offices of Ashutosh Industries, the executive assistant came running to greet him and escorted him to Ashutosh's office. Even though he was a service provider and Ashutosh Industries was his client, Rakeysh had an aura about him that commanded respect. He called it the 'Aurora Aura'.

∞

'Hello Mr Aurora,' Ashutosh said as he stood up to greet him.

Rakeysh took off his shades slowly, folded them and took

Ashutosh's extended hand. 'Hi,' he said with an authority that came naturally to him.

'Welcome to my office,' Ashutosh said.

Rakeysh settled into his chair.

'You sounded worried on the phone. What can I do for you?'

'Worried,' Rakeysh smiled. 'I am not worried, Mr Rana. I came here to understand from you if you are satisfied with our service.'

'Of course, Mr Aurora,' Ashutosh said. 'We are more than happy with your exceptional services. No reason to complain. I would have called if there was any reason to worry.'

'But I heard a disturbing bit of news,' Rakeysh said.

'I am sorry, but I don't understand.'

'I learnt that you recently signed a contract for safety services with another firm?'

'Oh, that!' Ashutosh's laugh started casually but quickly turned into a giggle when his eyes met the stern gaze of Rakeysh Aurora. He gathered himself, 'That's got nothing to do with your services, Mr Aurora. They are just some new kids on the block with a different proposition.'

'Kids?' Rakeysh had tried but failed to get any details about his new competition. 'What is it that they are offering that G-Force couldn't?' He had a lot of difficulty in keeping the irritation out of his voice.

'Accident rescue services,' Ashutosh said.

'But we also have accident services included in the package that you have availed,' Rakeysh reminded him. 'What was the need to hire these guys on top of that?'

'You do?' Ashutosh was genuinely surprised. 'I wasn't aware of that. What did your company do when accidents happened at Ashutosh Industries in the last three years? They have cost us more than three crore!' His tone, measured now, had just a hint of aggression.

'Mr Rana,' Rakeysh said, trying to be calm, 'someone has to contact us in the event of an accident. The helpline numbers are displayed on the windshields of all of your vehicles. For worker accident response, we have shared our helpline number with your operations team. Once we get information on an accident, we offer a complete solution post that. No one contacted us regarding the accidents that took place in your company.'

'Oh,' Ashutosh said. 'It's unfortunate that the accident victims couldn't call your helpline.'

Rakeysh was finding it difficult to hide the edge in his voice. 'How will these guys do any better?' he asked.

'Look, Mr Aurora. It's not my job to explain the business model of your competitors to you. I am not revoking your contract so I don't see the cause of worry that brought you here.'

'But it can't be just that,' Rakeysh persisted. 'You signed a significant contract with them.'

'Yes, and they are selling themselves cheap, if you ask me. They saved my life and our COO from being castrated while they were here.' He let out a short laugh. 'They showcased the brilliance of their service twice in a matter of months. To think I was about to let them go...'

Rakeysh nodded and rose from his seat. 'Thank you for your time, Mr Rana,' he said and shook hands with Ashutosh. He realized he wouldn't learn anything more from him without antagonizing him.

Back in the comfort of his car, he thought about what Ashutosh had told him—twice in a matter of months. There were no coincidences in Rakeysh Aurora's dictionary. He was becoming increasingly sure that his competition had stage-managed whatever they had pulled off. He had to understand what these guys were doing and he would have to get them before they became a bigger problem for him. One client was a mere drop in the ocean for G-Force but the situation had harmed his reputation.

And that was unacceptable.

# 20

# Why walk when you can fly

The windswept evening was pleasant and serene. The horizon was clear of smog and they could see further than they could on most days. The recent rains had bathed the dusty trees and shrubs, which now stood at their sparkling best. They were chilling with drinks at Nick's house, sitting in his large balcony listening to slow and melodious music. The team had done considerable legwork in the past weeks and the coming weeks would be even busier. Natasha was dancing alone, slowly, a wine glass in hand. Rasiq watched her, lost in his thoughts, envying her peace.

'What's bothering you?' Nick asked. He was sitting next to him.

'Delivery of the devices will start in three months,' Rasiq said.

'That's a good thing, right?' Nick said. 'Fits the timeline we gave Ashutosh Industries as well. Why don't you tell me what's really on your mind?' he nudged Rasiq and looked at Natasha.

Rasiq rolled his eyes. 'It's not that,' he said. 'I think we have everything needed to service Ashutosh Industries except speed.'

'Speed?' Nick quizzed.

'Yeah,' Rasiq said. 'We have to make sure we reach the incident site quickly. That's the only way to be effective. I am not too sure our ambulances match the response times I have in mind for DareDreamers. Not in the Delhi traffic.'

'We will be ahead of the industry standards for sure,' MD Vyom joined the conversation.

'Yes, but let's look at the entire turnaround time,' Rasiq took a tissue paper from under the pizza boxes and drew a timeline:

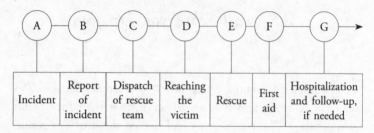

| Incident | Report of incident | Dispatch of rescue team | Reaching the victim | Rescue | First aid | Hospitalization and follow-up, if needed |
|---|---|---|---|---|---|---|

'Precisely,' Natasha chimed in. 'We expedite A to B and B to C considerably and do a better E and F. That's the premise of our mission, isn't it?'

'Yes, that's absolutely right. But we are missing a speed advantage in C to D, don't you see?' Rasiq said. 'If we have speed on our side, no one can match us. And as a corollary, if we don't have speed, we risk wasting all the other talents that we have.'

'Hmm,' Nick said, appreciative of the problem Rasiq was struggling with. 'How do we get speed then?'

'I think we'll need a helicopter,' Rasiq shared what was on his mind.

Nick started laughing. 'You're kidding, right?'

Rasiq shook his head, 'Just daring to dream.'

'You know how much it will cost?' Nick had an incredulous look.

'What happened?' Halka looked up from his laptop, pausing the song that had been playing on a loop all evening—'Truly Madly Deeply' by Savage Garden.

'Rasiq wants a helicopter,' Nick chuckled, beckoning him to join them.

Halka stared at Rasiq wide-eyed.

'We have one client right now. At our current rate of monthly expenses, we'll barely get through two months as it is,' Nick reminded Rasiq the statement of accounts they had been through last week.

'I realize that it's important,' MD Vyom said, 'but let's go slow, Rasiq. We have just started setting up our operations with the two ambulances and the fire engine. We can scale up gradually. Maybe after we have a few more clients?'

'Wasn't that always the plan?' Natasha said. 'To take it slow?'

'Guys,' Rasiq said, raising his hands. 'Think about what would happen if someone died because we didn't get to the accident site on time? Will we be as chilled out then? We'll beat ourselves up with guilt, won't we?'

'You're right,' Halka said, 'but people can die even if we get there in a helicopter.'

'Valid point, Halka,' Nick raised his mug and looked questioningly at Rasiq.

Rasiq inhaled deeply and stood up. 'Doing your best and losing is very different from being shoddy and incompetent. I'm not comfortable giving our second best. It's not my style. I have to have a clear conscience and the present set-up isn't up to my expectations.'

'Okay, for the sake of discussion—what do we need to get a chopper?' Arjun asked. 'Let's see if it's even feasible.'

'I don't know,' Rasiq replied, honestly. 'But I think it's at least worth a look into. And it can be made feasible,' he paused, and then added cautiously, 'if we talk to venture capital firms to raise the capital we need for the chopper.'

'But that's exactly what we didn't want to do in the beginning!' Nick protested. 'What about the plan?'

'Plans change, Nick,' Rasiq sighed. 'We need to keep evolving and adapting.'

'To your whims?' Nick retorted. 'Because nothing else has changed since we decided not to approach the VCs.'

Natasha tried to grapple with Rasiq's sudden and abrupt change of thought, 'Rasiq, you were the one who said that VCs might exert undue control. They might force us into decisions we won't like to make. You wanted ownership and control. What about that? Are you now telling us that the months of delays that we all endured together before we got the first contract were not needed?'

Rasiq was quiet. 'I don't know,' he shrugged. 'Saving lives became a reality for me after we won the contract, Natasha. And now, I don't feel comfortable being half-in. I think we need to go all in now.'

There was silence as the group thought about what Rasiq was saying.

'One thing is clear,' Arjun interrupted the silence before it grew to be awkward. 'If we are getting the helicopter, the office premises that I saw in Manesar would be perfect. We can convert the lawn into a helipad.'

∞

'I checked the lease rate on an Mi-26,' Nick said the next morning.

'What's that?' Rasiq asked.

'It's the only chopper that'll work for us.'

Rasiq smiled. 'You are coming around?'

'I don't know. But you should know what we need if you are thinking about it.'

'I appreciate that, Nick.'

'The lease is close to 1.2 crore a year,' Nick said.

'And running costs?'

'Those would dent our income by another eighty lakh a year. I have made many assumptions, but that's the ballpark.'

MD Vyom who had caught on to the conversation was shocked. 'That's huge.'

'Not really,' Rasiq assured. 'We need to work out the sales impact of having a helicopter. If it gets us more than two crore of annual business income, then it's worth it.'

'Yeah,' Nick conceded. 'But that's the classic chicken-and-egg case. You won't have additional sales without the chopper and you can't lease it without the additional business. No bank will give us a loan that big.'

'Yup,' Rasiq agreed. 'But that's where a VC comes in. To break this chicken-and-egg problem for start-ups.'

'That's your call,' Nick shrugged.

∽

Rasiq met several venture capital firms over the next few weeks to explain their business and the need for cash. Most were not interested in a non-technology start-up because it did not guarantee astronomical returns. Rasiq wasn't disappointed by the lack of success. The venture capitalists that sought enormous returns were not a good fit for DareDreamers either. The problem, however, remained.

'What's it, puttar?' his dad asked him when he saw the worried look on his face. Rasiq had his suit jacket across his chest and was lying on the sofa, still wearing his shoes, thinking with his eyes closed. 'I am seeing you suited up after a long time—you look smart!'

'What's the use of looking smart pops,' Rasiq said. 'I am stuck. I just got back from another failed meeting with a potential investor. I feel like a beggar.'

'What are you begging for?'

'We need a helicopter,' Rasiq said. 'It will cost us 1.2 crore a year for ten years to lease one out. We don't have the money and no venture capital firm is interested in partnering with us. Those interested are asking for far too much of a share in the business.'

'It's a very big toy you want but I'll give you the money,' his father smiled.

Rasiq sat up in surprise. 'What did you say?'

'I said, puttar, that I can help you out with the dough.'

'This is not a joke, pops! How will you manage so much?'

'We can raise a loan by using this house as collateral,' he father suggested. 'It's worth, I don't know… three, maybe four crore. You should be able to get a loan to cover the first two years. Then you'll need to step up the business.'

Rasiq fought the lump forming in his throat. 'You'll do that for me?' he said with some difficulty.

'I am doing it for myself, puttar,' his father chuckled. 'You promise me a good spread over my investment and I am sorted.'

'What sort of spread are you looking at pops?' Rasiq smiled, wiping his moist eyes before his father saw his tears. 'We can muster 4 to 5 per cent above the bank loan rate, I think, but I will have to check with the others first.'

'We can always negotiate, puttar,' his father said. 'But I don't want any ordinary spread. I want a cheese spread!'

'What?' Rasiq enquired, not able to understand.

'I have Amul cheese spread in mind,' his father said. 'I like that one the best. Besides, what will I do with 4 to 5 per cent?'

Rasiq couldn't hold back his tears this time. He laughed to avoid an embarrassing scene and quickly wiped his cheeks. 'Isn't it risky, pops?'

'You are risky, Rasiq,' he said. 'If we didn't think twice before having you, why should we start worrying now?'

Rasiq hugged his father. 'I gotta run now and tell the others,' he said. He picked up his jacket. 'You are the best, popsicle!'

'I know, I know,' his father said. 'But can you also buy some M-Seal on the way?'

'Sure,' Rasiq said. 'Is something leaking?'

'Your eyes,' his father said and burst into laughter. 'That was a good one!'

Rasiq smiled, ran back to his father and hugged him again before leaving.

The proposal cheered the team. They were glad to be free to proceed without compromising their vision.

'But who's going to fly the thing?' Natasha asked. 'Not Rasiq for sure,' she laughed. 'He crashed a Harley Davidson!'

'For sure,' Rasiq laughed. 'But it would hurt a little less if you also acknowledged that the crash is why we are together!'

'Well, you crash a chopper and we'll all be together in the afterlife too,' Natasha giggled.

'I can help with that. I might know the right guy for the job.' Halka grinned.

'What are you hiding behind that grin?' Vyom asked.

'I am going to poach a friend who works at G-Force. He hates it there, but the money has been too good for him to quit. If we can offer him the same money and a good life, he'll join us in a heartbeat.'

'G-Force? You worked there before?' Natasha asked.

'Yes,' Halka said.

'That's why you acted like a joker at the mention of the name at the meeting with Mr Ashutosh?'

'It's an old wound but a deep one.' Halka's face had a pained expression.

'Get this guy then,' Arjun said. 'And let's get the Manesar office space as well.'

∽

The team moved into the office in Manesar, opting to live on the premises as well so they could all be ready to jump into action at a moment's notice. Nick installed Internet and Wi-Fi connections. They tested the computers and communication systems thoroughly. Each device had a back-up for a breakdown.

They completed the formalities with the bank and the chopper leasing agency. Meanwhile, they received the first shipment of the devices from Vision IT. Over the next ten days, they fitted their accident alert devices on all the trucks and cars of Ashutosh Industries. They also installed manual triggers in the manufacturing facilities and trained the staff on using those devices. Nick wired the triggers to all smoke detectors and fire alarms to avoid the duplication of effort in time of emergencies.

They recruited Aslam, Halka's friend from G-Force, to pilot the chopper, which arrived a week after the devices were installed at Ashutosh Industries. He turned out to be a skilled driver on the road as well.

The first thing Rasiq noticed about Aslam was how fast his eyes moved. They darted around at impossible angles as they drew information and visual cues from all directions.

'Aslam here is the best driver in the world! With him, I feel safe going at even two hundred kilometres per hour. I manage to scare myself at forty when I am driving,' Halka beamed.

'No one calls me Aslam,' he spoke fast, much like his driving. 'They call me Asylum.'

'Because you are a crazy pilot?' MD Vyom asked.

'That's right!' Aslam replied instantly. He had a mad energy about him.

They laughed and shook hands, 'Welcome on board.'

# 21

# On the enemy's radar

'You look distraught,' Rakeysh Aurora's friend told him one evening when they met for dinner at Rakeysh's house.

'I haven't been sleeping too well,' he conceded.

'What's bothering you?'

Rakeysh hesitated. He didn't want to ruin the evening by talking about his business worries. He never spoke to others about his struggles. He believed in projecting success. This evening, however, he wasn't able to participate in the conversations given his state of mind. He had been downing his drinks in sullen silence.

'I haven't seen you this quiet in a long, long time,' his friend continued.

'There's a new company that's bothering me,' Rakeysh finally admitted.

'What new company?'

'I don't know who they are,' Rakeysh said. He took a sip of his whiskey. 'Some sort of accident rescue solution providers. What I do know is that they hurt my reputation by landing a deal with one of my clients.'

'You've got to be exaggerating,' his friend said. 'How is that possible? You provide the best safety and security services in the country. And accident rescue isn't even your thing.'

'Why does everyone keep saying that? We have accident

rescue operations,' Rakeysh slammed his fist down on the table.

'Relax, tiger,' his friend said, not intimidated by his demeanour. They had known each other for a long time and it isn't easy to browbeat old friends. 'Tell me what's worrying you.'

'I need to find out who these guys are,' Rakeysh said. He took another swig. 'I believe that they are charlatans and I need to expose them before they poach any more of my clients.'

'This is bordering on an obsession, Rakeysh,' his friend said. 'It's a young, unknown company with probably just one client and you're planning to take them on right away?'

'I didn't build this business by waiting for problems to happen before I addressed them,' Rakeysh said. 'One needs to be proactive. Nip the problem in the bud.'

His friend shook his head. 'I'll say again that your obsession is unhealthy. You don't even know if this is a problem yet.'

'What I don't understand is what they are waiting for.' Rakeysh ignored his friend's advice. 'It's been more than two months since they signed their first client and they haven't done anything since. I can't understand their game.'

'Did you get your men to look for them?' his friend asked, opening another bottle of wine.

'Yes, but no success.' Rakeysh took a big gulp to finish his drink.

'Maybe they folded? Start-ups need more than passion to stay afloat.' His friend poured Rakeysh and himself a glass.

'I hope so for their own good. But I doubt it. I need to find them soon.'

'All right then, take this,' he said, handing him a business card from his wallet. 'You can't tell anyone you got this from me. I think this guy can help you out with your problem.'

Rakeysh took the card from his friend. Narad Money,

Public Relations Consultant, RDX Pvt. Ltd.

'What does this guy do?'

'I can't say more. You'll have to meet him and find out.'

Rakeysh nodded and pocketed the card.

# 22

## *Epic Shit*

*V*ibhor would often tell people that he was fond of elephants, which was, of course, a lie. Or rather, a half-truth. The real word was love. But he knew that most people would not be able to understand his feelings. To avoid ridicule, Vibhor refrained from publicly using the only word that described his beautiful relationship with his elephants. But when he was alone with them, he never shied away from telling them how much he loved them.

He had created a small sanctuary on the grounds of his sprawling farmhouse in Sainik Farms in Saket where he housed five of these giants. Now fifty-five years old, he gave five days of the week to his business. But his weekends were reserved for his beloved tuskers. He could finally afford the little luxuries of life.

But despite being at the peak of material success, Vibhor was often the butt of jokes among his friends. Even his employees made fun of him behind his back. But the only thing that hurt him was the attitude of his wife towards his passion.

'You have time only for animals because you are an animal yourself,' she cried. Vibhor was beginning to classify the outbursts as her weekend tantrums. She had threatened to leave him several times if he did not change the object of his affections. But Vibhor knew that deep down, Payal loved him and would never leave him even though she did not share or appreciate this particular interest of his.

'Please don't leave me,' he begged. He played the appeasement game with her. 'I will even let you ride on my elephants every week.' He offered her the ride only because he knew she would never accept it on account of her loathing. He thought it was cruel to ride animals that were meant to roam free. He called the treatment 'inelephant', a play on inhuman.

'Can you think of nothing beyond your stupid elephants?'

'My dad taught me to think big and this is the biggest I can think,' Vibhor joked. 'Besides, elephants are one of the most intelligent creatures with gigabytes of memory.'

'If you care only for them, why did you marry me?' Payal retorted. 'You should have married them!'

'Payal, there are two ways we can spend more time together,' Vibhor reasoned. 'Either I make a sacrifice and spend time with you the way you want me to or we can meet midway and both of us can be happy.'

Payal was silent.

'We have done it your way all these years, darling,' Vibhor continued as carefully as possible. 'Can you not let me do the things I enjoy, on alternate weekends only, for the coming years?'

'Your idea of spending time together means dealing with elephantine proportions of shit. Literally.'

'Wait! That reminds me. We have a problem.' Payal's sharp retort reminded him of Tusker, his white elephant. He was constipated and had not evacuated his bowels for two weeks.

Payal shook her head and sighed.

Vibhor placed his hand gently on her shoulder, 'Listen, let me give Tusker his medication and if he shits, we will go anywhere you wish.'

'But you said the same thing two weeks ago!' Payal protested.

'Tusker hasn't been shitting since! Neglecting him while we enjoy ourselves in a restaurant would be cruel.'

'Can't Balram take care of it?'

'He has been trying, Payal. His ideas are not working. Plus, he is insensitive towards my elephants. He is more of a halwai than a mahout.'

'He is not insensitive. He is normal,' Payal lashed out. 'Anyway, it seems this weekend will also turn out like the last two!'

'I have a hunch he will download today. The pressure has been building...I can sense it.'

'That's all that I have sensed since we created this zoo. The stink doesn't go away even if I spray a whole bottle of room freshener in the house. Hurry with your medication, will you?'

'You get ready,' Vibhor said. 'It shouldn't take me long.'

∽

He gave Tusker laxatives and then waited patiently. He followed it up with a thirty-litre bucket full of berries, figs and prunes.

'Hurry, this wait is driving me crazy,' Payal hollered from the window on the first floor of the house two hours later.

Worried for Tusker and harried by his wife, Vibhor climbed a ladder while Balram held it in place. He then administered an enema to the elephant.

Finally, his wish came true. More than four hundred kilogrammes of elephant faeces came flying out of Tusker in a torrent. Unfortunately, Vibhor was right under the deluge when it started to pour. The ladder fell and he and Balram were knocked out.

The thick, solid waste formed a coffin of sorts for them.

When Payal looked out of the window to shout angrily at her husband, she was horrified by what she saw. A huge pile of brown slush and in the midst of it, two people writhing in agony.

'Oh my god!' she gasped as she grasped what had happened. Then she reached for her handbag and pulled out her iPhone to retrieve the email she had marked as spam that very morning.

Quickly she dialled a number.

'DareDreamers? I received your email today regarding your services. We have an emergency here...'

∞

'What do we do? Do we accept this job?' MD Vyom thought aloud.

'Monkeys, we need monkeys,' Nick said. He spoke quickly and his heart was racing.

'Let's grab our equipment,' Natasha said.

'We are taking the ad hoc case then?' MD Vyom asked no one in particular as the group jumped into action.

'Of course,' Rasiq shouted from his station. 'DareDreamers don't shy away from an SOS call.'

They were airborne in less than 180 seconds.

'We need to make a pit stop at the Delhi ridge,' Rasiq had to shout over the noise of the helicopter. Asylum pointed towards his headset and signalled to Rasiq to use the one placed near his seat. Rasiq wore it quickly. 'We need to stop at the ridge to catch a few monkeys. It's their favourite playground in Delhi.'

Asylum nodded and gave him a thumbs up.

'We can't land here, Rasiq,' Asylum informed him when they reached the ridge. 'It's not allowed. And besides, there is too much tree cover!'

Everyone was wearing their headsets now.

'It's alright,' Natasha said. She had pulled out a bag of nets. 'Just go as low as you can and try to hover above the trees. I'll catch the monkeys.'

Asylum looked at Natasha in shock. He did not ask

questions, however, understanding the time sensitivity. He brought the chopper down as low as he could.

The cars on the Simon Bolivar Road slowed as people looked up at the chopper curiously.

Natasha leapt out onto a tree directly under them, a harness securely fastened around her waist. MD Vyom, sitting at the edge of the chopper, was so carried away watching Natasha that he nearly fell from the helicopter and Halka had to grab him by his arm. MD Vyom kept his free hand over his heart and breathed a sigh of relief. Natasha looked up and gave them a thumbs up. She climbed halfway down the tree and opened out the net she was carrying. They saw her nab two monkeys in quick succession.

Inside the chopper, Arjun grabbed a net and withdrew four arrows.

'We need them alive,' Nick said.

Arjun was concentrating and did not reply. He inserted the four arrows into the four corners of the net and picked up his bow. He arranged the arrows on the bow such that they fanned out to make an arc.

'Grab my safety belt,' he told Halka.

Halka grabbed his belt from behind and Arjun leant out of the chopper at an insane angle.

Rasiq was looking tense.

Arjun shot all four arrows together. The net spread out in mid-air and landed over a group of five monkeys, ensnaring them. Natasha moved swiftly to the monkeys and took the arrows out of the net. She closed the mouth of the net and secured the monkeys. She waved at Arjun, impressed, before she set after catching a few more monkeys of her own.

Nick and Rasiq had prepared two more nets with arrows and Arjun set about executing the shots.

Six hundred seconds gone.

'Time up. Let's go,' Rasiq said.

Natasha unhooked her harness and tied all the nets with their captured monkeys to it. Nick threw down a rope ladder, which Natasha grabbed and climbed up nimbly.

Rasiq signalled to Asylum to fly to their destination.

Halka pulled up the nets with their cargo of monkeys till they were level with the landing skids. He then secured the rope to the door of the chopper. They could hear wild screams from the animals; it was no doubt an ordeal for them.

'How many do you reckon we caught?' Nick asked Halka.

'Close to forty, I think.'

'Enough!' Nick said. 'Let's hope they are hungry.'

They landed at the Sainik Farms residence nine hundred seconds after the call. Rasiq worried if they were too late.

They loosened the nets when the chopper was a few metres above the ground. The monkeys climbed out of the nets and sniffed the air before rushing towards the elephant shit.

Seeing all the monkeys, Tusker panicked and ran amok. He could have crushed all living things in the vicinity, but Halka leapt out of the chopper and grabbed the chain tied to the elephant's feet to try and immobilize him. He had, however, underestimated the might of the rampaging elephant and got dragged along with the chain. Tusker stopped for a moment and reversed his direction to start charging towards Halka, who used the moment of Tusker's confusion to run towards a tree to tie Tusker's chain, restricting his movement.

In under a minute, the monkeys made short work of the upper layers of the shit, gobbling their way through the pile. Their favourite dish had been made extra special thanks to the berries, figs and prunes that Tusker could not fully digest. They screamed in fright when their digging revealed the bodies below.

Natasha, Arjun, Rasiq and Nick sloshed through the shit and dragged out the two unfortunate, unconscious men.

MD Vyom administered CPR on Vibhor and Nick on Balram. The two men coughed and vomited as they regained consciousness.

They turned their attention to Payal, who had been crying inconsolably as she watched what was happening from the window of the house, too afraid to be near the elephants. They gave her the thumbs up.

'Can we get some water to clean them?' Rasiq shouted.

'Pond,' she squeaked pointing to a large water body in the distance.

They carried the two men to the pond and washed them, as well as themselves, as best as they could.

Half an hour later, sanity prevailed. The monkeys were still busy, feasting on their food.

'How can I thank you? How can I ever repay you?' Vibhor's voice was charged with emotion. Balram sat quietly on the ground, still shaken by the near-death experience.

'This is what we do for a living, so it was literally us just doing our job,' Rasiq said.

'If your job is working miracles, then yes, you were doing your job. That was some mind-blowing stuff!' Vibhor said.

'But what was it that you did? I mean with all these monkeys?' Balram managed to ask.

'What you saw was coprophagy,' Nick explained. 'It means consumption of faeces. Monkeys enjoy eating elephant faeces. This peculiar trait of theirs was our only chance in this freak accident.'

'But you could have called the fire brigade. It would have been so much easier with a powerful jet of water.'

Nick shook his head. 'You lived for this long only because

the shit was porous; water would have clogged the pores and you would have suffocated.'

'Wow,' Vibhor said.

Payal hugged Vibhor. 'Easy,' he said. 'You are squeezing me half to death.' Payal laughed with difficulty, between her sobs.

'Thank you for that rescue,' Vibhor said again as the team began retrieving the nets to recapture the monkeys. 'Apart from paying you for what you did today, I want to engage your services for my company too.'

'You have been through a lot. Rest today and we can discuss these things later,' Rasiq smiled.

Vibhor nodded, still breathing heavily. 'Okay. Would it be possible for you to come to my office tomorrow?'

∽

'I am dropping the MD from my name,' MD Vyom announced on their way back in the chopper.

'What? Why?' Rasiq asked him, surprised.

'It's not dead weight anymore, thanks to you, Rasiq,' he said. 'I don't need to keep reminding myself of it anymore.'

Rasiq's smile morphed into a wide grin. 'It's all your doing, Vyom,' he said his name tentatively without the MD for the first time. 'All the thanks for that should go only to you.'

The next day, Vibhor signed a five-year contract with DareDreamers for the Delhi operations of his Tuskman Group. He paid them upfront for their services. They had enrolled another big corporate client.

## 23

## *The low-level rendezvous*

*N*arad Money turned out to be a short and slimy-looking man with a protruding belly that was evident even under the thick overcoat he wore to ward off the chilly end-December weather. The semi-dark office in the basement of a dilapidated building looked more of a den than an office. The room was sparely furnished and without any personal touch that gives offices their character. The only window was shuttered up. It didn't have cabinets, file drawers, not even a computer.

'Hi, Mr Narad. I am...'

'Rakeysh Aurora. Your reputation walked in ten minutes before you.' Narad's bald head shone like a large, freshly polished golden egg under the vintage interrogation lamp, the only source of light that hung over his large table, placed oddly, in the centre of room. He leapt from his seat to shake hands with Rakeysh, who looked amused by the man and his mannerisms. The little flattering, didn't hurt either. 'Tell me, what can I do for you?'

'You can begin by explaining your name,' Rakeysh said. He was now comfortably settled in the chair opposite Narad.

Narad laughed. 'I get that a lot. It's not my given name. It's a name I chose. Much like yours, Mr Aurora. I worship money and I don't like to pretend otherwise.'

Rakeysh liked that Narad did not 'sir' him. It showed confidence and some semblance of self-respect. Maybe he would be right for the job, Rakeysh thought.

'What's your real name?'

'It's Narad Money,' Narad said with a broad smile. 'Would you say your real name is Rakesh Arora without the "y" and "u"?'

'That man died twenty-five years ago,' Rakeysh snorted. He had flinched at the mention of his old name. He touched the many rings on his fingers to reassure himself. 'He's a ghost.'

'It's the same with me. I have forgotten the man I used to be before I became Narad Money.'

'Okay, then. That settles it. Now to business. This company of yours, RDX, what does it do?' Rakeysh asked.

'It's a PR firm. We were known as Reputation Development Xperts before.'

'Oh! I think it was a mistake to come here... Sorry,' Rakeysh said, beginning to rise from his chair.

'Wait! You haven't heard me out. We no longer use that name for our company,' Narad Money said quickly. 'We decided to use the abbreviation alone. Do you follow?'

Rakeysh smiled and settled back in his chair.

'Incidentally, we are also Reputation Destruction Xperts,' Narad elaborated. 'Most PR agencies build the reputations of their clients. But my take was fresh. You can build reputations in two ways—develop your own reputation or destroy that of the competition. It's all relative, isn't it?'

'Yes. Besides, destroying reputations is easier than building them,' Rakeysh Aurora added.

'Exactly! And there is a lot more money in it. If there is a speck of dust on a white canvas, I will find it. If there is none, I will create it. If that doesn't work, I will create an illusion of dust and sell the idea to everyone till they start seeing it.'

Narad was not a straight man by any stretch of the imagination. He was as shrewd as his friend had told him. He was as crooked as the finger Rakeysh needed to get the ghee out of the box.

'Anyway, tell me, what's been giving you those bags under your eyes?'

Rakeysh's eyes grew cold and his nostrils flared.

'I call a spade a spade,' Narad said.

Rakeysh tried to ignore Narad's jibe and told him what he knew about the start-up and their first deal.

'Okay,' Narad said once Rakeysh was done. 'You need me to find out who these guys are? Simple enough.'

'Just for starters,' Rakeysh said. 'I also want to know who they are targeting next as a client.'

'You got it,' Narad said. 'So that we can expose them when they are making their dubious pitch?' Narad asked.

'Exactly,' Rakeysh emphasized. 'You catch on quickly.'

'That I do,' Narad chuckled. 'Leave all your worries in my able hands, Mr Aurora. But Mr Money needs some money to start working on your case.'

'How much?' Rakeysh asked.

'RDX offers a contract, perfectly legal, for ten lakh. That's for the "development" part. But if you want RDX's destructive power, it will cost you another fifty lakh—under the table, of course. I hate it when the government profits from my brilliant ideas.'

'What's the advance?'

'Fifty per cent.'

Rakeysh Aurora wrote a cheque for five lakh and handed it to Narad.

'I'll draft the contract for this in the next few days and send it to your office,' Narad's voice had lost its eagerness.

'Don't look so disappointed. The rest is under the table, as you suggested,' Rakeysh said.

Narad smiled and breathed easy. He bent and saw a briefcase under the table. He laughed nervously. 'You came prepared with the exact cash?'

'I too do my research before meeting people,' Rakeysh said. 'And I am usually right in my analysis of them.' He leant across the table so his face was mere inches from Narad's, 'Also, under the table money should never be given over the table,' he whispered.

Narad raised his eyebrows. 'Why are you whispering?'

Rakeysh rose to leave and pointed at the cameras in the office. 'So that you won't con me for the next guy, who comes to you with a fee over my head,' he said. He opened his jacket to show Narad a small metallic device clipped inside. 'It's a voice frequency scrambler for your audio recording devices.'

He walked out. Narad gulped hard.

## 24

## *The affair of the minister of home affairs*

*T*he lights were dim and the music was loud and foot-tapping. More than the alcohol and the food, the guests were enjoying the music and the New Year's mood. They danced crazily to the DJ's beats as strobe lights blazed across the dance floor.

The team members were all deeply settled into their groove when Nick got the call.

'Private number' flashed on the screen, making Nick suspicious.

'DareDreamers,' he had to scream into his phone as he made his way to a quieter corner. The decibel level in the pub had reached a crescendo as it was nearing the celebratory stroke of midnight.

'Can you come over quickly please?' a muffled voice spoke. 'I'm suffering from a serious condition...' the voice indicated pain. 'I think only you can help me.'

'What can we do for you?' Nick gulped down the remains of his beer.

'I can't explain it over the phone. Please come immediately. This is an emergency. Hurry please!' the panic in the voice was evident.

'Are you an existing client?'

'No,' the voice was strained. 'Please help me.'

'But you didn't even give me a name.'

'I can't give it over the phone.'

'It's the standard operating procedure at DareDreamers. You have to give us your name and location, at least, before we can accept your case. Ordinarily, I would glean all the necessary information from the phone number, but you are using a private number.'

'All right, if you insist. But can I expect secrecy?'

'Of course! You don't have to worry on that count.'

'Thanks,' the person at the other end paused. 'I'm Adhishek Suri.' When there was no response, he added, 'The home minister.'

Nick's eyebrows shot up. 'But you are a Cabinet minister with the entire government machinery at your service. Why call us, sir?' Nick stood erect, an involuntary, Pavlovian reaction to authority that four years in IIT had ingrained in him.

'As I said, I have a strange medical situation. And only you can help. I wish to keep this private. Can you please come to the presidential suite of the Taj Mansingh hotel?'

'Sure, sir. We'll be there in about three hundred seconds.'

'Thanks.' The phone went dead.

Nick returned to the dance floor and saw the rest of the team enjoying the celebrations, which he now had the misfortune of ruining.

'DareDreamers! It's show time!' he sent a group SMS.

One by one they checked their phones and stopped dancing, fighting their desire to continue having fun, which clashed with their sense of duty.

'Shit!' Natasha protested as they headed towards the exit as fast as they could. The debriefing could take place on the way.

As they piled into the van, Nick told Asylum the name of the hotel where they were headed. Asylum hit the pedal and the speedometer leapt to 120 kilometres per hour within a few seconds.

'Emergency. Seems medical! Home minister's in trouble. Won't say what,' Nick spoke in abbreviated sentences as they zipped towards their destination.

'Home minister?' Rasiq asked in disbelief. 'Are you sure?'

Nick nodded.

'We never seem to be able to catch a break! This is the third time this year. I was so dying to party!' Natasha voiced her thoughts. She was not easily impressed after having worked closely with most of the big names in Bollywood.

'We were sad when nobody knew us and we had no work and now we are sad because we have too much work. When was the part where we had balance? Did I blink and miss it?' Vyom said.

'I've been sitting idle for so many years. Trust me, work upsetting fun plans is far better than having no work at all,' Arjun recalled his past.

'Or doing meaningless work,' Halka added his two cents.

'Congratulations Rasiq for running a highly motivated sweatshop. Are you proud of your leadership?' Natasha laughed. She called the ambulance to the Taj Mansingh hotel.

∽

When they reached the hotel, they were met by a man who looked every inch a policeman in plainclothes. He escorted them to the minister's room.

The soft lounge music playing in the lobby and the long, quiet corridors of the hotel seemed jarring when juxtaposed with the tension in the air.

Two Black Cat commandos stood at the door of the hotel room they were led to. The tall policeman in plainclothes stopped outside and made a call.

'Who is the doctor among you?' the man asked as soon as he hung up.

Vyom stepped forward.

'For now, only you can go in. Others can join you if they are needed.'

Rasiq nodded to Vyom who seemed hesitant. The doctor entered the room and was plunged into semi-darkness.

'Thank god you are here. Please come in,' an agonized voice came from the far corner to his right as his eyes struggled to get accustomed to the darkness.

'I can't see a thing,' Vyom complained.

A bedside lamp was turned on. Vyom saw the familiar face of the young minister emerge from the blanket.

'This is most embarrassing!'

'What happened?'

'Will you swear the doctor's oath of secrecy?'

'I am already bound by it. Taking an oath twice makes no sense.'

'Then come closer and have a look.'

When Vyom approached the bed, he saw a woman's head emerge from under the blanket.

He looked at them, confused. 'What is the problem, exactly?'

'We are... locked,' the minister said. He seemed deeply embarrassed. 'It happened while having intercourse.'

'Can you explain how it happened?'

'That's it. While we were having sex, we got locked. I tried to withdraw, but couldn't. We've been trying to free ourselves for over an hour but to no use,' Adhishek said. He was sweating despite the cold. 'There are people outside waiting for me. My family too. You have to help us, doctor!' The authority with which he delivered sound bites on the news channels was not in evidence tonight.

'Have you faced something similar before?' he asked the woman.

She began to cry.

'You will have to answer if I am to help you.'

'I have always had difficulty in having sex. And today... Oh my god! My reputation is ruined!'

'I have never seen such a thing before but I think I know what has happened. If you will allow it, I would like to bring in my colleague, Nick, to confirm my theory.'

'What? Is that really necessary?' Adhishek pleaded.

'I wouldn't ask otherwise,' Vyom said. 'My course of action here is entirely contingent on the hypothesis and I would like a confirmation before proceeding.'

'Is this fixable?'

'If my theory is right, yes,' Vyom said. 'Otherwise, we might have to take you to the hospital in our ambulance.'

'I'll call for him,' Adhishek said, picking up his phone.

‰

Nick did a quick search on his tablet to confirm Vyom's theory.

'You are suffering from a rare occurrence, called penis captivus. Just one or two documented cases in the world, apparently,' Vyom confirmed the diagnosis to Adhishek.

'If it has a name, it must have a treatment too,' the frown on the minister's face transformed into a look of hope.

'Yes. I will need a strong muscle relaxant. If her muscles relax, maybe you will be freed.'

'Maybe? And if that doesn't happen?' The woman's voice was shrill.

'Then we might have to go for a surgical cut and stitch.'

The minister's face registered horror. The woman began to cry again.

'Please get the medicine. But not a word outside. No one from my security detail knows what's happening inside. They only know that we are working together on a confidential government project.'

Vyom wrote down the names of a strong, injectable muscle relaxant and a steroid on a piece of paper before handing it over to Nick. 'They are both in the ambulance,' he told Nick who dashed outside. He waited in the hotel room with the minister to monitor the situation.

'What's up?' the team asked Nick as he was sprinting through the lobby.

'A side effect of having an affair in the Ministry of Home Affairs,' Nick giggled at his joke.

'Don't tell us short stories. Narrate the entire episode,' Halka's voice boomed.

'Not now,' Nick said without stopping. 'Work to do.'

∞

Nick returned with the required medication.

Vyom cleaned the woman's upper arm with an alcohol swab.

'I'm scared of injections. I'm afraid I will scream,' the woman said when she saw Vyom preparing the shot.

'Then let me cover your mouth,' the minister said.

'I can't let you do that, sir. Because if she makes any sudden movement, I may not be able to administer the injection properly.'

'Then try not to scream please,' the minister said.

The woman nodded. She turned her head away, bracing herself for the pain.

'That's all,' Vyom said while removing the syringe.

'Did you give me the injection already?' The woman couldn't conceal her surprise. 'I didn't feel anything!'

'Yes. The amount of pain that people experience depends on how a doctor administers the injection. For me it's an art,'

Vyom said with pride.

'I can't afford a surgery, doctor,' Adhishek said. 'Apart from the possibility of a physical loss, I stand to lose my reputation.'

'I've done all that I could have. We'll know in about half an hour,' Vyom said. 'Please try and stay calm till then. And you can wait outside now, Nick. I'll call if I need anything.'

Nick nodded, leaving the room, albeit a little reluctantly.

Vyom stood by the bedside, carefully observing the woman. In under three minutes, her eyes had a glazed look before they closed. Her lips went slack as the effects of the medicine started to kick in.

'Will she be alright?' Adhishek asked. He was worried about the woman's safety for the first time since his panic had set in.

'I gave her a slightly higher than normal dose to prevent a surgical intervention as far as possible. I will have to watch her in case her heart rate becomes irregular. If that happens I will administer a dose of steroids to revive her,' Vyom said, feeling her pulse.

'The second injection?' the minister asked.

Vyom nodded.

He took a seat on a stool near the bed.

∞

Outside, Nick had briefed the team.

'Shit!' Arjun said.

'Yeah, but man is this a humdinger of a case. There are only two or three recorded cases of penis captivus in the history. And I had a ringside view of the whole thing. Well, almost the whole thing,' Nick spoke fast in his characteristic style.

'But how did it happen?' Natasha asked.

'There's a condition that some women have. It's called vaginismus in which the vaginal muscles spasm involuntarily in the event of penetration. Much like how the eye shuts when an object comes towards it.'

'I think it's patently disgusting, what the minister did,' Halka said. He was looking at Rasiq who had been unusually quiet.

Rasiq found it hard to meet Halka's eyes as he was reminded of his similar transgression not too long ago. 'People should know better, shouldn't they?" he said. But his voice lacked the usual confidence.

'We don't judge,' Natasha said, sensing his discomfort.

'We need to take this to our grave and there can't be any record of this,' Nick emphasized. 'Minister's request.'

∞

'Yes!' Vyom heard a muffled scream after about fifteen minutes.

'You saved us doctor!' the minister said in a hoarse whisper. 'I am free from the lock! Thank you!'

The minister grabbed a towel lying beside the bed, wrapped it around his waist and rushed to the washroom. He emerged several minutes later in his business suit and walked over to the bed to cover the woman with her clothes.

'How long will it take for her to revive?'

'Three to four hours, but we should take her to the hospital to monitor her condition. We have an ambulance here.'

'Please ensure that she gets top-notch care.'

'You get nothing less from DareDreamers, sir,' Vyom said.

'Consult your team members on how much I owe you and I'll get the cash delivered to you. But the media cannot hear about this incident. It will ruin my marriage and my reputation. Please.'

'Your secret is safe with us, sir. You have nothing to worry about,' Vyom reassured the minister for the nth time that evening.

'You won't believe me if I tell you how horrible I have been feeling throughout this ordeal. I have promised myself that I will take the lesson I learnt today seriously and will not repeat this ridiculous behaviour,' Adhishek said. 'But what do we tell the people outside?'

'The lady suffered a minor concussion,' Vyom said. 'She received it when she slipped in the bathroom. It caused her much pain for which I have given her an injection. She'll be all right in a few hours but should be taken to the hospital for overnight monitoring.'

'Thank you once again, doctor,' the minister said.

❦

'Phew! That could have turned out much messier than it did.' Vyom wiped his forehead. He was sweating on the first of January at 3.00 a.m.

'Then he learnt his lesson cheap!' Natasha said.

'Yeah,' Vyom said. 'He seemed genuinely repentant though.'

'Calamities have a way of putting things in perspective,' Halka said.

'That's beyond the scope of our job, guys,' Nick said. 'It's not in the syllabus!' He laughed at his own joke. He was still high on the excitement of witnessing a unique case.

'How much do we get paid for this?' Rasiq asked, smiling at Nick's idiocy rather than the humour in the joke.

'We have to decide,' Vyom grinned. 'He'll get the cash delivered.'

'What do you mean?' Nick asked.

'Maybe he's just ensuring that he buys our silence,' Arjun said.

'Whatever is the case,' Rasiq said. 'We did our job well today, guys! Now let's go and resume the party—we have to cover a lot of lost ground!'

# 25

# Fury at discovery

'*I* have found them,' Narad informed Rakeysh on the phone a week after he had accepted the assignment. 'Did you know they have an Mi-26 chopper? They were seen capturing monkeys in the Delhi ridge last week, using some serious stunts. The girl leapt from the chopper into a tree!'

'Are you becoming a fan?' Rakeysh snapped. 'They did that in broad daylight to impress people. It must have been a street-side trick to fool the audience.'

'Be that as it may,' Narad chuckled, 'they have no media coverage despite those antics in broad daylight, do they?'

'Your doing?'

'You bet,' Narad said. His confidence seemed to bounce back. 'They did win another client though—the Tuskman Group— they saved the life of the proprietor.'

'And?' Rakeysh said, ignoring Narad's attempt to fish for a compliment. 'Anything else to report on?'

'No "good job, Mr Money", or "that was fast, Mr Money"?'

Silence greeted Narad's words. He thought he could hear Rakeysh's breathing getting faster and louder.

'They are a weird bunch of people,' he said quickly before he pissed off his client.

'Give it to me straight, Narad,' Rakeysh demanded.

Narad was surprised at the seeming arrogance behind

Rakeysh's use of his first name. Ever since Narad had started working for him, Rakeysh's attitude increasingly betrayed a sense of owning Narad.

'They have leased an office space in Manesar,' Narad went on, his tone now sombre. 'We believe they are a team of six: four boys, one middle-aged man and one girl.'

'Hmm,' Rakeysh said. 'You have anything else? Names?'

'Yep,' Narad said. His grin was mischievous. 'They call themselves DareDreamers. Does that ring a bell?'

There was silence on the phone.

Narad continued. 'Rasiq, the founder, is an ex-investment banker from IIT Delhi and IIM Ahmedabad. There's another engineer from IIT Delhi—Nick, they call him. Then there's a kid from the mountains—Arjun—but I couldn't get any background on him. The middle-aged man is a doctor. Calls himself Vyom. The girl, Natasha, used to be a Bollywood stuntwoman.'

'Don't know any of them,' Rakeysh was perplexed. 'They are all nobodies.'

'I saved the best one for last,' Narad said, feeling emboldened. An involuntary chuckle left him despite his struggle to control his excitement. 'He's a bodybuilder by the name of Halka,' he said.

'Who's Halka?'

'You don't know him? He used to work at G-Force.'

'I don't know everyone who works at my company,' Rakeysh fumed.

'But he's not everyone,' Narad said. He was now enjoying Rakeysh impatience. 'He's the one you fired for a personal reason...'

Rakeysh remembered. 'That man!' he exploded. 'Him?'

'Absolutely, 110 per cent sure,' Narad reassured him. 'He is also the one who poached Aslam—the pilot who recently quit G-Force. He's with DareDreamers now and is flying their chopper.'

'That bastard,' Rakeysh growled. 'I'll meet you at your office to discuss this further.'

Narad could hear the phone smashing against a wall or the floor and he jerked the receiver away from his ear at the loud noise. He disconnected the call and took a deep breath.

'This means a lot more money for Narad Money!' he smirked.

# 26

## *Airborne viral love*

'Guys,' Rasiq said in the meeting he had called one afternoon, 'business is doing pretty well. The basic infrastructure is in place now. Over the last three months that we have been in operation we have been able to manage all incidents efficiently. There have been three chopper deployments, a couple of ambulance deployments and our firefighting services have been pressed into action once already. We have arrived at the locations quickly, executed our SOPs efficiently and there have been no casualties thus far. So overall, a good show, I would say.'

The team beamed with pride.

'However,' Rasiq said, 'our profitability remains a concern. The chopper continues to be a big overhead and we haven't been able to offset its costs.'

'But we kicked off the operations at the Tuskman Group last quarter,' Natasha pointed out. 'That will help, won't it?'

'Sure,' Rasiq agreed, 'but it won't be enough. And even if we double our deployments over the next three months, we will still be underutilized.'

'That's true,' Nick said. 'So far, we've been busy with the backend work. But that's not going to go on forever. In fact, that should be going into autopilot mode any day now.'

Rasiq nodded, 'I am wondering if we should consider a B2C expansion?'

'You mean a proper business to consumer marketing?' Nick reiterated.

'What's that?' Halka asked.

'As a business house, we have been approaching only businesses like Ashutosh Industries and Tuskman Group. I believe that we should now approach individual consumers who may need our services and can afford them,' Rasiq explained.

'And who would these people be?' Arjun asked.

'Owners of premium cars like Audi, BMW and Mercedes who won't mind paying for additional safety cover, maybe,' Rasiq said. 'The point is we have to earn more revenues with the already existing infrastructure.'

'But should we limit the number of independent clients?' Natasha asked.

'For now, we can go for an additional 5,000 consumers, on a trial basis, to complete a decent first year.'

'And if we get a better response then perhaps we can even expand our operations. More ambulances, nurses, firemen! Even an additional chopper,' Arjun said with enthusiasm.

Halka didn't seem too happy with the idea. 'I think we should wait,' he said. 'We might sign on more clients than we can service properly.'

'But the probability of multiple clients needing our services simultaneously is low,' Nick objected.

'Halka,' Rasiq said. 'I was worried about that too. That's part of the reason why we have not marketed ourselves aggressively over the past few months. But we must break even or risk going bankrupt soon.'

'And all this state of the art, super expensive infrastructure is also idling away,' Natasha said.

'All right,' Halka conceded. 'If you feel strongly about this then let's do it. I am also getting bored with not having much to do.'

'And the best part about the direct sales approach is that we can stop anytime,' Vyom said. 'The moment we feel we have enough clients we can stop the sales operations.'

'That'll be the day,' Natasha exulted. 'I love the optimism!'

∞

On a Friday morning, Rasiq and Halka were heading towards Gurgaon to ink the deal with their B2C sales agent. As they turned towards Cyber City, their car shook as the road beneath them rumbled.

'An earthquake. Pull over!' Rasiq shouted.

Ahead of them, traffic had come to a standstill.

They heard shouts and screams and jumped out of the car to see what had happened.

What they saw shocked them. Up ahead, the road had caved in and a crater, about ten feet deep, had formed. It had sucked in a few cars and they saw people scrambling out of their cars, shocked and surprised.

What was truly appalling, however, was a deep crack—a fissure with a fathomless depth, anywhere between a hundred and five hundred feet—that had formed inside the crater. One lone car was stuck perilously between the walls of this crack, almost vertically, with the bonnet facing downwards, staring into the abyss. It seemed about to plummet any minute into the depths, which were waiting for the car like a predator for its prey. A crowd had gathered around the crater, peering down at the crack.

Rasiq dialled a number on his mobile. 'Rasiq here. We need the chopper and the team, right now! You have my location. I can cast the scene here from my phone camera.'

'Are you alright?' Rasiq asked Halka who had been staring at the hole as if in a trance.

There was no response from Halka.

Nick made a video call to Rasiq and he showed him the accident scene.

Seven minutes later the helicopter zoomed over the crater. Nick dropped two headsets and Rasiq and Halka put them on.

'I need to do this,' Halka said over the headset. 'Throw the harness.'

Asylum lowered the chopper and Natasha threw the entire length of the harness down. Nick looked at the crater with awe and curiosity from the helicopter. Halka grabbed the harness and plunged into the crater. The cries for help that were emanating from the car stopped almost instantaneously. Halka perched on the lip of the crack and rappelled down its wall slowly, moving closer to the car. One wrong move and he could send the car hurtling down into the pit.

'Don't be afraid,' he assured the girl, when he was level with her, but still a few inches to the side. 'Remain calm.'

'I am not afraid anymore,' she said.

When Halka tried to open the door of the car, it slid a few metres down, without warning. The crowd gasped, even as a few insensitive people began to film the imminent disaster.

Halka noticed that the fragile walls of the crack, coated with loose sand, were beginning to give away under the weight of the car.

'Pull me back!' Halka shouted and the chopper started moving.

'Just a few metres, you idiot!' Halka shouted, extremely agitated, when Asylum pulled him up a lot further than he needed.

'I am not a mind reader,' Asylum retorted.

'Careful guys,' Rasiq said over his headset. 'Let's stay focussed on the job. Is the girl all right?'

'For now,' Halka replied. 'Asylum, can you make me circle slowly around the car?'

'No,' Asylum said, his voice still irritable. 'The car is too small. I can't make such small, precise movements with the chopper. What's the plan?'

'I need to make sure the car won't slip when I open the door.'

'Asylum,' Rasiq intervened. 'Move the chopper slightly forward to give Halka some horizontal momentum to swing. Halka, analyse the situation and decide how you want to pull up the car.'

Asylum moved the chopper a little, swinging Halka like a pendulum. Halka observed the points where the car was supported by the walls from as many angles as he could.

'The front end of the car is stuck for now, but the grip is very flimsy,' Halka reported. 'I can't land on the car or open the door. It's too risky.'

'Let's tow the car with the chopper,' Rasiq said.

'I'm lowering the metal chain,' Natasha said as she threw it down from the chopper.

'The front tow hook is not accessible at all,' Halka said as he grabbed the chain, 'and there's no rear tow hook.'

'You'll have to tie the chain around the rear axle,' Rasiq spoke slowly into his headset.

Halka exhaled nervously. 'I need to work fast,' he said.

'Be careful,' Natasha said. She was itching to be down there herself.

Halka made fast, but careful and deliberate movements as he went under the car to tie the metal chain to the rear axle of the car.

'Pull up, Asylum.'

'We can't pull the car up,' Rasiq said. He was in the best position to direct the operation as Halka was too close to the car and the others were too far away in the chopper. 'It's wedged at an impossible angle for that. The pull will require a lot of thrust and that might break the axle.'

'Okay,' Halka said. 'What do we do then? We can't pull it up and we can't open the door or it will slide down!'

'Asylum,' Rasiq had an idea. 'Pull up just enough to make the metal chain as taut as possible. Move very slowly.'

Asylum inched the chopper up, as instructed. Halka told Asylum when to stop.

'Can you maintain a slight upward thrust, Asylum? Just enough to hold the car in place without pulling it up?'

'Yes,' Asylum said focusing all his attention on the task. 'It's done.'

'The car won't jerk the chopper now, Halka. And even if it skids when you open the door, the upward thrust from the chopper will prevent it from diving into the depths' Rasiq said, breathing a sigh of relief. 'All yours now.'

Halka steadied himself next to the car and carefully reached for the door on the driver's side. But the minute he opened the door, the loose soil under the car fell away from the walls of the crack. The car started skidding down and pulled the chopper with it, just a little bit, before Asylum stabilized it. The car was now hanging like a pendulum. There was a collective scream of anguish from the crowd, which was unaware that the Mi-26 was a workhorse capable of pulling much heavier weights.

Halka moved closer to the driver's seat of the car and cut the seat belt pinning the girl to her seat. He extended his hand slowly to reach the girl who was holding the steering wheel tightly.

'Let go,' Halka instructed.

She left the wheel, shutting her eyes. Halka slowly pulled her out of the car. 'I have her. Pull us up now.'

Natasha released the metal chain holding the car. The car skidded down into the crack and disappeared. The earth had swallowed it. Asylum pulled the chopper up slowly, raising Halka and the girl out from the abyss.

'Good job, guys!' Rasiq exulted as he punched the air with his fist.

The crowd cheered and whistled as it applauded the duo emerging from the crack. Halka held the harness in one hand while his other arm was securely around the girl's waist. The girl held on tightly, her face buried in his chest.

Even after Halka released the harness and they stood on solid ground, the girl continued to cling to him. Halka put his other arm around the girl as they stood in a silent embrace with all the mobile phones of the crowd pointed towards them.

Halka could feel the rapid fluttering of her heart against his.

'Tell me when it's over,' the girl said.

'It's over,' Halka replied. 'But don't let go just yet.'

The girl pulled her face back from his chest and looked into his eyes without letting go. Halka lowered his lips and kissed the girl with his eyes closed.

Natasha lowered Nick from the chopper with a harness and a security belt. When his feet were safely on the ground, Nick removed the safety belt with hands that were shaking slightly. He forgot his fear quickly as he rushed to the edge of the crater and stared at it in awe.

Rasiq walked towards Halka and the girl. 'Ahem,' Rasiq cleared his throat as he neared the duo. 'This isn't part of the rescue operation.'

Halka let the girl go. 'This is Achala,' he had to shout over the noisy crowd gathering around them. 'The girl I told you about.'

Rasiq was taken aback, 'Truly Madly Deeply?' he was reminded of the Savage Garden song that was Halka's favourite and the one he listened to in an endless loop in the memory of his lost love.

Halka nodded.

*What a coincidence!* Rasiq envied. *How many times do you get to save your damsel when she is in distress? This is poetic!*

Rasiq escorted Achala, who was still shaking, away from the crowd as they applauded Halka and wanted to take selfies with him.

The cameras kept clicking and flashing at a smiling Halka who was demonstrating a new depth to his patience. Rasiq offered Achala some water, an energy bar and a chocolate from his car. The chopper pulled away from the scene.

'Like I suspected, it's a sinkhole,' Nick said as he approached Rasiq.

'A sinkhole?' Rasiq looked surprised.

'Yes. It can occur when the water table is drastically lowered. With so much construction activity going on in Gurgaon, builders are using all the groundwater they can lay their hands on. The government has tried to intervene, but it is too little too late. Besides, the rainwater clogs in every street here, even when there is a drizzle, eroding the earth beneath and making the ground fragile and collapsible.'

'You mean it was a disaster waiting to happen?' Achala's voice quivered.

'Yes! Exactly,' Nick said. 'It was a miracle you survived. Good work, the way you conducted yourself, without panicking.'

Achala smiled, 'I knew I would be fine as soon as I saw Halka,' she said.

Nick smiled. 'You'll be a celebrity as soon as one of these guys uploads the video.'

Her smile vanished faster than it had appeared as her thoughts drifted to her father.

Part Three
..................................................
Too Many Juicy Carrots

## 27

## *Viral dis-ease*

*R*akeysh had been sitting immobile and quiet across from Narad for what seemed like ages. Narad was beginning to feel the queasiness of a prey in the grip of a python.

'So now I pay to watch that asshole bouncer kiss my daughter in public? Wow,' he said, clapping slowly. Rakeysh had seen some of the videos that had been uploaded to YouTube and had garnered more than a 100,000 views within a day. 'Some progress I have made since I met you,' he finally exploded. Narad wondered what this meeting would have been like had it happened ten years earlier. Maybe Rakeysh's hands would have been around his neck by now. He was glad to have skipped meeting a younger Rakeysh.

'Oh! That's what is bothering you! This generation of children will do the exact opposite of their parents' wishes—'

'I did not come here to discuss parenting with you. Besides, what do you know about parenting?' Rakeysh demanded. 'Have you done anything since we last spoke? Or have you spent your time researching ways to invest the advance I gave you?'

'Easy, easy! These things take time. My men are shadowing the partners at DareDreamers, and each day we are learning more and more about how they operate, which will help us identify their weaknesses. We will come up with a foolproof plan soon. I am already working on it.'

'Are you incubating the plan by sitting on it? Or will it require you to move your ass too?'

'Only asses move their ass, Mr Rakeysh. Smart guys move their minds. Impatience is a dangerous thing. Halka and his team will pay a heavy price for that public display of affection, I assure you. Revenge will be yours, but it would do you good to remember that it is a dish best served cold. Currently, the temperature at which you are operating seems closer to the boiling point,' Narad said.

Rakeysh shook his head, his anger flaring. He took in a deep breath visibly trying hard to keep it in check. 'You said you are working on a plan?'

'Yes,' Narad said. His eyes gleamed when he spoke, 'I'm trying to kill one bird with two stones.'

'I expect more of action and less of your clichés, Narad! You are testing my patience now,' Rakeysh fumed. His face glowed with rage and Narad could feel it's heat.

'I didn't use a cliché. The cliché is to kill two birds with one stone,' Narad croaked, his bravado evaporating under Rakeysh's boiling fury.

'Just get the job done!' Rakeysh thundered. He stormed out of the office, unable to bear speaking to Narad anymore.

# 28

## *Two to tangle*

$B$acked by the publicity from the sinkhole rescue, DareDreamers signed a few more clients. While they couldn't make it for their B2C meeting that day, they were approached by an insurance company which proposed a reduced accident insurance premium for the clients who installed the ARA devices on their cars and homes.

They hired more staff to run their expanded operations. Besides the three operators to monitor the devices and telephone lines, they employed two people to manage their accounts, renewals and finances. On Rasiq's insistence, they hired a data analyst, Arnab, as well. His job was to calculate the savings to their clients and crunch data generated by the ARA devices installed on the fleets of their steadily growing clients. He could highlight risky driving habits and inform their clients. They planned to use this to conduct customized training programmes for drivers to ensure disciplined driving to avoid accidents.

With these additional people, they now had a small-scale enterprise.

∽

'When are you going to bathe next?' Natasha demanded.

'What? That's none of your business!' Nick stretched his arms and yawned.

'If you stink up my air, then yes, it is!'

'Man,' Nick complained. 'It's like I'm living with my mother again.'

'Aah!' Natasha shouted. 'You take that back now Sriniketh!'

'Not gonna,' Nick laughed.

Natasha chased him and he dodged her. She leapt from the centre table and landed on top of Nick, throwing him off balance. She grabbed him by the collar.

'All right,' Nick conceded defeat. 'I'm sorry, I'm sorry.'

'About what?'

'For calling you my mother. I take it back. Please don't hurt me,' Nick pleaded.

'That's better,' Natasha smiled with satisfaction and released Nick.

Nick winked at Rasiq.

'I can't believe I am living with a bunch of teenage boys. It's a nightmare.'

'Or a fantasy?' Nick winked.

Natasha shook her head in disgust. 'Your idea of a fantasy,' she said. 'Not mine.'

The ARA alarm went off. They rushed to the on-duty phone operator's terminal. The video footage was of a bus full of kids. The bus seemed fine, but the driver had beads of sweat on his forehead, his face taut with palpable tension. The GPS locater indicated the bus was in Mussourie.

'How did this school get hold of our device?' Arjun asked.

'It must be the school in East Delhi run by the Ashutosh Foundation. The contract covers his allied businesses in Delhi as well,' Nick recalled installing the devices in the school's buses.

'But they are in Mussourie,' Vyom said. 'Our contract doesn't cover the area.'

'Technically,' Nick said.

'We are not turning down this request,' Natasha said.

'What's the issue?' Rasiq spoke, his mouth close to the microphone.

'The brakes have failed! The handbrake is working a little, but it will burn out any moment. I don't know how to stop this bus. There are fifty kids and two teachers on board.' The driver whispered, he did not want to create panic in the bus.

'Can you shift to a lower gear?' Asylum asked.

'No,' the driver replied. 'We are going downhill and the speed has been increasing. The bus might overturn if I try and force a change of gears.'

'Aerial distance between Manesar and Mussourie is 220 kilometres,' Nick said. 'Approximately forty-five minutes by chopper.'

'Slow down, Jeevan! We are going too fast. These are mountains, not an F1 track!' A teacher's shout came through the microphone.

'We are coming, Jeevan,' Rasiq assured him. 'Stay calm and focused.'

'Keep the speed in check with the handbrake, but use it only occasionally to avoid a burnout,' Asylum said.

'I am trying, but please hurry!' Jeevan pleaded.

'Come on, let's go,' Halka shouted.

Within a few seconds, they were airborne. Nick's phone rang. 'Yes?'

'We have another critical alert,' the phone operator informed him. 'I am sending the live feed to your phone.'

'Now what?' Nick looked up sharply. The others looked on as the blood drained from Nick's face when he pushed a few buttons on his phone to look at the feed from the second accident. The team huddled around him.

The video footage was from an overturned transport truck

on a highway near Narela in Delhi. There were three men inside. The device signature showed the truck belonged to a logistics company they had signed up just a few weeks ago.

'What do we do? They are in the opposite direction!' Nick despaired. 'The truck falls under our committed service area.'

'Looks like they are alive right now,' Vyom pointed on the screen to one of the guys who was moving a little. 'If we fly them to a hospital, they might live. But we need to get there ASAP.'

'Should we split?' Halka suggested.

'Are you going to take a cab to Narela?' Vyom said, irritated with Halka's suggestion.

'We need to decide fast,' Natasha said.

'We shouldn't have signed up so many clients so fast. It was a mistake!' Halka's face broke into a frown.

'All right, let's sit here and discuss whose mistake this is!' Arjun said, losing his patience.

His reprimand stunned them. Arjun had never spoken rudely to anyone before.

'Come on, Rasiq,' Natasha poked him. 'Tell us what the right thing to do here is?'

The poke drew Rasiq out of the freeze he had got into. 'We go for the kids.'

Asylum stepped up the speed and the chopper hummed in protest as it notched up three hundred kilometres per hour, the top speed of the Mi-26.

'Nick, call the hospital nearest to the accident site and tell them to dispatch an ambulance,' Rasiq shouted into his headset. 'I am also asking our ambulance to rush to the truck, as a backup measure.'

Nick's eyes were moist when he looked at Rasiq. He wiped them and pressed a few buttons on his tab to locate the nearest hospital. He dialled the number but couldn't speak. He choked.

Arjun took the phone from him and spoke to the hospital. He gave them the location of the accident.

'We couldn't have done anything more,' Vyom said. He placed a comforting hand on Nick's shoulder.

'Yes,' Rasiq heard Natasha say. But her voice lacked conviction.

Rasiq didn't say anything. He stared out of the chopper. *Oh my god! The worst has happened. What were we doing? Hoping to be lucky and thinking accidents would happen in manageable sequences that fit our business model?*

'These are more than fifty lives, including kids,' Halka remarked. 'From a purely rational perspective, that's more valuable than the three men in the truck.' Even he knew that his argument was hollow.

*My gut always told me that we could only serve one of two— the humanitarian or the business perspective. One is about to be compromised now*, Rasiq thought.

'Maybe the ambulance will get there in time,' Vyom hoped. 'We alerted them before anyone else. A to C was done very fast,' he said, recalling Rasiq's timeline. 'We gave them a much better chance than they would have had in our absence.'

They discussed their rescue plan on the way.

'I am going to puncture the tyres,' Arjun informed. They had discussed and differed on the options. 'Asylum can keep me as close to the bus as possible.'

'I don't think that's a good idea,' Nick protested. 'The bus could spin out of control if the tyres burst and it might skid into the valley.'

'Not if I burst all four tyres simultaneously.'

Everyone was silent. The risk associated with the move was immense.

'We can't rescue fifty people one by one using the chopper

and Natasha's skills,' Halka said. 'Arjun is right, I see no other option.'

'But shooting at the tyres might mean instant death for all fifty of them,' Vyom expressed his doubt.

'If you have any better ideas, let me know!' Arjun drew his pistols.

'If we can find a straight, uphill section of even a hundred metres, the increased friction from the flat tyres might be enough to stop the bus,' Asylum gave his opinion.

⁂

They located the bus hurtling down the mountain. It made a risky overtaking manoeuvre and the car in front of the bus nearly rammed into the side of the mountain, trying to get out of its way to avoid a collision. They could see the driver of the car hurling abuses.

Asylum spotted a hairpin bend after which the bus would move uphill for more than a few hundred metres. 'There,' he said into the mic, 'That's our only shot.'

'Okay,' Arjun shouted over his headset, leaning over to him. 'Level with that road.'

Asylum lowered the chopper into the valley. The move was risky and they were glad they were in an Mi-26. An ordinary chopper would have been difficult to control in the valley winds.

'I can't go any lower,' Asylum said. 'Too dangerous!'

'Arjun, I will lower you in a harness to the level of the bus,' Halka said.

'You should really think about this again,' Vyom said.

'I know what I'm doing and I understand the risks,' Arjun said. He clicked the safety off on his pistols.

Arjun jumped out of the chopper, his harness held by Halka, who lowered him.

'Enough,' Arjun instructed over the mic.

Arjun was now in position and readied himself to take the shot. The bus was about a kilometre away from the bend.

'We will puncture your tyres after you make the approaching hairpin turn,' Nick spoke over the tab to the driver of the bus. 'There's a straight and uphill section after that where you can slow down and stop the bus with the handbrake and shift to a lower gear. Brace for impact!'

'Arjun!' Natasha screamed as she saw a truck approach the hairpin bend from the opposite side. Everyone had been focused only on the bus and had missed the truck. Now, it was just seconds away from hitting Arjun, who was suspended in mid-air, right in its path. Since he was beyond the bend, the truck driver couldn't see him.

Asylum was paralysed with fear. It was too late now for an evasive manoeuvre anyway. There was no way they could avoid the collision.

Natasha ran the width of the chopper and jumped horizontally in the air from the opposite door of the chopper with a harness in her hand. Gravity provided her the angular momentum she needed to swing like a pendulum towards Arjun. She grabbed him right in front of the truck, which had begun its panic honks, as it ate away the dangerous inches between them. Her momentum carried them across the truck's face as it whizzed past them in a blur. She then twisted with a sudden jerk using her body as a shield to cushion Arjun from the impact against the mountain wall.

'Aargh!' Natasha screamed with pain as she was dragged against the jagged edges of the mountain, the impact tearing her clothes and the skin of her left arm and back.

'Natasha!' Arjun's eyes widened with surprise and horror as he tried to grapple with what was happening.

'Focus, Arjun,' she said. The adrenaline pumping through her veins ensured she didn't pass out. She couldn't afford to. Not yet.

She wrapped her legs around Arjun as they swung back away from the mountain. She used the two ropes to steady them so that Arjun could take the shot. 'You have one chance at this,' she said, 'make it count.'

The children, who had seen what had happened, were now screaming in fear.

Arjun closed his eyes to gather himself. Beads of perspiration broke out on his forehead.

'Now!' Natasha instructed Arjun, as the bus came up on the uphill section right in front of them.

Arjun opened his eyes, took aim and fired both pistols, one held in each hand, in quick succession. Two simultaneous shots from each pistol, four hits. All four tyres exploded and the bus wobbled forward in shock, like a giant boxer dealt with knockout punches. Its death run gradually rolled to a stop.

'It's going to roll backwards, down the slope once it stops,' Rasiq shouted. 'I don't trust the handbrake to hold it.'

Halka quickly tied Arjun's harness to a peg in the chopper. He then positioned himself so he could take a running leap out of the chopper; he leapt and landed on the roof of the bus as it came to a momentary halt. He rolled off the roof but managed to land on his feet. Quickly, he ran behind the bus and pushed against it as it started rolling back. He skid a few metres, his shoes tearing with the friction against the road, but together with the handbrake, his force was enough to stop the bus.

The kids rushed out, a few of them crying. Some threw up as soon as they got out of the bus. But they were alive. Not much mattered besides that. Jeevan got out last and immediately ran to pick up a couple of bricks lying by the roadside, which he wedged under the rear tyres to prevent it from rolling back. Halka could then let go of the bus.

Arjun pocketed the pistols and held Natasha while they were still suspended. 'You can let go of your rope,' he said. He hugged her tightly, securing her in his powerful arms as she felt her strength fade away. She released her hold. Arjun's clothes were drenched with Natasha's blood. Her cuts were deep.

'You almost died there,' she said, half conscious.

'I know,' Arjun said. 'Thank you for saving my life. Missed the stupid truck in all the excitement.'

'I always knew men were idiots,' she said. 'Too much testosterone... Plan little, act more. Never a good strategy. Especially not in risky endeavours,' she gritted her teeth to stifle the pain she felt.

'But you did the same, didn't you?'

'It's different with me. I have a lifetime of practice,' she tried to smile but it took an effort. 'Also, I couldn't let you die.'

Arjun's heart was now racing faster than before which he didn't know was even possible. 'Why?' he asked, his voice quivering with anticipation.

'I love you, you idiot, that's why,' Natasha smiled.

They hugged each other tightly. Her wounds hurt, but she felt a sense of calm overwhelm her in his embrace.

Arjun felt her breath on his neck and the warmth of her embrace. Natasha pulled back just a little and kissed him on the cheek. He moved his lips closer to hers and Natasha moved the rest of the distance to meet his. They kissed while still suspended from the harness.

Nick, Rasiq and Vyom pulled them up. They were grinning. The mic had caught the declaration of love. Rasiq wondered if Arjun would ever have made the first move. And had he not been in mortal danger that required Natasha to intervene, would she have ever confessed her feelings? *Near-death experiences do liberate people from the burden of inhibitions,* he thought.

Vyom cut open the sleeve of her shirt and inspected her injuries.

'Will I live, doctor?' Natasha looked at him with mock worry.

'Yes, you will,' he laughed, cleaning her wounds first with water and then with alcohol swabs from the first aid kit. 'But you'll need multiple stitches. Till then this bandage will have to do. I am giving you a shot of painkillers.'

'Let's check on the other accident,' Rasiq said.

'Already did,' Nick said. 'One ambulance will reach the site in about five minutes, they said. The men in the truck don't look good. They're not moving.'

'The ambulance isn't there yet?' Vyom could not hide his surprise.

Nick shook his head. 'But there's no sense in us going there now. Is there?'

'I don't think so,' Rasiq said. 'Their lives are in the hands of the hospital. By the time we reach Narela they will already be in the hospital.'

They flew the chopper to the Mussourie helipad. From there they took a taxi back to the bus.

'I'm sorry, guys,' Arjun broke the silence.

'What for?' Vyom asked.

'I was rude just before the mission,' Arjun said. 'I was tense.'

'Don't worry about that,' Vyom replied. 'No big deal.'

'You were quite intense there, Arjun,' Rasiq said. 'Not tense. And whatever helps you bring your A-game works with this group. What we pulled off is unbelievable. And Natasha, you have my heartfelt respect. We would have lost Arjun had you not risked your life like that.'

'Desperate times call for desperate measures,' Natasha said.

She held Arjun's hand tightly.

The teachers rushed towards them to thank them when they got out of the taxi. Rasiq pushed Arjun and Natasha to the front of the group. 'You are today's heroes.' Rasiq made a gesture of V for victory with his fingers, as he saw Halka in the distance tending to the kids.

Their success, however, didn't make them happy. The thought of the accident at Narela preyed on their minds.

∞

Rasiq's phone rang early the following morning, waking him up. 'They didn't make it,' the vendor relationship manager of the company that owned the truck involved in the accident informed him. 'Your ambulance took them to the hospital, but they died en route.'

'All three of them?' Rasiq asked.

Nick walked into his room as he had heard the phone ring. He was wearing the previous day's clothes as he hadn't bathed.

'Put it on speaker,' Nick said.

Rasiq complied.

'Yes, all three of them are dead. The doctors couldn't save them.'

Nick and Rasiq looked at each other.

'I am sorry,' Rasiq said.

'It's not your fault,' the manager said. 'You did your best.'

*No, we didn't. Had we flown there directly, we could have saved their lives with Vyom's first aid and a quick ride to the hospital.*

'I will understand if you want to cancel the contract,' Rasiq said.

'We might have to do that,' the voice on the other end said. 'Even though your ambulance was the first to arrive there. It actually arrived before the local hospital's ambulance, which I am given to understand had been alerted by you mere seconds after the accident. I mean,' he hesitated a little, 'had your chopper been on legitimate business it would have been alright, but it was deployed outside your service area. That was a clear breach of the contract.'

Rasiq realized that the client must have heard about their involvement in the school bus rescue in Mussourie.

'I understand,' Rasiq said. 'We couldn't help it.'

'These are difficult choices, Rasiq,' the guy said. 'Cancelling your contract is purely a business move. Personally, I am impressed by your other rescue.'

'But the families of the deceased won't be so kind,' Rasiq said.

'Just one last thing before you hang up,' the voice said. 'I don't know if it is important, but the police suspect there was a minor explosion in the truck and are investigating it.'

'What?' Rasiq said. Nick was staring at him in shock. 'Are there any suspects?'

'No, not yet. But they believe that it's likely that it was foul play by a relative with whom the truck driver had a longstanding feud.'

Rasiq was lost in thought.

'Are you still there?'

'Yes,' Rasiq said. 'Thank you for updating us on that.'

Rasiq hung up and got up from his bed. 'Didn't you sleep at all?' he asked Nick.

'No man. I couldn't because of yesterday,' Nick shook his fists in the air. 'I can't stop thinking about how ridiculous it is that the six of us are tied down to one helicopter.'

'We can't afford to lease another one,' Rasiq pointed out. He put his hand on Nick's shoulder to console him. 'It scares me too. People's lives depend on our services and to think we may not be able live up to what we promise...'

'The probability was so small, yet it happened,' Nick said. 'And here we were thinking that we have worked out the maths. That's exactly why the six of us must be capable of splitting up and reaching separate locations if needed. Screw the probability. We will not make the same mistake again. That's why I was up the whole night. I was working on an idea.'

'What idea?' Rasiq asked.

'I am going to build jet packs,' Nick said.

'What?' Rasiq said. 'You do know that none of the designs work, right? Not as a practical, everyday use vehicle.

'I know,' Nick agreed. 'They don't last more than fifteen minutes or one needs a parachute to land when the fuel is used up. Not convenient, besides being risky.'

'Imagine one of us landing on a busy highway and getting knocked down by a speeding car,' Rasiq said.

'But maybe I can do it. I have been trying to figure out the science behind it. I'm confident I can make them work much better.'

Nick's conversation seemed to be more with himself than Rasiq. He left the Manesar office a few minutes later to retire to his labrary.

Rasiq realized that the flight of imagination which Nick was trying to take was from the runway of remorse. There was no way he could make jet packs. It was a wild pursuit his hurting friend needed, to calm himself.

# 29

# Desperation—the source of machination

$R$akeysh's immensely successful run over the past twenty-five years was losing steam like an outdated product from James Watt's laboratory. For the first time, his carefully crafted numerology compliant name, the gem-laden rings on his fingers, the feng shui locket and talisman around his neck had all failed to work their magic.

The Super Six, as the newspapers had named them, were bigger than cricket these days.

It wasn't the setback of a few crore rupees that bothered him. That was an insignificant amount. Besides, he had retained the contracts for other security services with the clients DareDreamers had bagged. It was the fact that his ego had taken a hit. He was not in the game to come in second. Especially not to a bunch of charlatans. Especially not Halka— the good-for-nothing, brainless giant who did not know his boundaries.

'The Mussourie School Bus Miracle was scripted by you?' Rakeysh shouted at Narad, as he entered his office.

Narad nearly jumped up from his seat. 'The plan was good, Mr Aurora. But it seems like they are not the charlatans we thought them to be. They had no clue about the accident and they still pulled off a miraculous save.'

'Why don't you buy a DareDreamers fanboy T-shirt? I heard

it's available on Amazon these days,' Rakeysh said as he moved restlessly.

'I told you that I was killing one bird with two stones, didn't I?' Narad said, unflustered. 'You haven't heard about the other stone yet.'

'What other stone?' Rakeysh stopped pacing. He reminded Narad of a tiger he saw in a cramped cage, in a zoo. Angry. Frustrated. Ready to jump.

'The one that hit the mark,' Narad exulted. He explained the Narela truck accident to Rakeysh. 'The company has cancelled their contract with DareDreamers. 'Wait till I add some fuel to that fire and use my machinery to make the world see it. They won't be heroes anymore once the media starts questioning their business ethics and drags their name through the mud. Their clients will desert them because sticking with a muddy buddy makes one look dirty too.'

Rakeysh nodded. 'Finally, it pays to have you...' his voice trailed off. A worrisome thought had just occurred to him.

'What happened, Mr Aurora?' Narad asked.

'Did you say that those men in the truck died?'

Narad nodded, uncertainly. 'Yes. But are you alright?' he asked.

The colour had drained from Rakeysh's face.

'Here, have a seat.' Narad pulled a chair for Rakeysh.

'It's nothing,' Rakeysh said, sitting down. He was taken aback by the deaths, but he could not afford to be weak now that he was so close to accomplishing his goal. 'Was there really no other way to do this?' he asked, knowing fully well that he was asking the wrong guy.

'If there was, I would have preferred a less murky path too, Mr Rakeysh.'

'What if...'

'You are focusing on the wrong thing, Mr Rakeysh,' Narad tried to loosen the grip of doubt on the old man. 'We are so close to achieving our goal. It's your goal. Think of a world without DareDreamers and these upstarts. Think about how peacefully you'll sleep knowing G-Force is the best security agency in the country again.'

'And what comes next?' Rakeysh asked.

'I'll finish the job,' Narad said. 'If you want, I'll spare you the details but I will need your presence in the closing act that I will stage in a few weeks. Victory is just a bend away.'

Rakeysh nodded weakly.

# 30

# What goes up, comes crashing down

*O*ver the next few weeks, a lot of their clients called up to enquire about the Narela accident. Rasiq had not expected the news of their failure to be spread so far and wide so fast.

'You seem worried,' Arjun asked Rasiq one afternoon as they were having lunch. 'Should we be worried too?'

'We have a problem,' Rasiq admitted, looking over his shoulder for Nick. He wanted to keep him out of what he was about to discuss because the Narela incident had affected him the most.

'Don't worry,' Natasha said. She took a spoon of biryani that Arjun gave from his plate. 'Nick's not here.'

'Still at his home?' Rasiq asked.

She nodded.

'But what's the problem?' Vyom asked.

'I have been getting calls from almost all of our clients since the Narela incident,' Rasiq said. 'I wasn't expecting the news of our failure to spread so far and wide so fast. They all seemed to question our abilities.'

'That guy who cancelled our contract! He must have called other clients and warned them,' Halka said, clearly upset.

'I really don't think so,' Natasha said. 'He was so nice to us even when he was cancelling the contract. Almost apologetic.'

'Yeah, I noticed that too,' Vyom said.

'But you never know these guys,' Arjun said. 'Maybe he was just being diplomatic.'

'Either way,' Rasiq said, 'I am not sure if we can do anything about it. We did fuck up. There have been some cancellations too.'

'What?' Halka said, 'why didn't you say that earlier?'

'Didn't they see the news about the Mussourie rescue?' Vyom said. 'How can they be so insensitive?'

'Is it serious?' Natasha asked.

'I am not going to lie to you,' Rasiq said evenly.

'Shit!' Arjun swore.

'What do we do now?' Halka said.

'I don't know,' Rasiq said. 'I am doing my best to assure the callers. Despite everything, we are still the best at what we do and nothing changes. And our ambulance still reached the site sooner than a local hospital.'

'Then what's the issue?'

'Some of them accused us of being more interested in carrying out Bollywood stunts that get us publicity instead of doing our jobs,' Rasiq said. His forehead was creased with deep lines as he remembered the humiliation he felt.

'Hey,' Vyom looked up and gave an excited shout when he saw Nick stepping into the office. 'Look who is back from exile!'

They stopped their discussion and smiled, glad to see him. They had barely seen Nick in the past few weeks.

'Come on guys,' Nick's grin was wide. Gone was the frown they were used to seeing after the accident in Narela. 'It's ready.'

'What?' Arjun was the first to jump to his feet. 'Already?'

'Arjun,' Nick said, 'I have never punched anyone in my life. But if you are trying to imply the task was easy, I wouldn't mind starting now.'

'No no,' Arjun said, backing away, smiling. 'I just meant that you seemed set for a long haul. This is sooner than I expected.'

They followed Nick's gaze as he looked out of the office window, his face lighting up as if he had seen the most striking girl ever in his life. The jet pack was leaning against the boundary wall.

'Where are the rest of them?' Halka asked.

'This is a prototype. I will make the remaining five if this works.'

'If this works?' Vyom looked confused. 'Do you have doubts? And you expect us to use this? Are you crazy?'

'I know it works,' Nick said. 'I mean, I have tested it for short distances. But I couldn't take the full flight.'

'Why? Don't trust your little demon, do you?' Asylum winked.

'It's not that. I'm scared of heights!'

'I'll do it,' Natasha offered.

'No,' Vyom said. 'Your wounds have not yet healed.'

'Let me give it a try then,' Halka offered. 'I'm a tough coconut to crack.'

'Are you sure?' Arjun asked, concerned for his safety.

'Of course!' Halka beamed. He strapped on the jet pack and Nick placed a helmet on his head.

'How's a helmet going to help if this thing crashes?' Halka asked.

'I don't know, but I do know that you are not flying without it,' Nick insisted. He explained the small set of controls on the joystick that was fitted onto the belt. 'This is a test flight. Don't go too high.'

'Wish me luck!' Halka said. He fired up the jet pack expecting a blast of hot air. All they could hear, however, was a gentle hum.

'It's electric, don't you look so surprised.' Nick said. 'I am not going to risk our lives with internal combustion on our backs!'

'We shouldn't have expected anything else from you, my friend,' Rasiq smiled.

Halka increased the thrust and rose from the ground. 'Wohooooooooo!' His squeals could be heard even when he climbed nearly a hundred feet.

'Go Halka, go!' Vyom shouted, most uncharacteristically. Everyone looked at him in surprise.

'This is brilliant!' Halka shouted. He pressed the joystick forward and accelerated at great speed. Next, he pulled the joystick back a little to slow down. Spellbound, the team watched Halka's crazy antics for the next fifteen minutes as he defied heights.

'I wish I were there!' Arjun lamented. 'He's having a ball!'

'He had the balls to have that ball,' Rasiq laughed.

'This is exactly what we needed to save us,' Natasha said.

'What do you mean "save us"?' Nick asked, still smiling at the trial.

'Nothing,' Vyom said. 'Just that we can avoid a Narela now.'

'I know it's not nothing,' Nick said. 'Come on, doc. I am big boy. I can take it.'

They looked at Rasiq, who shrugged in frustration.

'Sorry,' Natasha said to Rasiq, but then she briefed Nick about what Rasiq had told them—the contract cancellations.

'But it doesn't matter anymore,' Arjun said. 'You see? That rocket is going to get us back into an even higher orbit of success.'

Rasiq, however, didn't share their optimism. He hadn't shared his biggest worry with them yet. They were looking at an imminent working capital problem. They might not be able to retain their employees or service their clients if things didn't change drastically. And quickly.

'Wohoooo, guys' Halka whooped. 'Coming back down now.'

As soon as he began his descent, he started spinning uncontrollably. He spiralled downwards and crashed to the ground.

'Halka!' Vyom ran towards him and was the first to reach him. The helmet had cracked and Halka lay unconscious. Rasiq quickly took off the jet pack.

Vyom ran his hands all over Halka's body.

'Doesn't seem to have any broken bones and there are no signs of an internal haemorrhage. I think he'll be fine. But we'd better hurry him to the hospital.'

∽

Halka regained consciousness thirty-six hours later. He had received surprisingly few and minor injuries.

Everyone cheered when he opened his eyes, and Achala hugged him. She had been by his side the entire time.

Nick, however, seemed to have lost his mischievous smile. He was subdued and blamed himself for testing the device too early.

'Hey…' Halka tried to laugh, but it hurt his ribs. He cringed from the pain before he continued, 'look at the bright side, man. I am alive and not kicking you!'

But Nick was in no mood for humour.

'I am sure you will make a better one,' Halka tried again to cheer him up. 'For a prototype, this was great. And you have to let me be the first one to try it again, since I am now an experienced hand.'

'I failed you guys,' Nick said. 'I had actually started believing that I had developed the perfect solution that could set us free. This is a huge setback. We are back to our biggest problem.' He left the room, a worried look on his face.

# 31

# Mind your mind

*F*or once, the call they received on their SOS line wasn't about an emergency.

'Can I speak to Rasiq, please? The founder of DareDreamers.' The voice at the other end was brisk and business-like.

'Hold on,' the operator said and handed the phone to Rasiq.

'Yes? How can I help you?' Rasiq said. He took the phone from the operator.

'I wish to meet you urgently regarding a pressing matter.'

'What's this about?' Rasiq asked.

'It's not something we can discuss over the phone. We need to talk, face to face.'

'Is it an emergency?' something about the voice unsettled Rasiq, but he didn't know what.

'No. But…'

'You called on our SOS number so if it isn't an emergency then I don't see any reason for us to meet you,' Rasiq answered.

'What if I said that this meeting is about addressing your biggest business worry, would you still ignore it?'

Rasiq became silent. *What could this be about?*

'Come to City Park Hotel in Pitampura at 4.00 p.m. today,' the man said. Rasiq's silence seemed to reassure him. The voice had acquired a hint of authority.

'We'll see,' Rasiq said. 'I need your name and phone number.

You seem to be using a private line.'

'Can we do this when we meet?'

'Sorry. No explanation, no show. That's our protocol.'

'Well,' the man at the other end cleared his throat, 'alright. I am Narad Money. M-O-N-E-Y,' he spelt out his last name, slowly. He then gave Rasiq a phone number.

Rasiq was amused, but he refrained from showing it.

'All right Mr Money,' he said. 'We'll see you at four today if we are not busy then.'

'We? No, no. I want you to come alone.'

'That's not possible. If it concerns the business you'll need to meet all the partners. That's the deal.'

'If I see you alone, I'll meet you, but I will leave if I see the whole team. The decision is yours,' the voice had a tone of finality and the line was disconnected.

∞

'What do you say?' Rasiq asked the team after he had briefed them. 'Do we take this crackpot seriously?'

'Did the voice sound familiar to you?' Natasha asked.

Rasiq shook his head, 'Something about him did not sound right, to be honest.'

'I don't know why you want to waste time meeting this loon,' Nick said. He had been grumpy since the failed jet pack experiment. 'I am not coming, so that's one less thing for you to worry about.'

'Yeah,' Vyom said. 'If you have a hunch this might turn out to be something, you should go and check it out. I see no point in the whole team going for this.'

∞

Rasiq entered the coffee shop of the City Park Hotel at 3.59

p.m. He looked around and was about to take out his mobile to call Narad when he heard quick footsteps behind him. He turned to face a man who smiled nervously.

'Mr Rasiq, I'm Narad,' the man said. He extended his hand with another smile. 'You decided to come alone, after all.'

Rasiq took in the appearance of the strange-looking man and shook his greasy palm. The eyes of that man were at best shifty, the face flat and emotionless, as though ironed by a steam press. Though his manner was extremely pleasant, something about him was disturbing.

'You are punctual and I appreciate that. Come,' he said, 'we have reserved a table in the far corner, away from all the noise.'

*We? He's allowed to bring more people, but not me?*

Rasiq followed him to a table occupied by an older gentleman who stood up as they approached. He was sharply dressed and sported a well-kept beard and a hat. As Rasiq shook his hand, he noticed the gentleman's fingers were studded with more rings than he could count. The man seemed to be sizing him up, like a bowler looking at a batsman before delivering the very first ball.

'I am Rakeysh Aurora,' he said with an air of authority.

*Achala's father. Halka's old boss. The CEO of G-Force*, Rasiq remembered. 'Rasiq,' he was curt, involuntarily.

'Thank you for coming to meet me today,' Rakeysh said.

'What is this about?'

'You have become a mini-celebrity of sorts, haven't you?' Rakeysh smiled. Rasiq sensed an undercurrent of intimidation in his tone and decided to let the old man do the talking for a bit.

Narad ordered coffee for all three of them to break the uncomfortable silence that ensued.

'Let me start by saying that the idea behind your start-up is solid,' Rakeysh said. 'It's way ahead of our times. Or maybe

I should say my time,' he let out a short chuckle.

Rasiq nodded along. *He's trying too hard. Silence does strange things to people. He's gone from intimidating to appeasing in less than sixty seconds.*

Rakeysh cleared his throat, 'I struggled for many years to arrive at my modest success. But your success has set a new benchmark for the industry.'

*Modest? Is he kidding me? G-Force is at least a billion-dollar company. His personal net worth must be around five hundred million dollars for sure. What is he up to?* Rasiq's mind was racing now.

'Thank you,' Rasiq said to the barista who had brought their coffees over.

Rakeysh had read Rasiq's micro reaction when he had uttered the word 'modest', and that was his in. 'Even my business model is modest compared to your offering,' Rakeysh continued. He tore open a sachet of a Sugar Free sweetener and added the white powder to his cup. 'I was just fortunate that I set up my business a couple of decades before yours, otherwise I wouldn't have stood a chance. But you see my modest idea had the possibility of being scalable, which allowed G-Force to grow and become what it is today.' He paused to pick up his coffee and gestured to Narad and Rasiq to drink too.

Rasiq's lip twitched as he was about to respond, but he held himself back. *What does he want? I can't give up my cards till I understand that.* He didn't pick up his coffee.

'You, on the other hand,' Rakeysh continued, 'are in a strange position with your business, aren't you? I mean, you are here today only because it nags you. Am I right?'

Rasiq was surprised. *How is he reading me?*

'You have great talent at DareDreamers, but you do not have an efficient delivery mechanism to deploy it across the country. Not at a pace essential to its success. You will either spread yourself too thin, or you will localize your talent to a small area, which would be a grave injustice to your vision. Not to forget, financially unviable.'

The summation was so true it forced Rasiq to give up his reticence, 'You heard about the Narela accident then? Is that what this is about?'

'Precisely,' Rakeysh said. 'You must be spending sleepless nights thinking of that time in the future when you will again have two, maybe three incidents happening in parallel. What will you do then?'

'If we had more choppers…' Rasiq started, but Rakeysh's laugh cut him off.

'I am sorry,' he said, 'but you know that these unique skill sets that your team have are hard to find. What if both the accidents need Halka? Or Natasha? Or Arjun?'

Rakeysh articulated Rasiq's business worry better than he had been able to himself. This was a first for Rasiq.

*Why wasn't I able to frame it? Is it because I am too close to the subject?*

Rasiq could sense Rakeysh's tentacles crawl up all the way inside his brain. He was thrown completely off balance. 'What is it that you wanted to meet me about?' he asked.

'I want to buy all your worries, Rasiq,' Rakeysh said. His voice was calm, business-like. He knew he had Rasiq right where he wanted him, but he was still treading carefully. He was close to putting an end to his miseries and could not afford a misstep. 'The moral responsibility of giving a hundred per cent of yourself to each and every client, especially when you are dealing with lives—it's something else, isn't it? I have been dealing with the pressure for twenty-five years, Rasiq, and trust me, it never goes away. You win some, you lose some. It's still just business for an ordinary man like me—I succeed 80, maybe 90 per cent of the time and I can live with that, albeit with some difficulty. Even my clients are happy because they save more than they pay for my services and it makes business sense to the bosses. But you, Rasiq, I know your type. That's never going to be good enough for you.'

Rasiq was silent for a long time.

'Twenty million dollars,' Rakeysh said. 'For DareDreamers.'

'That's a generous offer,' Narad said. Rasiq had a feeling that Narad had been sitting there all this while just to come in at that moment and say that.

'Thank you for the offer,' Rasiq said. 'And the coffee,' he pointed to his full cup. 'I'll think about your proposal and...'

'No hurry,' Rakeysh said, as he rose. He flashed a broad smile. 'It was a pleasure to meet a smart, young mind like yourself. I have no doubt that you will succeed in whatever you put your mind to.' He and Narad shook hands with him and left.

Rasiq remained rooted to his seat, thinking. He couldn't have pitched it better to himself.

∞

'No one is perfect, Rasiq,' Halka said. He threw his hands up in the air in frustration. He had taken the news of the meeting the hardest. 'But we are the best among the best. Yes, all our rescue missions will not be successful. But didn't we always know that?'

'And Rasiq, if we do our jobs, the success rate of rescuing people from the accidents that do come under our purview will be much higher. We have seen it with the rescue missions we have undertaken, right? Path-breaking things that have never been tried before have helped save lives,' Natasha said.

'No organization has a hundred per cent strike rate,' Vyom pitched in. 'We have come this far, we can go further too. We are better than the alternatives. And you know why? Because there are none.'

'If the world listened to people like Rakeysh,' Nick looked up from a sketch he was making, 'there would be no doctors because they would either have to have a hundred per cent success rate with their patients or not be doctors at all. No teachers because everyone in their class would have to do well. No lawyers because they should either win all their cases or not be in their line of business. And you know only one lawyer out of two in a case can win.'

'And coming from Nick,' Arjun said, 'right now, that means a lot. DareDreamers can kick more ass with us than with Rakeysh. We are the bloody DareDreamers!'

'He's offering twenty million dollars,' Rasiq said. 'That's almost three million dollars apiece, give or take, after accounting for the chopper debt.'

'That is peanuts compared to what we will earn eventually,' Halka said confidently. 'That guy is not a fool. If that's the first figure he offered, then our company is worth much more.' Halka's voice cracked from all the shouting.

'Are you sure you are not looking at him with shades of the past, Halka?' Rasiq asked.

Halka erupted with anger. 'No,' he said, 'in fact, it's only because of my experience with him that I am able to see through this guy. If you are seriously considering this offer then you are the one who is not able to see things clearly.'

'Well,' Rasiq said, 'that's subjective. It's neither here nor there.'

Silence. Halka threw his strong arms in the air.

'You told me that what we are doing is more meaningful than winning medals for my country, didn't you?' Arjun asked. 'Did that include selling our business to someone else? How can you put a price on something that's purely emotional?'

'Can you tell me what is going on in your head, Rasiq? What happened to you there? Why does this guy have such a hold over you?' Natasha was perplexed.

'He brought up all the demons that have been haunting me since the Narela incident,' Rasiq said, his head hung low. 'This dream is too big for us. Bigger than all of us combined. I love it like you do, but I also realize that we are hopelessly ill-equipped to handle it. Nick too has been uneasy, so he tried to develop a jet pack. But he failed. And we will too,' he paused, shaking his head. 'I mean, on the one hand we could be putting lives at risk by expanding the business but on the other, there's the risk of bankrupting the business if we don't expand. We are in a deadlock.'

'I knew it. That man has us by our balls. Did you ever stop to think that if he knows so much about you and could get inside your head, then he must have done something to be in that position? I don't trust him one bit,' Halka said.

'Halka, you are not helping any of us by being unreasonable. If I know Rasiq well, you are pushing him even further away from what you want,' Nick warned.

'He is thinking logically and what you keep bringing up is an emotional argument,' Natasha said.

'Guys, let's cool it. We can't tackle the situation using personal agendas as a basis. Nick wants to prove himself with the jet packs and Halka has a grouse to settle,' Rasiq's head was beginning to throb with unprocessed thoughts. He looked at Arjun and said, 'And it's different from winning medals because lives are involved. We aren't performing in a sports arena, but are facing the harsh realities of life and death, literally. An error won't result in a bronze or a silver or no medal at all. It will cost lives.'

∞

The next day, Rasiq got another call from Narad, this time on his personal number.

'This is to inform you that Mr Aurora thinks he undervalued the worth of your company and has upped the bid to twenty-five million dollars. But please understand that this offer doesn't have an infinite shelf life. It comes with a short expiry date of thirty days, which he has negotiated with a lot of difficulty with the board members of G-Force. Please think it through carefully. After thirty days, the sum would have to be invested in another acquisition G-Force has been considering for a while now.'

Rasiq was slightly taken aback. 'Yesterday, Rakeysh said there's no hurry, and now we have only thirty days?'

'What can I say,' Narad said. 'He told me that it was the board's decision and beyond his control. He did apologize for it.'

'And you forgot to tell me that he apologized?' Rasiq said. He was sure Narad was making things up on the fly.

'Hey, I am just the messenger,' Narad said before hanging up.

Rasiq shook his head.

❦

Three days after his meeting with Rakeysh, Rasiq sat with the team to discuss the matter.

'I have thought long and hard about it and concluded that it's best to sell. I have spent these past few days thinking of alternative plans to make our start-up a failsafe one, but I failed. Just six of us cannot cover the NCR, leave alone the entire country. Even with the jet packs we can't do two simultaneous missions that both require Halka or Natasha. The bid has now gone up to twenty-five million dollars and even if we don't work we can spend the rest of our lives comfortably. Not that we will sit idle.' He looked around to gauge their reaction. When he did not get any, he continued, 'We will think of another brilliant idea. One that won't involve human lives.'

'Tell me Rasiq, you worked at an investment bank. You must have made any number of business pitches. Were all of them successful?' Natasha asked.

'That is exactly the point,' Rasiq banged his fist on the table. *Can't they see? Are they blind?* 'I can digest the loss of a few million rupees, but I can't stand the thought of having blood on my hands because of our incompetence or inability to reach in time.'

'But what of the blood we save from spilling? Doesn't that count? Without us, Ashutosh would have died. And so too would Vibhor and his mahout. Achala would have perished. Should I go on? We are dealing with accidents; how can we give a hundred per cent guarantee?' Vyom's voice was shrill. 'That bastard threw the bait and you swallowed it. He played the guilt card and now you can't think of anything else.'

'I have to believe that Rakeysh will be able to save lives too,' Rasiq said. 'He'll take over our business model and back it with all the resources that G-Force has at its disposal. DareDreamers won't have to struggle to stay profitable and won't have to worry about bankruptcy. Otherwise, he wouldn't be paying such a huge price for it. He'll have our devices…'

'But he won't have the kick-ass rescue team,' Nick said, 'because none of us will work for that guy. 'And what is DareDreamers without the DareDreamers?'

'Are you trying to give a moral twist to your amoral greed?' Natasha asked, her stare cold and accusing.

'Yes Rasiq,' Vyom said. 'I too want to hear the answer to that question. Is it all about the money for you now?'

'You haven't stopped thinking about the money since he gave you the number, have you?' Nick said.

'Fuck you all!' Rasiq screamed. 'If that's what makes this

discussion easier for you, please go ahead and believe that. I am okay with all of you hating me if that's what you need to do to move beyond DareDreamer. I will accept all of these ridiculous accusations and you will do good by trying to remember that start-ups get bought all the time,' he said, 'even though they are all created with passion.'

'I don't think any of us want to sell, Rasiq,' Natasha said.

They all voiced their agreement.

'Now what are you going to do?' Halka looked at Rasiq. The tension in the air was palpable.

'I am still out. Either you can take your share or continue to work for DareDreamers once it's acquired by G-Force. Or else buy me out and stay independent.' *This is getting uglier than I imagined*, he thought, *but he was too far gone with the idea of selling the business and could no longer see a way back.*

The silence in the office was deafening. Images of the bustling, happy place of his dreams came to his mind, but his anger cut through those memories till there was nothing left but emptiness.

He got up and left.

# 32

## *Dream over?*

'What did you say? You are selling out your bestseller? Oye, have you gone mad?' His father was furious. 'You make us happy, then you make us sad. You make us happier again, then you make us sadder. Why do you keep ruining your future?'

'Dad, I am selling it because it isn't fool proof,' Rasiq said.

'You have already made a fool of yourself. And the proof of that will find you someday and haunt you for the rest of your life.'

Rasiq patiently explained his reasoning to his father.

When he finished, his father reached out to touch the left side of Rasiq's chest.

'What are you doing?'

'Just checking. You do have a heart and it beats after all. Does it not speak to you anymore? Or has your mind found a way of shutting it out entirely?'

Rasiq exhaled in frustration.

'You can rationalize anything, Rasiq. That's a gift and a curse of an overtly analytical mind. But I think there may be too much noise in your head right now. Since you have already decided to quit, why don't you take a break for a couple of weeks? That will give you enough time to come back and close the deal with Rakeysh if you still want to do that. What say?'

'But where will I go?'

'France, of course. You found yourself there when you went

last time, didn't you? Why not go and search again?'

❦

A week later, as he packed his bags for his trip to France, there was a knock at the door.

Nick. He did not smile, nor did he give Rasiq his usual bear hug. His face was gaunt and it was obvious he hadn't been sleeping too well.

'I just finished work on the jet packs,' he came straight to the point, barely able to conceal his anger. 'Even though yours is no longer needed, I did spend your share of the money on it as well.'

'Selling DareDreamers was never about having a jet pack,' Rasiq said.

'I know. Take it as a farewell gift,' he said, wiping a tear that had escaped to run down his cheek. 'Our friendship ends today, Rasiq.'

He threw the jet pack on the bed.

Rasiq stared at the floor, unable to meet Nick's eye. *He'll never understand. None of them will.*

'I can't believe that we now have to save our company from you, Rasiq. Not Rakeysh, but you! I curse the day you came to my home with the idea for this start-up. You screwed with my head Rasiq, like you screwed with everyone else's. All of us were fine till you showed us a dream. You have woken up, but we…'

He did not finish the sentence or even wait for Rasiq to respond. He stormed out of the room.

Rasiq's chest contracted with pain. He wished life was simpler than this.

❦

France without Mihir, Kshitij and Sandra did not feel the same at all. Still, given what he was going through, he found it serene and peaceful. His father was right. He needed the silence. He needed to cool down. The insulting accusations heaped upon him by his team members had infuriated him. Fortunately, that was behind him.

For the entire first week, he just strolled around the quiet town of Nantes, soaking in the pure, unpolluted air, the laid-back life that felt like an antidote to the hectic life he had led. He enjoyed his favourite French food, rich with a variety of cheese, and endless cups of coffee. He visited the Cathedral a few times as well.

On Friday, he rented a car and drove to Brittany. The three-hour drive turned out to be a trip down memory lane. The postcard worthy landscapes sprang alive with memories of the carefree time he had spent with his friends and Sandra as they pedalled their *vélos* across the town. It was as if he had pressed the play button of a movie player inside his mind. Perhaps that was the closest he had been to bliss.

He stopped at several places, drinking in the magic of France and decided he would settle there after selling his business. He would earn a PhD from a French university and become a professor. Perhaps, he could finally start to live for himself.

❧

He reached Brittany at ten in the morning and headed straight to the canals. He surprised a fisherman ready to begin his day by hiring his boat for a generous sum.

In the next ten minutes, he was racing across the waters in the motorboat.

'Slow down a bit. I'm in no hurry to get anywhere,' he grinned at the fisherman. When the man didn't understand, he repeated in French, '*Baissez la vitesse un peu. Il n'y a aucune hâte d'aller à quelque place.'*

The man nodded and smiled. '*D'accord,*' he bowed, politely. '*Tu parles parfaitement bien français!*'

Normally, he would have loved to chat with the fisherman in French, but today he needed to be alone and settled into a comfortable quietude.

The balmy day, the uncrowded sea and the gentle lapping of the waves gave him the peace he sought. Like a meditation. He could spend not one but several lifetimes in France.

∽

From Brittany he headed to Chamonix, in the Alps, on Kshitij's recommendation, who was in the US on business and couldn't meet Rasiq.

The Aiguille du midi cable car from Chamonix took him to the 3,700-metre-high platform on Mont Blanc. He stood in the glass room, a marvel of engineering, looking down at the thousand-metre-deep abyss under his feet, which were safely planted on transparent glass.

As he stood observing the view, he realized that he was not close to the summit of Mont Blanc, as he had earlier thought. It was almost another thousand metres to the top.

He had a sudden desire to go to the summit and experience the richness of the beauty around him, without the constraints of the glass. He wanted to feel the chilly air brushing against his cheeks.

He remembered the jet pack that Nick had thrown at him. Thankfully, he had had the sense to pack it. He saw the chance to realize his impulsive desire.

He rushed back to his hotel in Chamonix, retrieved the jet pack and strapped it on. He realized that it didn't look very different from a backpack of the kind tourists typically carried, with the exception of the joystick in the belt. He was sure he could get away with it in France as if it were a radical new fashion. The pack felt light. He read through the instruction manual on the way to Mer de Glace, which was a short walk from his hotel.

It was around 6.30 p.m. and already dark. He smiled as he walked among people. No one had any idea of the special power he had. *Is that how superheroes would feel if they were real?*

The desire to fly seized him. He began to look for a secluded place from where he could take off so he wouldn't invite unwanted attention. There would no doubt be permission issues. He finally found an isolated spot around a bend in the mountain road.

He pressed the ignition switch. The gentle hum was deceiving since he knew, from Halka's trial, how powerful it was. He manipulated the joystick and to his delight, he rose slowly into the air. He hovered a few feet off the ground for the first minute and then tested the landing which Nick had managed to fix. *Perfect!* He took in a deep breath and rose very high this time, nearly disappearing into the dark sky. There was a remote chance someone might see him, but he was too thrilled to care.

Rising higher, he felt the wind slapping against his face. The joy and exhilaration he felt in that moment made him forget all his worries. He wanted to hug Nick for this marvellous creation.

He began his descent gradually. As he was heading back to his secluded spot, he saw a woman bending over the rails that bordered the abyss. She was inclined at a very precarious angle. From the way her back was heaving it looked like she was retching. *Is she ill? Throwing up?* Before he could ascertain, he saw her climb on the railing.

*Oh my god! She's planning to jump.*

He turned the throttle on his jet pack and started accelerating towards the woman. He was amazed at the speed with which he moved. He estimated it was more than eighty kilometres per hour. As he neared the lady—in a matter of seconds—he shouted out to her. She was now standing on top of the railing with her arms outstretched. Her eyes were closed. Rasiq shouted out to her a few more times, but she was deaf to the world around her. He pressed on the joystick further, but she jumped before he could reach her.

Before he could think, he was instinctively diving down the valley at great speed. He caught the woman in her free fall and locked her in his powerful grip. He then switched to the ascent mode and they began to rise. The terrified woman still had her eyes tightly shut.

It took her several seconds to realize that she wasn't dead and was, in fact, heading up instead of down. She opened her eyes, saw Rasiq and shrieked, more out of shock than fear. Thankfully, they had reached the spot from where she had jumped and Rasiq landed them gently.

'Let me die, let me die!' she screamed the moment Rasiq left her. He had to immobilize her using a grip he had learnt from Halka.

'Why are you trying to kill yourself?'

'Let me go! I wish to die!'

'I am calling the police, you can do what you want in their presence,' Rasiq took out his phone.

'Please don't. Don't add more misery to my life.' Her body became limp as she gave up struggling. 'Release me, I can't breathe!'

Rasiq eased his grip on her. She stumbled and sat on a nearby wooden bench, sobbing. He let her recover.

'Why?' he asked softly when she had regained her composure somewhat.

She lifted her face from her hands and looked out into the

distance, her eyes dazed. 'I threw away my husband's winning lottery ticket. It was for a 100,000 euros prize money. He keeps buying lottery tickets, it's his hobby. And he is careless with his papers, never throws anything out, so the junk keeps piling up. He doesn't even dispose of his old lottery tickets. Thinking that he never wins, in a fit of anger, I cleaned up his room while he was at work today. He called me a few hours ago to tell me that he had finally won the lottery after a decade of trying...' her voice trailed off.

'Did you tell your husband about this?'

She shook her head. 'Daniel will go wild when he finds out what I have done.'

Rasiq sat next to the woman and hugged her to console her. 'You have to talk to your husband. It's easy to imagine the worst when your emotions are heightened. He may not react the way you are expecting him to.'

The woman looked up as she wiped her nose with her handkerchief. She kept shaking her head.

'Alright,' he said, 'now I can't leave you till you talk to your husband.'

'Why?'

'Because I can't be sure if you'll try to kill yourself again.'

'Don't you have anything better to do?' she asked. She began to sob again.

He accompanied Angela—that was her name—back to her house where they waited for her husband to return from work. Angela sat like a clock that had stopped. Still and without movements, hoping time would stop too and she would never have to face the dreaded moment.

'You know,' she said, 'he was never a gambler, but when he turned twenty-seven he started buying one lottery ticket a month. Never two or more. I used to laugh because I felt there was no way we would ever win the lottery.' She started sobbing again.

The doorbell rang and she looked up in fear. 'It's him. He's here.' Her eyes reflecting a mix of terror and shame.

Rasiq caught her hand reassuringly. 'Come, let's bring him in. One step at a time.'

∞

Daniel broke into a smile when Angela opened the door and hugged her.

'We won! We won!' he shouted as he lifted Angela off her feet and twirled her around. When he calmed down, he saw Rasiq and looked at him curiously.

Rasiq gauged from the man's kind eyes that he loved Angela. This was the moment he should know.

'I am Rasiq and I caught your wife mid-air in her drop to death about an hour ago,' he said.

The man's face crumpled with confusion as he looked at Angela, who began to cry.

'What? Why? What happened?' Daniel asked overwhelmed with confusion.

'She wanted to end her life because she threw away your winning lottery ticket.'

'What's happening Angela?' Daniel walked with faltering steps, like a man hit on the head. He flopped into the nearest chair, looking at both of them uncomprehendingly. The picture of happiness that had played in his head all the way to home was turning rapidly into a nightmare.

Rasiq could understand his confusion and disorientation. It was too much to absorb for a man who had expected to come home to nothing but unbridled happiness.

'But why, Angela? Why would you want to commit suicide

over money? I don't understand!'

Angela struggled against her sobs and said, 'I couldn't bear to see your disappointment. You won the lottery after thirteen years and I ruined it for you.'

'Oh my god!' Daniel said. He finally gathered the strength to stand up. Tears welled up in his eyes. 'You don't even know why I started buying the lottery tickets.'

Angela looked at him in confusion.

'Remember our second anniversary? We stopped outside a jewellery shop in Paris because you wanted to look at the diamond necklace displayed on the window,' he paused, a hint of a smile playing on his lips as he turned the past in his head. 'You looked at it for a long time before we finally walked on. And when we passed the store a second time, you looked longingly at it again.'

'Yes, I think I remember,' Angela said. 'What has that got to do with...'

'I went back to that store the next day. The necklace was for 40,000 euros. I knew we could not afford it in our lifetime. So, I started buying a lottery ticket every month. I hoped to buy the necklace with the winnings. For you, Angela. I won, but what would it have meant with you gone?'

Angela tried to speak but no words came out of her mouth. She rushed to embrace him and buried her head in his chest, her back heaving.

'Daniel, Angela,' Rasiq said, interrupting their moment. 'My job here is done. I think I should take your leave.'

Daniel walked up to him, 'Thank you, Mr Rasiq,' he pronounced his name with a French accent. 'I can't thank you enough. You said you caught her mid-air?'

Rasiq smiled. 'Yes,' he said, 'I am sure Angela will tell you all the details.'

'Oh, many times over, I am certain,' he braved a smile, fighting back his tears.

'Rasiq, can you wait for just a moment please?' Angela said.

'Sure.'

She returned with a bottle of a rare, 1954 vintage Bordeaux red wine. Tied to the neck of the bottle was a small note that read: 'To the flying angel from heaven who gave a new lease of life to our love.'

Rasiq knew he would never drink that special bottle of wine. It, along with the note, was a precious souvenir from France that he would always cherish.

He thanked them and left.

Love. A powerful emotion that he too had experienced. Not just with Sandra, Mihir, Kshitij and Ruchika but others too. On his walk back to his hotel, Rasiq remembered his friends. Nick, Halka, Natasha, Vyom, Arjun and Asylum. He missed them. None of them wanted to sell their enterprise, even for a fortune; it was hard to find such passionate people. Rasiq confessed to himself that he had overlooked their emotions and happiness and had given importance to only himself—his worries, his problems. And maybe the money too.

He had spent his days in France planning and thinking about the past, himself and his future. The others, who had contributed towards making that life even possible, had not mattered. No, he thought. I can't do that. That's not who I am. He thought how happy Nick would be when he found out that his jet pack had helped save a life.

He involuntarily picked up his phone to call Nick, but stopped. He knew Nick wouldn't take his call.

∽

A couple of days later he boarded his flight to Delhi.

Sitting in the window seat, he couldn't sleep. He stared outside at the absolute darkness, thinking of his trip.

*It's easy to imagine the worst when your emotions are heightened,* he remembered telling Angela. *Is that what I am doing with DareDreamers? Imagining the worst?*

*No, it's a real fear.* He thought of the conversation with Rakeysh. *It is real.*

*Define real. The probability of two Halkas or two Natashas being required at once is inconsequential. Besides, didn't I just pull off a daredevil stunt? Surely, Natasha would have done it better, but the jet pack makes even me a superhero. Isn't this exactly what we needed to ensure our operations go smoothly? A little training perhaps for everyone, more skillsets? More DareDreamers like them? Possibilities open when the mind steps out of fear-zone into the dare-zone.*

Before he could continue the conversation, he drifted into a sleep. He glided into a limbo between the thoughts that preoccupied him and his dreams.

Rakeysh was wearing a black magician's robe and a ridiculously tall hat.

'Let me buy your worries…' he whispered while moving his bejewelled fingers over Rasiq's face.

*No. This can't be real. This can't be magic,* his logical mind protested.

*Unless…*

'If he knows so much about you and can get inside your head, then he must have done something to be in that position. I don't trust that guy one bit,' Halka's words rose from the depths of his subconscious mind as he struggled desperately to get out of the clutches of the sinister magician.

Rakeysh's fingers continued to move over his face in a mesmerizing dance.

Rasiq started feeling helpless. He felt trapped. He started sweating.

'You know how magicians fool you,' he remembered his father telling him when he was a kid. 'They will use their non-stop yapping to draw your attention away from where the action is. While you are distracted, looking with all your focus but in the wrong place, they will make their move in plain sight.'

*I have been looking in the wrong place. Our conversation is not where I'll find the answer.*

Rasiq could feel Rakeysh's tentacles digging deeper into his brain. He shouted in agony.

'Hello,' the guy in the seat next to Rasiq's shook him.

Rasiq opened his eyes and came back into reality, bright white light flooding his eyes.

'Can you please not shout in your sleep?' he said. 'And please shut that window.'

Rasiq squinted his eyes as he looked at the open window. He saw only clouds outside. He shut the window and realized that he had an intense headache. The pain from the dream had crossed over to the physical world and he felt disoriented. He wiped the sweat from his forehead, understanding a little about what he wanted to do when he landed.

'Do you need anything, sir?' The flight attendant hovered over him, concerned.

'Water please.'

'Are you unwell?'

'On the contrary, I think I just got a little better,' Rasiq smiled, mysteriously.

∽

He went straight to their office in Manesar from the airport. They had two days left to make their decision and there was

no time to waste.

They all looked at Rasiq as he dragged his bags in. They were seeing him after four weeks.

'What brings you here?' Arjun asked.

'Can we all meet?' Rasiq asked him.

Arjun shrugged and gathered the others in the conference room.

The sense of gloom he had left them with still prevailed.

'Have you come to collect your share?' Halka enquired. 'Or have you come to rub salt in our wounds because we will be working for Rakeysh in a couple of days?'

'Neither, actually,' Rasiq said. 'I have come to tell you that I am not selling my stake in DareDreamers. I was an idiot and you were right.'

There was a confused silence as the rest of them looked at each other, unsure of what Rasiq was saying.

'But for now,' he continued, 'we are going to ride out our challenges, whatever it takes. We are going to make our great company greater. And I am really sorry, guys, for putting you through hell over these past four weeks. I know you won't feel like it, but I could really use a hug right now.'

'Are you kidding?' Natasha said. Her brooding face transformed into a smile that made her look exceptionally beautiful. She jumped off her chair. 'This means we get to keep the company! This is the miracle that we have been wishing for each minute of each day for the last four weeks!'

They hugged and shouted and laughed like old times.

∽

His father was gardening when Rasiq got home. He went straight to him, touched his feet and hugged him.

'I'm not selling DareDreamers, dad!' he said. 'And I need

your blessings to make it even more successful.'

'I knew you would make a U-turn without giving an indicator!' No one could surprise his father enough for him to forget to make his terrible jokes. 'You were tired and had to take a break for a bit. I can understand that. Now get up and win this race. It's the one that matters.'

His mother came out to join them and Rasiq hugged her.

'Our blessings are always with you.'

∽

The next day he dialled Narad's number.

'Good evening Mr Rasiq, I was expecting your call but not until tomorrow. I hope everything is alright?'

'Yes. We are good. I wanted to speak to Mr Rakeysh.'

'Very good,' he said. 'When would you like to meet to finalize…'

'Can you take him on the call right now? Patch him in?'

'Sure,' Narad broke into a chuckle. 'He would be happy to hear it directly from you.'

There was silence for a few seconds.

'Mr Rasiq? I hear you've made your decision before the deadline,' Rakeysh said. 'The board would be glad to hear this.'

'I am sorry, Mr Rakeysh, but we won't be selling DareDreamers,' Rasiq said.

There was a silence on the call. Rasiq smiled, thinking what must be running through their heads at this point.

Narad cleared his throat. 'You are turning down a very generous offer, Mr Rasiq. Have you thought it over carefully because there is still time to reconsider…'

'Have you thought about what you will do when you have two, maybe three incidents happening simultaneously,' Rakeysh interrupted Narad.

'I am grateful for your concern, Mr Rakeysh. If you must know, we now have jet packs for that.'

'What are jet packs?' he asked, confused.

'I am sure you'll be able to google that after the call,' Rasiq said. 'If there's nothing else…'

'I am sorry,' he said, 'but you know that these unique skill sets that your team have are hard to find. What if there are two accidents need Halka? Or Natasha? Or Arjun?'

Rasiq laughed, 'You are using the exact same words, Mr Rakeysh. Did you seriously mug these things up?'

'Be that as it may…'

'There are many more DareDreamers, Mr Rakeysh,' Rasiq said, interrupting Rakeysh. 'We are not the only ones in the world. We'll find our kin to fill in.'

Rasiq hung up and finally felt free from the chains with which Rakeysh had him tied for so long.

He was ready to pursue what he loved.

The rest would follow.

## 33

## *Terror without error*

'*T*urns out it was a foolish idea after all,' Rakeysh sat down opposite Narad, trying hard to remain composed, but the call from Rasiq had hurt his pride immensely. 'A foolish idea from a foolish man.'

'But we almost got them, didn't we? I don't understand what made them change their mind, Mr Aurora. Something must have happened at the last minute.'

'Either we are messing with the wrong bunch,' Rakeysh said, rubbing his forehead with his palm, trying to ease away his worry lines, 'or you are an ineffective operator. Which one is it?'

'It's a process, Mr Aurora,' Narad said. 'You have to respect the process.'

'Said every loser with little clue about what they had to do,' Rakeysh said, brushing Narad's response aside. 'Admit it, they are too clever for you. They are always a hundred steps ahead of you.'

'You underestimate me,' Narad said. 'We have just started, Mr Aurora. You can't deny that I am very thorough in my understanding of how they operate. I will now use their strategy against them. You must give me some more time.'

'What do you have in mind this time?' Rakeysh asked.

'Trust me, you don't want to know,' Narad's confidence returned as he saw Rakeysh was still hopeful and interested.

'And why is that?'

'Because you will want deniability for what's going to happen next. I'll need more cash, though,' Narad said. 'What I am going to do is risky and it'll have costs associated with it.'

Rakeysh shook his head. 'I do need to know.'

'Don't worry, you will soon see that the money you paid me was well worth it. And it's only a fraction of what you were willing to pay them.'

'The plan, Narad,' Rakeysh reiterated.

'Have you read *The Almighty* by Irving Wallace?' Narad asked. Rakeysh nodded.

'Great! When the guy's paper was not doing too well,' Narad continued, 'what did he do? He devised a unique strategy. Instead of waiting for news to happen, he started creating sensational news. He engineered incidents and kept his unsuspecting correspondents stationed near the incident sites, well in advance. Naturally, his correspondents were the first to report the news to the world. And soon, his paper became the most successful one in the country.'

'Yes, but what does that have to do with our DareDreamers problem? You want me to diversify to the news industry?'

Narad realized that Rakeysh was hooked. Yet again, he thought, feeling almost giddy. He took out his e-cigarette and inhaled deeply. It made him feel like Sherlock Holmes without risking lung cancer and leaving his money behind without enjoying it. 'No, Mr Aurora,' he said. 'In my plan for DareDreamers, I want us to go a step further, like in the book. I have something in mind.'

Rakeysh nodded, a slow smile spreading across his face.

'Ideas rule this world and ideas mean money, Mr Rakeysh. I know I have not delivered, but deliver I shall. It's only a matter of time. Meanwhile, there are expenses…' Narad trailed off meaningfully

'How much?'

'I will need another twenty-five lakh for now.'

Rakeysh nodded, 'I'll have it delivered this evening. But no jeopardizing lives, Narad. I am still not going to okay that.'

'I promise there will be no loss of lives,' Narad said. He kept his hand over his heart.

'Now, go get these guys. Make them pay for turning down my generous offer. I can't wait to get that boy Halka out of my life for good. I can't bear to look at his face.' He cringed as the images of Achala's rescue flashed through his mind.

'I know, Mr Aurora,' Narad said. 'But that isn't going to be easy. That boy Halka,' Narad made air quotes, 'has a physique to die for. He could give many celebrities with their chiselled bodies a run for their money.'

'Really? I always thought his upper body was like a giant triangle pointing to his dick,' Rakeysh's eyes looked like red pools of malevolent thoughts.

Narad laughed as Rakeysh left.

'Interesting.' He put his feet up on his desk and took a drag from his e-cigarette. 'Meet the new Armstead from *The Almighty*,' he smiled.

∞

Over the next few days, Narad immersed himself in the dark side of the Internet: the playground of criminals, paedophiles and terrorists, where illegal activities flourished under the cover of anonymity.

It takes special skills to penetrate this dark zone. Special references have to be dropped through a trail of coded messages that signal the anonymous criminals to make the first contact.

He checked an anonymous IP address that had been given to him by an acquaintance. He landed on what seemed a very ordinary and unremarkable site that sold parts from junk planes.

'I need a Fiat 6000 FC engine,' he left the message. The Fiat 6000 FC engine was non-existent. It was a footprint he left for someone to contact him. Someone who would trace his IP and reach out to him.

∽

Later that week, as Narad was checking his Facebook account, he received a ping from a guy named My Mood.

'Hi, brother,' the chat window said. Narad clicked through the guy's profile but found nothing useful.

'Hi,' Narad pinged back. 'Do I know you?'

'No,' My Mood replied. 'But I knowing all about you.'

'I am sort of famous,' Narad wrote, 'so I am not surprised.'

'I famous too.'

'How?'

'Because I knowing that you looking for me.'

'Yes. I am looking for a friend. I mean, who isn't?'

'I not here for franship,' the guy wrote. 'It's about the other thing you wanting.'

'Are you Al-Q?'

'Shut the fuck up man! Big brother is always watching. Be careful with this stuff!'

My Mood's sudden switch to good English surprised Narad. 'But I didn't use the full name!' he wrote.

'You must be insane to think no one will get the drift with that lousy abbreviation. We don't use that name anymore.'

'What do you use?'

'Are you for real? Meet us and we'll talk,' My Mood typed and sent an angry emoji. 'Do not forget to bring your brains along.'

'Okay,' Narad responded, chastised.

'If you happen to be standing below Kotha No. 12, GB Road at 10.00 p.m. tomorrow, we will pick you up,' My Mood wrote.

'It's a date!' Narad responded.

There was no reply.

My Mood was gone. His account was deleted immediately and there was no trace of him anywhere.

'These guys are good,' Narad said aloud to himself, impressed.

∞

Narad reached GB Road—the hub of Delhi's flourishing sex trade at 9.50 p.m. the following night. He could barely control himself, he was so excited. He ignored the giggling, garishly made-up prostitutes who solicited him from the caged windows of their semi-dark dungeons.

After waiting for more than thirty minutes, just when he was beginning to worry and wonder what he was doing there, a Maruti Omni van stopped in front of him and the door slid open. Narad was pulled inside quickly and a gunny bag was thrown over his head. His neck hurt from the whiplash.

Ten minutes later, the van stopped. Narad was pulled out and carried down a long flight of stairs, like a sack of wheat. He was installed on a chair and the gunny bag was finally pulled off. Narad blinked and looked around. He was in what looked like the basement of an old building. He inhaled deeply and said, 'You guys shouldn't keep your pick-up spot ten minutes away from your office. It's easy for someone looking for you to sweep a small radius like that.'

A man dressed like a peon, complete with khaki green Nehru cap, walked up to Narad slowly. 'We know,' he said, 'but petrol prices have gone up and it's a drain on our margins. Cost-cutting is the buzzword these days.' He was rubbing his right thumb in the palm of his left hand, crushing and mixing chewing tobacco presumably. He clapped his right palm lightly over the mixture, gathered it up and put it under his lip. He then ran his fingers over his moustache.

'Now,' he said, 'what brings you here?'

'Where am I?'

'This is the office of KyaFayada. What do you want? I won't ask again.'

'I need your help in creating an incident,' Narad said.

'Are you from a news channel?'

'No, why?'

'We get requests from a lot of news channels who want to create news and be the first ones to report it,' the peon said.

'Seriously?' Narad asked, shocked.

'Yes,' the peon nodded. 'It's been three decades since *The Almighty* came out and they still think it is original,' he stopped nodding and started shaking his head. The transition was seamless, Narad noticed.

'Take this,' he handed Narad a slip of paper. 'Take the lift on the right and go to the seventh floor.' He spat out his tobacco and the long red slurry of spit, betel and tobacco landed at the foot of a pillar. Narad followed the trajectory. He noticed massive red stains on the pillar and the floor.

'What's this?' he asked, looking at the piece of paper the man had given him. It had the number '57' written on it.

'It's your token number,' the peon said before spitting again.

∽

When Narad stepped out of the lift on the seventh floor, he was taken aback by the sight that greeted him: a long, snaking queue of fidgety, sweating people. Plaster had chipped from the walls and lay on the floor in a powdery dust that ruined his polished shoes. At some places, the bricks were visible. A musty, moulding smell hung in the air.

'What's this queue for?' Narad asked a young man.

'Controlled Terrorism,' the man said.

'What's that?'

'First time?' the man asked.

'Yes,' Narad replied, feeling embarrassed.

'The desk where you apply for small-scale attacks.'

'Oh,' Narad said. 'I didn't know they were so organized! What's your token number?'

'Forty-five,' the man said.

Narad walked to the back of the queue.

Forty-five minutes later, the line hadn't moved an inch. His shirt was drenched with sweat and his nostrils were full of stench from all the people standing around in the corridor. Suddenly, a podgy man walked out of the lift holding a briefcase. His appearance evoked a collective sigh of relief. The office had begun to function.

Narad waited patiently for his turn for close to five hours. There were still a few people before him in the queue.

At 4:00 a.m., the podgy man rose abruptly from his desk and packed up his briefcase. People pleaded with him to process their requests, but he ignored them and walked briskly towards the lift. 'Come tomorrow,' he kept repeating.

Narad followed the man and jumped into the lift behind him.

'Hi, I am Narad,' he said.

The podgy man remained silent.

'Let me know how I can get my request processed,' Narad said. He pushed a bundle of 2,000-rupee notes into the man's pocket.

The podgy man stared at Narad, his brows knitting. He suddenly broke into a smile. 'I am Mangal Deshpande.' He extended his hand and Narad shook it. 'It's nice to meet people who know the way things work. Let's talk in the canteen in the basement.'

∞

'This is the good stuff,' Mangal said. He sipped on his large peg of Glenfiddich on the rocks, studying Narad. They were sitting in a secluded corner on the ground floor of the building. 'Now tell me, what do you need?'

Narad set his drink down. He explained to Mangal what he wanted the outfit to do. 'Do you need anything else?' he asked.

Mangal smiled. 'I will give you a whole list, but that depends on how it's to be done.'

'I have a few ideas about how to make it truly beneficial for my client. And don't worry, he'll spare no expense,' Narad replied, making a cross on the wet circles made by their frosty glasses on the table.

# 34

## Landing safely into trouble

*I*t was 3.00 a.m. when their SOS line rang.

'It's a lady from the Ministry of Civil Aviation,' the operator came running into Rasiq's room.

'Wake everyone up,' he told the operator, taking the phone from him. The operator nodded and left.

'Yes ma'am, this is Rasiq.'

'We don't have time for introductions so I am going to get straight to the point. We have an emergency. There's been an incident on an international flight bound from France to India.'

'What happened?' Rasiq asked.

'Both pilots passed out after consuming their meal,' the voice on the phone spoke quickly. 'It's flying on auto-pilot for now, but we need to land the plane safely before the fuel runs out.'

'Where is it?'

'It's over the Arabian Sea. Without the pilots, it drifted off course and is now low on fuel. All attempts to revive the pilots have failed,' the woman said. 'Can you help us?'

'Of course,' Rasiq said. 'We need...'

'Come to the Air Force Station at Palam quickly,' the woman said. 'A team from the Air Force is struggling to devise a plan.' She hung up.

Rasiq turned to face the rest of the team, which had gathered around him by then. 'We have to get to the Palam Air Force station ASAP.'

∽

Asylum flew them to the Palam Air Force station.

Nick identified the squadron leader from the stars on his uniform. They introduced themselves, as they walked.

'Do you have a plan?' the squadron leader asked.

'Yes.'

'Let's discuss it on the way.'

Rasiq detailed the plan while they were airborne in a C-130J Super Hercules. The interior of the Hercules plane was built like a vault of solid steel. The tough, ruggedly built, all-weather aircraft had a long history of successful use in rescue operations.

'The timing needs to be perfect. The door of the passenger aircraft cannot remain open longer than a few seconds,' the squadron leader said. 'The sudden loss of pressure can lead to many complications.'

Rasiq nodded, 'We will try to execute the operations quickly.'

'Do you think you can pull this off?'

'We know this is risky, but that's what we do,' Rasiq said. 'In case we fail, you will have to exercise the grim option of a cabin crew member trying to land the plane.'

'Hope it doesn't come to that. Let's do our best!' the squadron leader said in his mission mode voice.

∽

The sky was cloudy and the weather turbulent. The Hercules flew at 0.58 Mach or 660 kilometres per hour, roughly twice the speed of their chopper. They intercepted the Boeing after a flight time of forty-five minutes.

'We have set up a communication channel with the cabin

crew in-charge. The passengers are not yet aware of the situation,' the squadron leader informed them.

'Mic test,' Rasiq said into his headset. 'Can you hear us?'

'Yes,' the flight attendant's shaky voice came through on their earpieces.

'You have to explain to her how to depressurize the cabin,' Nick shouted over the hum of the engines.

'She will be doing that,' the squadron leader pointed towards the young engineer accompanying them. She was reading an aircraft manual. Unfamiliar with civil aircraft machinery, it was taking her time to get through it. Time that they didn't have.

'I guess I should go and help her,' Nick offered.

'You know the specs of the aircraft?'

'Yes,' Nick said. 'I upgraded my knowledge on the way.'

'Why are we depressurizing the cabin?' Arjun asked.

'One can't open the door of the plane if the cabin is not depressurized,' Nick explained. 'The door is pressure locked, you could say.'

Nick slipped into the chair next to the engineer and assisted her in relaying the instructions for depressurizing the cabin to the cabin crew incharge, who acted swiftly.

The passenger oxygen masks were released and the cabin began depressurizing.

'Though the cabin pressure will fall gradually to match the outside pressure level, even a minor difference of air pressure can create suction that could rip you out of the plane when the door opens. Hold fast, hold tight,' Nick cautioned the cabin crew in-charge.

'Ninety seconds to rendezvous,' the squadron leader's voice had an urgency to it.

Natasha and Halka had strapped on their jet packs. Halka had tied Asylum to himself using a harness and a safety belt.

'Stay calm,' Halka said. 'You are in safe hands. And we are going to make it.'

Asylum grinned nervously. 'Flying a plane is different from sliding along a precarious rope tied between two planes. This may end with a new landing experience for me. One that involves a 40,000-feet bone-crushing drop.'

'We have parachutes for that eventuality,' Halka reminded him.

Natasha secured one end of a strong cable inside the Hercules. The other end of the rope was in her hand—it was a long cable to avoid the Air Force plane getting yanked by the Boeing or vice versa. The daredevilry she was about to attempt was her most difficult one yet—live action at 30,000 feet. She would fix the rope for Halka to glide into the plane with Asylum.

'We are flying next to the plane now, at the same speed. You need to jump in ten, nine, eight...' The squadron leader started the countdown. All eyes were now on Natasha.

The door of the Hercules opened and they saw the other plane a few hundred metres away.

'Three, two, one, now!'

Natasha took in a deep breath before jumping from the plane and immediately switched on her jet pack. She accelerated towards the Boeing. 'Open the door now!' Natasha commanded.

She was now close to the aircraft, but the door didn't open, as planned. 'Open it, damn it!' she screamed.

At that moment, the door opened and they saw an ashen-faced cabin crew in-charge, trembling in fear. Natasha steered the jet pack to the direction of the open door and switched off her jet pack, seconds before she was near the aircraft. Her momentum carried her inside the aircraft. She had completed the stunt with exquisite timing and precision.

Natasha slipped through the door and skidded to the other

end of the aircraft. She rose quickly and secured her end of the cable inside the Boeing. 'Halka, jump! Now!' she instructed over the headset and pulled at the cable to make sure it was taut.

Halka hooked his safety belt to the cable and jumped out of the Hercules with Asylum securely strapped to him. They slid along the cable connecting the two planes, which were stationary relative to each other. Halka fired up his jet pack and propelled them along the cable towards the Boeing. They landed safely inside seconds after Natasha. Natasha unhooked the cable and closed the aircraft door.

'Rendezvous successful,' Natasha reported on the communication channel as she closed the door.

'Re-pressurize the cabin,' Nick's voice came through their headsets. The cabin crew in-charge swung into action.

Asylum rushed into the cockpit. He took charge of the plane and contacted ground control for directions

The plane had critical fuel level and the engines could die anytime.

Asylum contacted the Delhi airport. 'We need clearance for an emergency landing,' he said. He had recovered his poise, now that he was in familiar territory.

'You already have priority clearance. Our ground crew is waiting for you. Wish you all the best!' ground control responded.

∞

Asylum flew the plane for what seemed to be the longest fifty minutes of his life. His gaze was constantly hovering on the fuel gauge. He sighed with relief when he landed the aircraft in a perfect touchdown at the Delhi airport. When he tried to taxi the plane towards the emergency team awaiting them, the engines spluttered and died. They had barely made it. The ground support rushed to the plane to assist the passengers.

A few minutes later, the Hercules also landed at the Delhi airport.

The team hugged each other as they met inside the airport. They were surrounded by a huge crowd and the journalists from news channels, who were cheering. Before the crowd could be silenced so that they could answer questions from the journalists, policemen in uniform swooped down on them, without warning.

'You are all under arrest for attempting the sabotage of this aircraft,' an inspector announced tersely.

Their jaws dropped as they could not believe what they had heard. Amidst the flashing cameras of the news channels, they were whisked away in a police van.

The next day's newspapers carried their photographs with damning headlines.

**Dare Dreamers: The rescuers or the perpetrators?**

**DareDreamers' Modus Operandi Revealed: They sabotage. They rescue.**

Their arrest was replayed endlessly on every news channel. Elaborate theories and explanations for their past heroics also came up overnight to tarnish many of their rescue missions as manipulations. The heroes had turned into villains.

Part Four

Fighting for the Carrots

# 35

# Guilty until proven innocent

'*H*ow very convenient!' the inspector said, dismissing their version of truth with the suspicion police personnel normally have of crooks. It was dawn by the time they had reached the Indira Gandhi International Airport police station and Rasiq thought that it must be afternoon by now. Inside the holding cell of the police station, however, time had stopped moving.

'Trust me,' Rasiq looked at the inspector through a haze of pain and anger, 'it wasn't convenient.'

Their interrogation had gone on for hours. The civil procedure had escalated to third-degree very quickly.

'Tell us how you drugged the two pilots,' the inspector shouted, yet again. The assault on their sensibilities was complemented by the assault on their bodies as the inspector's baton came crashing down on Rasiq's shin. Both the mental and physical assaults were aimed to beat them into accepting the police's version of reality.

Rasiq and his team had borne the violence for a long time and were now numb from the incessant assaults. The inspector gestured to his subordinate who struck another blow on Rasiq's back, causing him to tumble forward off his chair.

The cops used every method, in the book and outside, to extort a confession from them. Rasiq's gaze fell on Halka's limp body.

Earlier, Halka had refused to take the blows from the cops without a fight and had hit back with a vengeance. He now lay unconscious on the floor next to them. They had shot him with a tranquilizer and hit him on the head with a rod before he had finally passed out.

The constable pulled Rasiq up and put him back in the chair. The others—Nick, Vyom, Asylum and Arjun—were still receiving kicks and punches. Vyom was wailing in agony. Rasiq could only hope that Natasha's fate in the women's holding cell was better than theirs. But he knew that it was only his wishful thinking.

*So much for risking our lives to save a plane from crashing. What a merciless thanksgiving.*

'We can keep doing this till you vomit the truth,' the inspector said. 'Confess to the conspiracy you hatched in France.'

'You can't torture us,' Nick whispered in his semi-conscious state. 'It's unconstitutional. You have no evidence against...' he screamed as they pulled his hair and slapped his face.

'Wow,' the inspector said, clapping his hands together. 'Aren't you the smart one? Teaching law to the police!' He lashed Nick with his belt, who howled with pain. Rasiq could see a deep gash on Nick's back. 'Let me educate you a little about your situation. You have been arrested under the Unlawful Activities Prevention Act,' the inspector said. 'You planned and successfully sedated the pilots, jeopardizing the lives of all passengers on that aircraft, not to mention property, so that this...' he kicked Asylum, '...this pilot of yours could pull off that stunt and make you famous and earn you a lot of new business.'

'I just landed the plane,' Asylum said, 'the girl and that guy,' he pointed towards Halka, 'pulled off the real stunt.'

'Sure,' the inspector said. 'But none of you are getting away anytime soon.'

'What?' Rasiq raised an eyebrow. 'UAPA? You are calling us terrorists after what we did? This is madness!'

'Where did you get that ridiculous idea?' Vyom managed with great difficulty.

'Is it really ridiculous?' a familiar voice said from behind.

Rasiq strained to turn around to see the man who had spoken. But he was hit again, before he could.

'Weren't you in France for three weeks recently? Enough time to plan this ghastly act, I would think,' the familiar voice continued.

'We've heard this story a million times now,' Rasiq said. 'It's just not true!'

'Tell us how you arranged for the meals of those pilots to be laced,' the inspector growled at them, repeating the question yet again.

'That's an insane accusation,' Rasiq screamed at the top of his voice. 'You don't have a shred of evidence to prove...'

The man who had spoken to them finally stepped in front of him. Narad Money.

'You?' Rasiq asked. 'What are you doing here?'

Nick and Vyom stared at the balding man, confused.

'I was keeping tabs on your business,' Narad said, 'conducting due diligence for the acquisition when I found out that you invented jet packs and went to France.'

'I told you about that!' Rasiq protested.

Nick's eyes widened with surprise. 'Is this Narad? The guy who was trying to take over DareDreamers? With that G-Force guy?'

Rasiq nodded.

Narad scoffed, 'Why would you tell me that you invented jet packs? Did you tell anyone else? No, I found that on my own. And I saw a clear pattern in all your missions. If you guys invested in making or buying something it better be put to good use.'

'You are twisting the facts to malign us…' Rasiq started.

'That's enough bullshit,' Narad said, cutting him off. 'I immediately told my client that you guys are a sham and they called the acquisition off.'

'I called it off,' Rasiq retorted.

'Sure,' Narad said. He turned to the inspector. 'He said no to twenty-five million dollars!'

'You be quiet now,' the inspector said, 'or you'll get another beating.'

'This is starting to make sense now. After the takeover bid failed, you couldn't handle it. Right? DareDreamers being better than G-Force doesn't sit well with you,' Vyom sneered.

'DareDreamers is and will always be the best at rescue missions anywhere on, under or above the earth,' Arjun said. 'You'll pay for this, Narad!'

'How modest!' Narad mocked them. 'I was surprised initially as to what sense does it make to go to France when you have just invented something that so many people in the world are struggling to make. But then I slowly uncovered the truth.' Narad paused. 'You remember that that's when I came and met you, Inspector.'

The inspector nodded. 'I'll see to it that you are rewarded, Mr Narad, for doing your duty as a responsible citizen.'

'I remember thinking how convenient that a mission emerged merely weeks after they became capable of executing it! By sabotaging the plane, they ensured that they were the only people in the world with working jet packs, who could save the day,' Narad said, his voice indicating his deep concern. 'I couldn't even sleep, just thinking about what was going to happen. I honestly didn't have any other option, inspector.'

'How can you be so spiteful? Just because we said no to your acquisition bid?' Rasiq asked, forgetting his instruction to be quiet in his pain soaked delirium. He was unable to fathom Narad's motivation to lie.

'He's all yours inspector,' Narad said, stepping away.

The policemen landed several punches on Rasiq's face. Blood dripped from his mouth when they stopped to rest their knuckles.

'How could you stoop so low?' Rasiq mumbled, numb to the pain from the beating now. 'You are the one behind this, aren't you, Narad Money?'

'The police found bomb-making and detonating equipment in Sriniketh's home and I am behind this! You guys are terrorists and there's nothing you can do or say that will change that truth,' Narad said.

'What else were you planning?' The inspector kicked Nick in the stomach and he doubled up with pain. 'What other means did you employ to pull off the other rescue missions? And what more were you planning with your terror laboratory?'

'It's a labrary. And every material in there has a bill of purchase. Do you think a terrorist would have such a thing?' Nick retorted.

'Are you implying we can engineer a sinkhole?' Arjun was furious. 'What about the rescue of the CEO of the Tuskman Group? Did we create that too? Listen man…'

'Narad Money,' he said. 'That's my name.'

'Your idiotic logic will belly-up on you. You are going to be the laughing stock of the country tomorrow!' Rasiq said.

'We have many hours between now and that invisible future,' Narad said. 'Enough to break you and make you confess to your crimes.' He turned to the inspector and said, 'Continue your duty, sir. Let me not stand in the way of justice.' His phone had begun to vibrate and he took it out of his pocket and stepped out.

'Yes,' Narad said as he picked up the phone.

'You promised you wouldn't jeopardize lives!' Rakeysh was furious.

'Calm down, Mr Rakeysh or you'll give yourself a heart attack,' Narad said. 'I promised that no lives would be lost and I kept my promise.'

'But that's not what –'

'I am not sure I understand why you are getting so worked up,' Narad said. His voice was bold and in control. He had completed the job and that gave him immense confidence. 'You wanted to believe that they are charlatans, but I realized that they are not. Rasiq told us about the jet packs which gave me the idea.'

Rakeysh was silent.

Narad inhaled deeply before speaking, 'In our first meeting I told you that I'll create an illusion of the speck of dust if I had to.'

'What happens now?'

'They are done for, Mr Rakeysh. They will rot in prison for the rest of their lives. Even if they somehow manage to prove their innocence, nobody will ever touch them.'

Rakeysh knew that he would never be able to condone Narad's method. But he also knew that there was nothing that he could do now. He was linked to Narad and any allegation on him, would mean an allegation on himself.

'Take this victory, Mr Rakeysh,' Narad said. 'Like most things in life, it's bittersweet.'

'A little sweet yes,' Rakeysh said, 'but too bitter.'

'You will make the final payment then?' Narad asked.

# 36

## *One good turn deserves another*

*R*asiq woke up to the sound of footsteps. If they had been able to see the sun, they would have counted the twenty days they spent in police custody, but time in the cell was a non-entity. He tensed for another round of brutalities and wondered when it would stop mattering.

'Your police custody period is over. We are moving you to Tihar Jail, till your case comes up for hearing in the court,' the constable kicked him. He recognized the signal for him to get up and obeyed without protest. The capability had left them by now. They had mastered the language of abuse.

They had been arrested on a non-bailable warrant and were at the mercy of the courts now.

A large crowd had gathered outside to watch as they were led to the police van. There were shouts of protest and through a vision blurred by pain; Rasiq saw his parents, Achala and many of the people they had recruited at DareDreamers. The crowd was kept in check by the police cordon.

The protest had attracted media attention, adding flavour to the sensational case. Nobody wanted to miss the big scoop.

'This is a conspiracy.' Achala's voice drifted to them as if from another time. They saw her talking to reporters from numerous news channels. 'If anyone thinks that DareDreamers manipulated the rescue missions, can they explain the sinkhole rescue? Tell me how anyone could have created that sinkhole from which they saved me? And I have with me here the passengers who were on board the rescued flight. Why is nobody asking them what happened?'

'Tell us your version,' the journalists responded.

'We saw the rescue mission from our windows. They could have lost their lives that day. It is hard to believe that anyone would go to that extent just to boost their business,' one of the passengers said.

The cabin crew in-charge who had helped them execute the rescue mission was also there. 'All of us survived a near-death experience that day. These allegations against our saviours are ridiculous. Is there anyone among us who believes they were behind the sabotage? Anyone?' she turned to face the passengers.

'No!' the passengers shouted.

'They are the victims in this case!' she said.

They watched the journalists scribble notes as they were whisked towards the police van. Natasha was in the van already, looking only slightly better than the rest of them. Arjun hugged Natasha who broke down.

His father came running towards the van, to hug Rasiq just as he was about to get into the van.

'Ask Arnab to go to Adhishek Suri for help,' Rasiq whispered.

'The home minister?' his father looked surprised as he watched them being taken away in the blue police van.

Rasiq nodded.

∽

They told Natasha about Narad's involvement in all this once they were alone in the transport van.

'Does this make sense to any of you?' she asked. 'Why would he be so pissed off after a failed acquisition attempt?'

'A very arrogant man,' Arjun said.

'Doesn't make any sense whatsoever,' Natasha said. She shook her head. She was not convinced.

Rasiq was thoughtful. *She does have a point. There has to be more to it than what meets the eye*, he thought.

∞

A day can be a very long time in prison. The conditions were filthy and cruel. The court procedures were tortuously slow—they might have to spend many years as under-trials.

The DareDreamers retreated into a shell of silence. Hope receded after the first few days and pessimism clawed its way back. They understood why prisons were hardly a place to reform people.

'Guys, I'm sorry to put you in this mess,' Rasiq said. Despair stared out of his eyes.

'Not your fault, Rasiq. Our fault. We became successful beyond imagination,' Halka said.

'You were the one who wanted to sell the company,' Arjun said.

'That would have in fact saved us from this turmoil,' Asylum's tone was one of regret.

'But even if we had to do it all over again, we would still not sell DareDreamers to that snake,' Vyom said. 'I would brave this end a thousand times over for the good we were able to do.'

'Don't talk about DareDreamers in the past tense yet,' Halka said.

There was silence as no one shared his optimism. Hope was a dangerous thing. But at least they were together in their misery. Rasiq wondered how Natasha was coping in the women's cell.

The initial days had been tough. The prison guards had beat them at the slightest pretext—not falling in line fast enough, reporting late for their meals, protesting their inhuman conditions and even talking to each other. But this changed abruptly, for no apparent reason. The guards mellowed down and became more considerate. Generous quantities of food were dumped on their plates instead of the frugal measures earlier.

They wondered at this sudden change but welcomed it. It made their life slightly tolerable.

A week later, they finally had visitors—Rasiq's father and Arnab, their data analyst.

'Oye…' Rasiq's father tried to crack a joke he had rehearsed several times on his way to the prison, but he couldn't go through with it when he saw Rasiq. He had lost the spring in his steps and his shoulders slumped under the burden of worry he was carrying. His face had the look of a man haunted by nightmares.

'Dad, get a grip on yourself. We have to be stronger than this.'

His father nodded. 'We are stuck in an endless legal loop. No one listens to us. The judiciary is ineffective, everyone is indifferent. I found out that some under-trials spend more time waiting for justice in prisons than serving their sentence.'

'Something will work out, pops. We are fine. You don't need to worry too much,' Rasiq said.

'I know. But who will console your mom? She doesn't eat or sleep well these days.'

'Why hasn't she come?' Rasiq asked.

'You are not allowed visitors,' his father said. 'I have been paying the guards for weeks now. They said they would make your existence in the jail less miserable and allow me to see you just this once.'

Rasiq fought the tears that were beginning to form. He had been so engrossed in his own misery that he hadn't even thought about how his parents were coping.

'They allowed me to bring Arnab after a lot of pleading. But it's important you speak to him.'

Arnab greeted them with a quick nod before speaking. 'Achala and I have been practically camping at Adhishek Suri's office these past four weeks. We were finally able to reach him a couple of days back.'

A little bit of light returned to Rasiq's eyes. 'What did he have to say about this?'

'Nothing yet,' Arnab said. 'But he was deeply concerned. I think Achala's arguments about the sinkhole case, which was fairly well documented by multiple videos taken from different angles, all of which are available on YouTube, coupled with the testimonies of the cabin crew in-charge and a few of the passengers on the plane you rescued made him believe that there was a genuine case to build for your defence. He might be able to make things move quicker and ensure that you get a fair and expedited trial. I still don't get why he's giving us the time of the day.'

Rasiq smiled weakly. 'We are not at liberty to share that,' Rasiq said. 'But let's just say that he can do a lot more than what he's doing right now.'

'I am not sure he would be willing to bend the system…'

'Not that, Arnab,' Rasiq said. 'He owes us. That's it.'

Arnab nodded, understanding. 'Well, if they conduct this investigation in a fair manner they'll see that there was no foul play in our missions whatsoever and they'll have to no option but to let you go,' Arnab said.

'But that could take years!' Rasiq's father began to sob.

*Foul play,* the word rung in Rasiq's head. *After that Narela accident, the police had suspected foul play with some explosion in the truck,* he remembered. *Is it possible that…*

*No, it can't be.*

*Yes,* he finally understood. *Narad and Rakeysh have been after us since then! With that accident, they tried to undermine our reputation. When that failed, they tried to acquire us preying on my insecurity from that one failure. When even that failed, they framed us on false charges of terrorism.*

*That's how Rakeysh was able to get to me in that discussion! He was the one who had set up that accident and knew what it did to me.*

*Fucking bastards!*

'Rasiq,' Arnab said. 'Is there anything more I can do to help?'

His energy was slowly coming back. His nostrils flared in anger and his eyes were full of a reinvigorated sense of purpose. 'Yes. I want you to pull the data from the ARA devices on the Narela truck accident and the Mussourie school bus that we rescued. For the Narela accident, there is a police report and an investigation into potential foul play—the cause of the accident was an explosion. See if you can find out something about the Mussourie school bus incident as well.'

'Why now? How is it linked to your case?' Arnab asked. He hadn't been privy to the partners' discussion on the possible foul play by Rakeysh and Narad. Rasiq brought him up to speed on everything—including the takeover bid and Narad visiting them in the holding cell on the night of the arrest.

'But sabotage is what they have brought against you,' his father said. 'How will more data on sabotage prove your innocence?'

'That was not one instance of sabotage, but two together. The people in the truck died because we couldn't get to them in time. If the police are trying to make us look like saboteurs who gain from our scheming, then those two simultaneous incidents were against our interests. We lost many contracts; why would we put ourselves in such a position?'

His father nodded. 'Yes. It only proves someone was trying desperately to ruin your reputation. And this is another attempt!'

'Not just that,' Rasiq was thinking fast now. 'Adhishek might not make much headway if he were to prove our innocence alone. But looking for someone else's involvement in the crime can make things a lot faster.'

'If there's any proof, it should be enough to point the investigation in the right direction,' Arnab said.

Rasiq saw a light sparkle in his father's eyes. 'Will you be able to get the ARA devices from those accidents now?' he asked.

'No,' Arnab said, 'but the data gets stored on the cloud.'

'Cloud nine?' Rasiq's father was back in form.

Arnab was confused, but Rasiq laughed, letting his anger take a back-seat. 'At least you got the number right this time!'

'I'll explain how it works on the way back, sir,' Arnab said.

'But I am a mechanical engineer,' his father said braving a smile. 'There was a time I made things work. Now it's the computer guys.'

∞

Over the next few days, the energy in the team was a little different. They allowed themselves to feel hope as they waited impatiently to hear an update from Arnab. However, the pain of confinement and their inability to prove their innocence chipped away at their will. When a fortnight elapsed without any news, they started losing that hope again.

'We are in the prime of our youth and doing nothing but watching the hours and days tick by. We are probably the best rescue team in the world, but here we sit, idling. Oh man, when will we be free instead of swinging from hope to despair all the time?' Arjun lamented.

Rasiq tried to keep his mind busy by reading books. The

guards had allowed them access to the Tihar library. Even though they had run out of things to talk about as a means of distracting themselves, a new and strange bond developed among them, born from sharing pain.

∞

One morning, as Rasiq was squatting in his cell looking for concealed images in the stark prison walls, he heard footsteps. A guard opened the door and looked at him curiously. 'You have an important visitor,' he said.

Rasiq was surprised to see that Nick, Halka, Arjun, Asylum and Vyom had also been rounded up. They were all being led to meet this special visitor. When they entered the visitation area, they saw Adhishek Suri, the home minister himself.

They greeted him and he gave Vyom a brief nod of acknowledgement.

'Sit down, please,' he said with a warm smile.

A sense of relief came over Rasiq. There was finally some movement.

'Okay,' Adhishek said, when they settled. 'After hearing what Arnab and Achala had to say about this episode and the accidents in Narela and Mussourie, I deployed a special investigation team and they operated in complete secrecy.'

'Did they find anything?' Halka asked impatiently.

Adhishek nodded. 'The flight crew in-charge told them that the flight was delayed by over an hour because there was a delay in the food delivery for the pilots. That was their first real clue. We then raised an Interpol investigation request for tracking the events in France leading up to the incident.'

'Interpol's involved now?' Nick asked.

'Yes, they looked through the airport CCTV footage for the ground staff member who delivered the meal packs to the pilots.'

'Did they find him?' Dr Vyom asked.

'Not at first,' Adhishek said. 'They identified him from the footage but he was, of course, missing. It took them a while as they interrogated the other ground staff members one by one to find him. They started tracing calls and finally tracked the guy down in Romania. They found records of several calls made to him from a private number over the days leading to the incident.'

*Narad Money*, Rasiq thought.

'Tracing the owner of that private number was the toughest part of the investigation. It took us several days to navigate the complex network of phones that ultimately led us to a man named Narad Money.'

The team looked at one other, unable to control their smiles of relief.

'Yes!' Arjun shouted. 'That bastard!'

'We shouted ourselves hoarse about his guilt and involvement in this, but the cops didn't listen to us!' Halka said.

'They did, eventually,' Adhishek said. 'And honestly, had Arnab not told us about your hunch, we probably would never have been able to crack it. Once the investigation team had a suspect, they could move a lot quicker. Searching is a lot easier when you know what to look for.'

'Is he under arrest now?' Asylum asked.

'Unfortunately, he has gone underground,' Adhishek said.

'Figures,' Rasiq said. 'But you must know that he was not acting alone.'

'Yes,' Adhishek said. 'But to prove Rakeysh Aurora's involvement, we will need to find Narad.'

'Oh,' Nick said. 'Is he missing too?'

'No,' Adhishek said. 'Look, I can understand your frustration, but this case needs to be navigated with the utmost caution. The police will have to face the music for years for your premature and wrongful arrest. But they can't make the same mistake twice. You understand, right?'

'No!' Vyom protested. He was furious. 'We are rotting here in jail because of that man. He ruined us. How can he roam freely? Where's the justice in that?'

'Justice will be served,' Adhishek assured him. His tone grave. 'It might take time, but we will not let this go.'

Asylum shook his head. 'That means we stay inside?'

'No,' Adhishek smiled. 'The investigation team argued your case at a special session of the court. The judge agreed that the arrests were made on circumstantial evidence which the new findings not only put to rest but also give the police a solid lead to pursue. The court has acquitted you of all charges. Delhi Police will also issue a formal apology to DareDreamers.'

They looked at each other in disbelief.

'You are to be released with immediate effect,' Adhishek said.

'Natasha too?' Arjun asked.

'Of course. In fact, she's already completing the formalities of her release. Ladies first, you see.'

'How can we ever thank you for what you have done?' Vyom said. His voice was hoarse with emotion.

'This is my thanksgiving for what you did for me, so don't even mention it. I am just glad that you all are free to do what you do.'

'Thank you, sir!'

'You can drop the "sir". I will always be Adhishek to you guys,' he grinned.

# 37

# RDX-ed

*B*efore fleeing, Narad took one last look around his office. He used to call it a den. Operating from this den he had single-handedly destroyed the reputations of several companies and individuals on way to making his millions.

He had never looked back because he had always believed in looking forward, to the future. But now that his immediate future was in question, he had the luxury of looking at his past.

He had congratulated himself on sending the upstarts who had founded DareDreamers to jail without a return ticket. It was one of his most successful operations. Until, that is, he learnt of the home minister's personal involvement in the case from his sources in the police department.

A full inquiry had been initiated.

He recalled the elation and pride he had felt in his last meeting with Rakeysh when he had collected his final payment.

'I never had much faith in you, but you surprised me,' Rakeysh had conceded with a smile.

That smile from the stone-faced Rakeysh was the first Narad had extracted. A milestone.

But now he needed to have another conversation, a very different one, with Rakeysh.

He called him and informed him about the events that had transpired more calmly than he had imagined he would be capable of. Now that he had shut down his business, he no longer had anything to fear from Rakeysh.

'The home minister is on our tail now?' Rakeysh fumed on the phone. He was not a pleasant man when he was angry. 'And yet you made this call?'

'This is just one of the many calls they will eventually unearth. I had no idea Adhishek knew them,' Narad said. He was unruffled. 'You have to believe me. The plan was brilliant. We had them and they were almost finished.'

'None of that matters now, Narad. Nothing can stop the hounds from uncovering the truth. Not if the home minister is personally involved. Your brilliant plan has backfired so colossally that it may ruin me and my reputation.'

'I didn't know it would turn out like this, Mr Aurora. I tried my best, but it just didn't work out. As it is, these things always have some risks associated with them.' Narad had nothing more left to say to defend himself. Rakeysh was right, of course.

'I do believe you,' Rakeysh said, calming down. 'Otherwise you wouldn't have acted so cocky and shown them your face when they were in the holding cell.' Narad wondered when he crossed the line between confidence and arrogance.

There was a prolonged silence before Rakeysh continued, 'I don't know for how long I will be safe. They will either make you croak or trace...'

'You don't have anything to worry about on my count,' Narad said. 'I am wrapping up my business. Hire the best of lawyers, if it ever comes to that and leave it to them.'

'What are you going to do now?'

'I intend to vanish without a trace and as long as they can't find me, they can't touch you. If they could, they would have arrested you by now. The investigation will stretch for a year or two and then people will tire and forget about this. They always do. There are always meatier, more current affairs for ministers to get behind.'

'I hope so,' Rakeysh said, but his confidence was evaporating quickly. His arrest and a life of imprisonment were becoming increasingly real for him. 'I hope to never see or hear from you again,' Rakeysh said.

The phone line went silent, dead.

The call was the last Narad made using his special SIM card. He set it on fire. He watched as the acrid smoke rose and disappeared.

# 38

## Discovering the shades of grey

*T*he DareDreamers team stepped out of the jail after completing the formalities for their release. A small crowd cheered them as they walked out. Halka had phoned Achala who had brought some journalists to cover the story.

It took them some time to adjust to the daylight, so accustomed had they become to the permanent semi-darkness that haunted their cells. And when they were finally able to see, they were greeted by Rasiq's parents and Achala, who rushed to meet them.

'Many assembled here are passengers you rescued. They were with me throughout this time,' Achala beamed as she hugged Halka.

Natasha emerged from the crowd, a lot frailer than how Rasiq remembered her. She had lost so much weight that her bones were visible. Arjun ran towards her as soon as he saw her and they embraced. They stood that way, without exchanging a word, for a long time.

'Man, we should find companions for ourselves. Else we might not have someone to celebrate with when we get out of jail the next time,' Nick joked with Vyom, Asylum and Rasiq as he hugged them, glad to be outside the cold prison walls. He didn't lose time in regaining his form.

Rasiq saw Arnab standing next to Natasha. He walked up to

him and hugged him. 'Thank you, Arnab,' he said, 'for having faith in us and not deserting us. It must have been hard for you. You could have easily found another job and put this behind you.'

'It was the only decent thing to do,' Arnab said. 'It was your plan, Rasiq. I just crunched the data. Like always.'

'You have to teach me how you do that some day!' Rasiq said.

'Whenever you want. And you won't find a better teacher than me,' Arnab said.

'I like your confidence,' Rasiq smiled.

'Of course,' Arnab laughed. 'Data is my last name!'

'It's Datta, D-A-T-T-A,' Rasiq said, spelling it out.

'Yeah, but in my dictionary, one of the "Ts" will always be silent because it is an information redundancy.'

∞

Achala came home late that night in a happy mood. There was a spring in her step that Rakeysh hadn't seen in the past several weeks, ever since Halka had been arrested.

'You seem happy,' Rakeysh said. He had started his preparations earlier in the day when he had seen the news of the partners of DareDreamers being released.

'Yes,' Achala said. 'I know you won't like it, but Halka was acquitted today! All the partners at DareDreamers have been released from custody.'

'Yes, I saw the news.'

'Did you see the interview I gave?'

'No,' he said. 'What interview?'

'I ran a campaign of sorts for DareDreamers. They were clearly innocent. My intervention got the home minister interested! Let me check the news,' she said, as she clicked the remote. 'There might be a rerun of it on some channel.'

Rakeysh was taken aback. He realized that Achala would be inconsolably upset and hurt if she were to discover what he had done. If the police ever caught up with him, she would also have to live with the fact that her actions were responsible for his incarceration.

He couldn't let that happen. She was the only thing in his life that was pure. He loved her more than he loved his business.

'Why didn't you tell me about it?'

'And you would have let me campaign for them? You hate Halka, papa. You wouldn't have let me step out of the house if you had any inkling of what I was up to.'

Rakeysh's practised nonchalance did not give away his thoughts.

'Papa,' Achala said, setting down the remote when she saw that her interview was not on any news channel, 'can you please forget the past and move on? Will you at least meet him once? He's evolved so much from the last time you saw him. Maybe it will change your opinion about him.'

'I can try,' Rakeysh said. 'But you have to promise me something.'

'Anything!' Achala said. A smile broke on her face. Rakeysh realized that he hadn't made her smile in a long time.

'You have to come away with me on a trip. We haven't taken a vacation together in a really long time.'

Achala smiled, 'Of course, papa! That would be lovely.'

Rakeysh understood that Halka hadn't told Achala anything yet. He now needed to move quicker on his preparations for laying low for a while.

∞

'Papa wants to go to Sweden with me for a vacation,' Achala told Halka at the DareDreamers office the next day. 'We had a good talk yesterday after a very, very long time. He even agreed to meet you and said that he would try and put the past behind him.' She was beaming with joy. 'Things are finally coming together for us!'

Halka gulped. He couldn't stop the frown from creasing his brow.

'What happened?' Achala asked, worried. 'Why aren't you happy? It's good news, right? Or are you worried about meeting him?'

'I have to tell you something, Achala,' Halka said.

'What?'

Halka told her all about the events of the past few months: the twin accidents, the takeover bid, Narad's involvement with her dad to attempt a buyout of DareDreamers, Narad's presence in the holding cell on the night of their arrest and Interpol's confirmation of Narad's involvement.

'I wasn't sure about any of this before we were imprisoned and then when we finally met yesterday, I was so happy to see you that I didn't feel like bringing this up,' he said.

But Achala wasn't listening anymore. She stood frozen like a statue, her eyes not even flapping. Her world crumbled as she grappled with the facts and tried to make sense of them.

'What does this mean?' she said after a long silence. 'What are you trying to tell me?'

Halka had no words to help her through her grief. He knew she would have to work through it on her own. He was too involved. Also, it was easy for him to hate Rakeysh—it was black and white for him. But Achala loved her father. She had to realize and come to terms with the fact that her father was a much darker shade of grey than she had ever imagined.

'Are you saying that he is a bad person?' Achala asked. She was struggling to absorb Halka's story. 'Even uttering this sentence is difficult…' her voice trailed off and tears started flowing down her cheeks.

Halka wanted to hug her and console her. But he understood that it would not mean anything to her right now.

'I need to leave…' she said as she ran out of the office. Halka could hear her sobs getting louder as she ran.

∞

Building things from scratch is much easier than rebuilding them from a negative balance. The partners at DareDreamers realized this the hard way. They had hit the road to meet with all of their corporate clients. Despite being exonerated, they had to reassure their clients that they were back for good. The letter of apology from Delhi Police helped, but most of their clients were hesitant to get involved with a company that had very recently been suspected of being a terrorist organization.

'I don't mind this one bit,' Natasha said after an unsuccessful meeting. 'It's a labour of love,' she said. 'I realize that now even more so than before. And no labour of love can be tiring or upsetting.'

Her cheerful outlook, however, did not result in conversions and they kept meeting with one failure after another.

The conspiracy theorists continued to raise questions about the home minister's keen involvement in the case. They kept digging into DareDreamers' past cases and came up with every conceivable 'alternative explanation' as to how they could have orchestrated the accident. In the absence of any other arrests in the case, the DareDreamers name had been cleared only on paper; their reputation was tarnished.

∞

One afternoon a few days later, Achala walked into the

DareDreamers office unannounced. She had changed visibly. Her eyes had dark circles under them and her smile, her brightest asset, was missing.

'I have decided to confront him with what we know,' she said without preamble. While she made an effort to sound determined, her eyes stared beyond the walls of their office, envisioning the grim scene in the future.

'Are you okay?' Halka held her hand. 'Don't you think we should wait?'

'Halka is right,' Rasiq said. 'We don't have any evidence against your father, Achala. Confronting him will do little good. All that you are likely meet is denial.'

'Adhishek Suri and the investigating team will nail him for sure,' Arjun said. 'They are already tracking Narad Money, a trail that will eventually lead them to Rakeysh.'

'I have met with these investigators, Arjun, when you were in prison,' Achala said. 'It's not going to be easy for them to find Narad. To begin with, that is not even his real name! It's not like he has an Aadhaar card with that name. He is not in any database.'

'Yeah, but they have a description. They know what he looks like.' Achala's argument had unsettled Nick but he did not wish to give up the sliver of hope yet.

'True, but he needs only a few minor surgeries like hair transplant and liposuction to look very different from those portraits,' Achala said.

'You do have a point,' Natasha conceded. 'And that's without considering other, more transformative operations. I have seen what these plastic surgeons are capable of. It's hard to recognize the core once it goes under their knife.'

'Besides, if they reach my father through Narad, he will be in a far worse situation than what he can manage if he cooperates with the cops. I need to make him see that.'

Halka saw her hands as they gripped the edge of the table. They had gone white.

'Fair enough,' Vyom said, 'but Rasiq's point remains. If the police can't arrest him for want of evidence, we can't confront him either!'

'I understand that. But I can get him to confess,' Achala got up. 'I will go on this Sweden trip with my father and I will try to appeal to him there.'

'It's not safe,' Halka pleaded. 'Please reconsider.'

'I have to go, Halka. In all probability, this will be my last chance to spend some time with him. If nothing else, I'll at least create some memories that I can hold on to while he is...' Despite her stoicism, she couldn't complete the sentence.

'You should go,' Natasha said. 'It makes sense to me. And maybe after you spend some quality time with him, you can talk to him about what he's done.'

Achala looked up to Halka, her eyes pleading, 'Can you come with me too? Please? Or join us a few days later. It will take some time for you to get your visa anyway.'

∞

'There's no way I am going,' Halka announced, more to himself than the rest, after Achala had left. 'I'm afraid that if I see him again, I'll beat him to a pulp.'

'Same here,' Arjun said. 'I mean, after what he's done to us, no one can blame us for feeling that way.'

'We don't beat people up,' Vyom said. 'We save them.'

'Well said, Vyom,' Rasiq said. 'Rakeysh needs to be saved, even if it is from himself.'

'The task is fraught with danger,' Nick said. 'The guy is most probably dangerous, despite how Achala might feel about him. We can't let her go alone. And we will all be at risk if we accompany her.'

'And Narad is on the loose too,' Vyom said. 'What if his men are trailing Rakeysh? They might strike if Achala succeeds in convincing Rakeysh to confess.'

'That's why it's a task for DareDreamers,' Halka said. 'You guys should all come with me.'

'What?' Arjun said. 'Who'll do the work here?'

'What work?' Natasha asked. 'We've had nothing to do since we've been out of prison.'

'I agree with Halka,' Nick said. 'I think we should all go—we could really use a vacation as well as solve our biggest problem.'

'Yes,' Rasiq said. 'If Rakeysh confesses, we will be in the clear. We would actually get many of our clients back. At this point, we have a mission to rescue ourselves.'

'Then it's actually important for all of us to go to Sweden?' Vyom asked.

'I think so,' Nick said.

'Man, I am beginning to like this assignment!' Vyom tried to bring in some cheer to boost the spirits.

# 39

## Skating on thin ice

*T*he temperature outside the airport building was an icy shock: -32°C. Everything was frozen, including a fountain, which seemed a bit odd to Rasiq. The many layers of clothing they wore was unable to block the ice-cold wind, which cut through them like a knife.

'How come you're not shivering?' Rasiq asked Natasha who was wearing the least number of layers. Only her nose was red.

'I'm used to such weather,' Natasha said with a shrug. 'Several of my stunts were shot at Everest and the Alps. Arctic conditions aren't a big deal for me.'

Rasiq looked sceptical.

'This is starting to look like a bad idea already,' Vyom was shivering, his teeth clattering.

Achala came to meet them at their hotel where they changed into their disguises. She had insisted they wear them.

'He is really scared right now and if he sees you, he might take a drastic step,' Achala said. 'It's important he doesn't know you are here.'

Rasiq knew the plan had merit even if he didn't like wearing a disguise. Rakeysh would freak out if he saw them and then there would be no hope of having a conversation with him. They had to tackle him carefully.

'I don't like this fat look,' Halka complained.

'Without it, your physique will be a dead giveaway,' Achala said. The expression on her face was stern. 'You can be recognized from a mile away.'

'And for a gun-wielding father-in-law, you will be a huge and easy target,' Nick said.

Rasiq gave him a look that warned him not to be insensitive around Achala. *This has got be the hardest thing anyone has ever done*, he thought. 'Are you sure about this, Achala?' he asked.

She nodded.

Halka was upset about this, but he understood that this was the best way to go about convincing Rakeysh to come clean. 'We'll be on the watch the entire time,' he said, holding Achala.

'He's not going to attack me,' she said. 'You don't have to worry.'

'I know,' Halka said, 'but don't forget the danger from Narad.'

They spent several days trailing Achala and Rakeysh in Sweden. They had installed a precision GPS tracker on Achala's watch so they knew where she was at all times. They were almost always within a single kilometre radius of her, but never close enough for Rakeysh to see them. They had also installed precision GPS trackers on each of their watches, all connected to a smartphone app, so that Achala could see where they were too.

'It seems Achala may not be capable of going through with this after all,' Natasha said one night when they were back at the hotel. 'And I, for one, don't blame her.'

'We need to give her more time. Please guys, let's be patient,' Halka pleaded.

Nick shook his head and took a deep breath to calm the anger simmering in him. He thought that they were taking too soft an approach towards a man who didn't think twice before hiring a slimy crook like Narad.

∽

On the ninth day of their stay in Sweden, they followed Achala to Narvik-Riksgränsen, one of Sweden's mountain lake resort areas famous for skiing and ice skating. They checked into a resort close to where Achala and Rakeysh were staying.

Rasiq and Natasha were the only ones not shivering. The rest huddled to share body heat.

'What?' Rasiq said when everyone looked at him questioningly. 'I adapt quickly, I guess.'

Natasha raised an eyebrow. 'You have a stronger constitution than I gave you credit for,' she said.

A couple of hours later, they sat sipping coffee at the resort's coffee shop, watching through their binoculars as Achala and Rakeysh donned their ice skates a few hundred metres away.

'This is just perfect,' Nick let out his frustration. 'The villain in our lives is having a ball with his daughter and here we are, hiding like thieves, waiting for the perfect time for his majesty, Rakeysh Aurora.'

'That's the worst analogy ever,' Halka growled. 'We are obviously hunters and he's our game. Does a lion think "I am hiding here like a thief" when he's watching his prey?'

'Patience, guys,' Rasiq said to everyone.

Halka too was on edge. He needed Achala to succeed. Predictability was the last thing he expected from the situation and they needed to be at their sharpest.

'I am sure he's not just having fun here. He must be meeting with his lawyers and advisers. He might be planning a fool-proof escape strategy,' Vyom said.

'Yes, I don't peg him as a guy who would waste time on vacationing,' Natasha concurred with Vyom's fears.

Rasiq looked worried.

❦

'You don't seem happy, Achala,' Rakeysh said. He was checking the buckles of his skates. 'You used to love ice skating. What's going on with you?'

Achala looked at her father, her expression blank. 'I guess people change,' she said.

Rakeysh sensed an undertone of implication in her words. 'Don't change too much though,' he said, not wanting to probe her too much. He got up and started skating slowly.

Achala followed him. 'Papa,' she called out to him. 'Can we talk about it?'

'About what?'

'When did you get in the business of taking lives?' she asked.

'I don't know what you...'

'You know perfectly well. Did you think Halka would never tell me what you did?'

'So you believe him? Not your own father?'

'My father chose his happiness over mine when I was in love. Halka chose my happiness over his when he gave up on our relationship. And I don't see you denying anything.'

'Alright!' Rakeysh said. He stomped his skate on ice. 'You want to do this now? Let's do it.'

Achala took a step back as she saw her father transform into an angry beast. He had never hit her, but looking at his fury Achala was scared he might start today.

'I contacted a guy who used,' he paused, searching for the right word, 'unconventional means. I did not do anything wrong apart from trying to stop my competition.'

'You paid him,' Achala said. She could no longer hide her disgust and anger either. 'You enabled him. You watched as this guy orchestrated an act of terrorism, risking the lives of two hundred passengers. You actually stood by when he killed three innocent people! Do you want me to go on?'

'Murder was never on my mind. But let it be,' Rakeysh said. 'You won't understand.'

'I won't understand? You told me that out of all the businesses you started and failed at, the only reason why G-Force worked was because you realized that you genuinely cared about saving lives. From that guy, who I proudly called my father, how did you become this guy? Do you understand yourself?'

Rakeysh was taken aback. He recalled the moment Achala had brought up. She had just stepped out of her teens and he was retelling her stories of his failed businesses. In his quest to bring down DareDreamers, blinded by his insecurities, he had lost sight of what motivated him to run G-Force as well as he did.

'I need you to confess,' Achala said. 'Halka and others are paying a huge price for what they did not do. It should have been you in the prison, not them.' Her voice cracked and tears started flowing from her eyes.

Ordinarily, Rakeysh would have wanted to hug her and tell her everything was going to be alright. He would have done whatever she was asking him to do. But not this time.

'They are out of the jail,' he said. 'I can't spend the rest of my life behind bars.'

Achala was aghast.

'You have to choose, Achala,' he continued. 'Are you with me or with them? We can get away, Achala. We can lay low till all this tides over. After all, that's why we are here. I have the best lawyers working on my case. I might get away scot-free.'

She shook her head, 'What have you become? A monster!'

'That's enough!' he raised his hand to strike her, but held back.

'Are you going to hit me now? Is that what it has come to?' Achala said.

Rakeysh was shocked. The words brought back the memory of Achala's mother. His head started spinning and he lost his balance.

He fell, shattering the ground beneath his feet. The ice on which he was standing was thinner than it should have been.

He was surrounded by a cold darkness that was not alien to him.

❦

A long time ago, he was Rakesh Arora, a simple middle-class man in love with a daughter of a rich man. She had married him against the wishes of her parents.

But time had played a cruel hand. He had been a man full of ideas but all those ideas bombed and they left in their wake a hefty debt. His wife was a software engineer at an IT firm and he used to laugh and say to his friends, 'She's the one who wears the pants in our house. As for me, I'm a dreamer. A kept man!'

After five years of bad ideas and repeat failures, the fights between his wife and him intensified.

'I'm tired of repaying your debts all the time for these flop ideas of yours. Why don't you get a regular job? What's this desire to own a great business?'

'I can't work for someone else, Sunidhi,' Rakesh said. 'Even the thought of it makes me cringe. I feel as if I am a slave when I am working for others.'

'Are you calling me a slave?'

'No, all I am saying that I can't do it! I will succeed in some business. My time will come, Suni.'

'Why don't you see you aren't meant for business,' Sunidhi said. 'In these years, you have done nothing profitable!'

It had hurt Rakesh to hear that and his shoulders slouched.

He sunk into the sofa, distress visible on his face.

'I'm tired, Rakesh,' Sunidhi said. 'Please make a promise to me today. This is the last idea you are pursuing. If this flops too, you have to get a job. OK? We have a daughter that we need to be thinking of. We should be saving up for her future, right?'

'Alright,' Rakesh said. Although he had said the words, in his heart he was sure his next idea would be a big hit. He knew he wouldn't have to take up a job.

But like every other time, he failed and found himself applying for a job to save his marriage. He got a low-paying job with great difficulty and lost it easily. He got another after two months and lost it again in a matter of weeks.

'You are a failure, Rakesh. Let's face it. You can't succeed in business or jobs. Everyone makes fun of you behind our backs. Did you know that? It's so humiliating for me.'

'That's funny,' Rakesh said. He was sick of her constant complaining. 'They make fun of me and it's humiliating for you? How does that work?'

But he understood. She had become the vice-president of her company and he could not hold even the lowest-rung jobs in an organization. An insurmountable status difference had existed between them even before marriage, but now the chasm threatened to separate them.

'Look. I have a business idea and this one will succeed, I am sure. You have spare money. Just lend me some,' he said. 'I don't see how anything else matters.'

'Shut up! I am sick of your foolish schemes...'

He had lost his cool and slapped her.

Sunidhi fought back the angry tears and looked Rakesh in the eye, fuming. 'So, this is what it has come to?'

Rakesh was filled with remorse. In that moment, he knew his life was never going to be the same again.

'You are a bitter man, Rakesh,' Sunidhi continued. 'You are an unsuccessful, bitter man and I could never have imagined things coming to this point. You can't take your frustrations out on me. I have paid through my nose to support you through all your failures. I will consider that as my settlement.'

She stormed out of the room.

'Don't leave me, Sunidhi. Please. I am sorry.' Rakesh had pleaded.

'Papa is right. You are a failure who begrudges my success,' she said. She was crying when she stepped out of the house.

'You have been talking to him?'

'Why not? He's my father and cares for me. What do you care? You treat me as the hen that lays golden eggs for your stupid schemes. I am through with you.'

He did not stop her.

Strange men had come to their house to pick up all her stuff because she had left without any of it. They created a mess of the house, but Rakesh did nothing to stop them. A few days later the divorce papers arrived for him to sign.

Her grief from her long relationship with Rakesh and the bitter separation thereafter wouldn't let her carry anything into her new life. Anything that once belonged to Rakesh, upset her. In this scenario, there was no room even for their daughter in her life.

Rakesh was relieved that she had not demanded custody for Achala. It would have broken him. While Sunidhi was busy climbing the corporate ladder, Rakesh raised Achala with love and care. She was the only bright spot in his dark life.

While earlier Rakesh had worked on impulse, he was now pushed against the wall. He couldn't imagine giving anything but the best to his daughter. With Sunidhi gone, their financial situation was precarious. He was the sole earner in that household of two. He realized that he couldn't afford the luxury of making mistakes.

In the past, he would start working on even a hint of an idea. He would invest time, money and energy in the project out of mere enthusiasm that had little to do with ground realities. He now understood the difference between working hard like a bull and working smartly. His fear of failure made him change his name by adding the 'y' and the 'u' because it was supposed to be lucky. He started wearing rings and lockets that would bring him success. He couldn't leave any stone unturned. He was desperate enough to employ anything that would get him there.

He started thinking ten steps ahead in every plan he conceived and was ruthless to his ideas. Only one shot to succeed. He needed to take it carefully. He zeroed in on the idea for a premium corporate security services company where he had the first mover's advantage in India.

His last gamble paid off and he became immensely successful as G-Force grew on the back of his patience, strategic planning and strong salesmanship. In five years, his business acumen came to be reckoned within the industry and his business started expanding. But before he could convince Sunidhi to come back, he heard about her second marriage.

How he wished his success had come in a few years earlier! Sunidhi's remarriage devastated him. It left a greater scar in his heart than their separation.

He didn't marry again. A couple of women had shown interest in him, probably because of his success, but he would never know. He didn't want to know. He lost himself to his work. And Achala. Work healed him, and Achala's love was the only real love he got from life.

His oxygen-deprived brain made him feel that he was in two places simultaneously. The past and this endless descent into a dark, watery abyss.

# 40

## Live another day

'Help!' They heard her scream at the top of her lungs. 'Halka! Help!'

'Achala!' Halka shouted, breaking into a run.

'Help! Guys help, please!' Achala continued to shout in panic.

'What happened?' Halka asked when he reached her. Achala stopped screaming and pointed to the ice. 'He...he's gone...'

There was a hole in the ice through which Rakeysh had vanished. Halka readied to jump in the water.

'Wait!' Vyom shouted. 'It would be suicidal to jump in like that!'

'We need a plan,' Arjun said, 'move off the ice as it might crack further with all of us standing here.'

Halka had to drag Achala away. 'Call the ambulance,' he told her. 'You can't help anyway standing on the ice.'

Achala nodded and quickly looked up the number for the ambulance on her phone. Vyom, Nick and Arjun walked back to firm ground too.

Natasha and Rasiq, however, had undressed and were now down to their full body, waterproof thermal suits.

'What the heck?' Natasha said. 'You stole my stuff!'

'No! I borrowed it from your wardrobe, Natasha. I even told you. Perhaps you were sleeping and didn't hear,' Rasiq tried his best to hide his smile.

'You'll answer for this, Rasiq,' Natasha said as she pulled her hood over her face. She shook her head and dove headfirst into the water while Rasiq was still contemplating the plan. *I can borrow her suit, but not her daredevil spirit.*

But he also knew that without an exit strategy, the move would mean certain death. At least one of them needed to act with caution.

'Rasiq!' Nick called out to him, reading his mind. 'Take my keychain! You know how it works.' He threw it towards Rasiq who caught it and took a deep breath before jumping in after Natasha.

The water was icy cold but the thermal bodysuit kept him dry. Nonetheless, Rasiq started panicking—he knew he wouldn't be able to hold his breath underwater for very long.

Fortunately, he saw Natasha swimming up towards the surface. She was towing Rakeysh. She soon hit the ice shelf over the lake and started banging her fist against it, but the ice refused to give way. She turned to look at Rasiq in panic.

Rasiq searched for the hole through which they had jumped but could see only a white expanse overhead. Nothing. No exit. They had lost their point of entry in the vast expanse of white ice that formed an unbreakable roof above them.

*Be cool*, he told himself to calm the rising panic he felt.

He swam up next to Natasha and reached up to place Nick's keychain against the ice. He switched it on. The ice started vibrating but nothing happened. Rasiq remembered that the vibrations were calibrated so they did not shatter a material, only dislodged anything adhering to it. The frustration coupled with panic knocked some of the air out of his lungs.

He saw Natasha struggling to hold her breath, but Rakeysh seemed gone. His face was as white as the ice. Rasiq looked at the keychain and saw there was an LED light glowing on a smiley face. Next to it, he saw a symbol of a skull. Rasiq switched the gadget on again; the LED on the smiley face blinked off and the LED on the skull turned on. He placed the keychain against the ice again, but nothing happened. The device had frozen and had ceased to work in the biting cold water. The LED lights also died seconds later. He turned to look at Natasha. She was losing consciousness and Rasiq grabbed her and Rakeysh, but he knew he too would run out of breath soon.

'The ambulance is on the way,' Achala said before her knees caved and she fell to the ground, tears streaming from her eyes.

'Something is wrong,' Nick worried. 'They should have been out by now. We need a new plan.'

'Here are their GPS coordinates,' Achala said. She was trembling with anxiety. She handed over her phone to Halka, who ran towards the coordinates and started punching holes in the ice. His hands bruised and bled under the gloves he was wearing.

'They are not here,' Halka shouted.

'The coordinates on the phone are not very precise,' Nick said.

'Arnab,' Arjun was yelling into his phone already. 'I need Natasha and Rasiq's GPS coordinates right now! Hurry up!'

'They are right next to you,' Arnab's voice came in clearly.

'Guide my steps to them as if I am blind! There's no time.'

'Walk twelve steps east,' Arnab said.

Arjun complied.

'Stop,' Arnab said. 'Turn ninety degrees north. Walk ten steps straight ahead now. Stop! You are right there.'

'Halka! They are here!' Arjun yelled.

Nick and Halka ran towards Arjun and smashed through the ice. They pulled all three out of the water.

Rasiq inhaled deeply and crashed on the ice next to Halka. Natasha and Rakeysh didn't move. They didn't look good.

'Quick! They need CPR!' Vyom yelled, 'Bring them here!' he said. Halka picked up Rakeysh, Arjun carried Natasha and Nick supported Rasiq as they walked back towards solid ground.

Vyom began administering CPR to Rakeysh while Nick started doing the same to Natasha.

'Move!' Arjun pulled Nick aside. Halka took off Natasha's shoes and Achala took off her father's. They started rubbing their feet.

'Come on, Natasha!' Arjun said. There was despair in his eyes as he looked at Natasha's death-white face. He continued alternating between pressing her chest and breathing air into her mouth.

'Come on! Come on, Natasha! Don't give up yet!' Nick said.

Natasha suddenly coughed out water and took a gasping breath. She continued coughing while Arjun hugged her, relieved that her ordeal was over.

'How is he?' she asked for Rakeysh.

'He's breathing, but he's suffering from acute hypothermia. His chances of survival look slim,' Vyom did not know diplomacy. 'I think he has suffered a circulatory arrest. His blood has stopped moving through his body.'

'No!' Achala began to cry. 'Please save my dad!' She held her father close to her body. Halka sat next to her and tried to console her.

The helicopter ambulance arrived and they rushed Rakeysh to the local hospital.

∾

'The situation is grim,' the doctors at the hospital said. 'He has acute hypothermia. His body temperature is down to 18° Celsius.

He has suffered a circulatory arrest.' The doctor confirmed what Vyom had already diagnosed.

'Please do everything you can to save him, doctor,' Achala said between sobs.

'Look, doctor,' Nick said. 'I know I am not a doctor, but there is something you can try. It worked for a Norwegian woman in 1999.'

'Did you read that on Wikipedia?'

'Yes,' Nick said.

'Thanks for letting me know,' the doctor snapped at him. 'Without Wikipedia, I don't know what I would have done!' He said sarcastically before turning around and walked away.

'Now you know why you are so irritating?' Vyom said. 'You can't tell doctors how to do their jobs.'

'Will one of you please tell me what's happening?' Achala asked, her face mirroring her anxiety.

'They will hook him up to a cardiopulmonary bypass machine and pass his blood through it. The machine will heat his blood before they pump it back into the body. There is still some hope, Achala,' Vyom explained.

'A woman survived thanks to the procedure after being in a state of acute hypothermia for eighty minutes. We have a chance to save him,' Nick said.

∽

Two weeks after the incident, Rakeysh opened his eyes. It was a miracle. He was shifted from the ICU to a room in the hospital.

'Thank god you're alive,' Achala kissed him on the forehead. 'You looked so dead when we brought you here.'

'Beta, I had to come back because I had to talk to you. Our conversation wasn't over.'

Achala smiled and held his hand.

'The doctor told me that some Indians rescued me. Are they still here?'

'Yes,' Achala said. 'They are waiting outside. Shall I call them in?'

Rakeysh nodded.

Achala walked them in. Halka walked in last. His heart was racing.

Rakeysh looked surprised, 'You guys?' he said.

'You brought them here,' he said. He turned to face Achala and smiled weakly. 'This was basically a checkmate? I shouldn't have expected anything less from my daughter.'

Rakeysh turned his gaze on Rasiq.

'I'm surprised that you rescued me. Why? Why would you save my life? After what I did...' his voice trailed off.

'We can't let people die,' Rasiq said. 'Even our rivals.'

'We are not judges,' Halka said. 'It's up to the courts to decide your guilt and your sentence. Our job is to make sure you make that court date.'

'Thank you,' Rakeysh said. A tear had trickled down his cheek.

'No need for that,' Rasiq said. 'We are glad you are alive and have recovered.'

'Well, not fully,' Rakeysh said. 'I have nerve damage on my hands and feet which will need intensive physiotherapy for months. Even then the chances of them working properly ever again are bleak.'

An awkward silence descended, which was finally broken by Rakeysh.

'I deserve worse though, don't I? But before we come to that, I have a question for Halka. You still love Achala, right?'

'Yes,' Halka said, looking at Achala.

'You know how many painkillers they have given me? I

don't think I have ever been in such a euphoric mood. Why don't you ask me now?'

Halka was shocked. Achala smiled weakly and motioned to Halka to walk up to her dad.

Halka got down on one knee.

'Oh my god,' Rakeysh said. 'You are horrible at this. You are not proposing to me!'

Halka stood up. 'I know,' he cleared his throat. He cast a glance at Achala and felt some of his confidence return. 'I wanted to ask you if you think it would be alright for me to marry Achala? We are deeply in love and the years I have spent away from her have been the worst years of my life. I don't want to be away from her ever again. With your permission, of course.'

Rakeysh smiled. 'Halka,' he said, 'I am sorry for the way I behaved earlier. You are a good-hearted, strong man and Achala is lucky to have your love.' He looked at Achala and Halka, 'You have my blessings.'

Achala moved towards Halka and hugged him. He lifted her up off her feet.

'Now, now,' Rakeysh said. 'No PDA, not in front of me, please. That's not much to ask for, is it?'

Halka let her go, but the smiles refused to leave their faces. They stood, holding hands.

'I wasn't always a monster,' Rakeysh said, more to himself than anyone else. 'Achala, it's important for me to know that you understand.'

'I know that papa,' Achala said.

'I was unnerved when I started losing business to DareDreamers. I couldn't handle it. I had succeeded with G-Force after so many failures, the fear of losing again was frightening. My business had been growing non-stop until you came along,' Rakeysh's voice choked a little. A silent tear slid down his cheek.

'But instead of competing fairly, I chose unethical means. I am sorry, Rasiq.'

Everyone in the room was sombre.

'I took this trip to chalk out my future course of action and evade my possible arrest,' Rakeysh continued. 'But…' his voice trailed off as he saw Achala crying silently. 'I am sorry, beta… I have to pay the price for what I have done, but first, listen carefully,' Rakeysh said, regaining his composure. 'I will have my lawyers draw up the papers for a proposal for a partnership between G-Force and DareDreamers.'

'What?' Rasiq was shocked.

'I believe I owe you at least that much,' Rakeysh said. 'We recently purchased a large office space in Lower Parel in Mumbai, which G-Force will lease out to you for a nominal cost. What do you think about it?'

'Well, I don't know,' Rasiq said.

'You could use our company's clients and services to…' Rakeysh started.

'No, I mean, I understand the synergies and the obvious advantages of the proposal. We could use your management team's experience and roll out DareDreamers' services as an add-on to your larger portfolio. Opening an office in Mumbai has been our dream since we started DareDreamers. But I am not sure why you are offering this to us…'

'Don't worry; you won't have to deal with me. You'll have to discuss the modalities of the partnership with Achala,' he said, looking at his daughter, who stood wide-eyed. 'Signing the partnership contract will be my last act at G-Force,' he said and paused, 'I will be appointing you as the CEO of G-Force and will resign from my post.'

Achala hugged him and nodded with understanding. It had to be done.

'I believe that surrendering to the police and confessing my crimes is the only thing left to do now,' Rakeysh said. 'I must pay my dues.'

Rasiq could feel himself tearing up, so he stared at the floor to avoid meeting Rakeysh's eyes. 'Thank you,' he said. He didn't know what else he could do. He realized that life did not always offer happy endings.

'I need to get some rest now,' Rakeysh said. He leant back on his pillow and closed his eyes.

∞

Rakeysh was sentenced to seven years in prison after he confessed. He also helped the police with Narad Money. He gave them all the information he had about him. They also drew a sketch of him from the description he provided and corroborated it with the description from the inspector who had arrested the team. The manhunt continued.

Once again, the news made to the headlines. The vicious attacks on DareDreamers began to taper off. The merged entity became a formidable presence in safety and security.

'We should start hiring quickly,' Rasiq said after presenting the budgets and outlays to the board, which now included Achala. 'Our clientele has huge potential for growth as nearly all of G-Force's clients could be enrolled under DareDreamers' accident rescue services with a nominal top-up.'

'Where do we begin?'

'I know one crazy innovator from a junior batch. He keeps emailing me about his creations. They rock!' Nick said. 'I'd be happy to mentor him. There's plenty of stuff we still need to make to be more formidable than ever before.'

'There are several talented daredevils, and not just in Bollywood,' Natasha said.

'I have a few archers in mind and will select those who wish to go beyond winning medals,' Arjun grinned. He had set up a training academy for archers who could not afford expensive training. He had hired international coaches to train them. He also supported their travel to global championships.

'I know two body builders who qualify,' Halka joined the conversation.

'I like the confidence!' Vyom said. 'I will go to AIIMS and see if I can recruit a few brilliant doctors. Maybe I can convince them to break free from the deadening routine of hospital shifts.'

'That's all well and good, but let's also diversify our skill set. I'll continue my search for DareDreamers in other domains,' Rasiq grinned.

# 41

# Back with a bang

'*H*ighly dangerous,' Nick muttered as he pored over the news on his tablet.

'What?' Rasiq asked.

'This news about an oil tanker catching fire in Lake Kivu,' Nick looked up from his tab.

'Of course, all fires are dangerous. Or are you trying to say something that we don't understand?' Rasiq asked, now familiar with the cryptic ways of Nick.

'The fire will heat the water for sure. But what will make this heating up different is that Lake Kivu contains very high concentrations of naturally occurring methane gas and carbon dioxide.'

'What's the scare?'

'The rising temperatures can force the dissolved methane and carbon dioxide out of the water,' Nick said. 'Like Halka opening a soda bottle after shaking it vigorously. Whoosh! Combustible methane bubbles out. Boom! Explosions. More heat. More carbon dioxide and methane. The lake becomes a self-perpetuating bomb, the explosions will travel to the shore and there will also be a release of a suffocating combination of deadly gases.'

'Theoretically possible. But has there ever been an incident like this?' Natasha asked.

'Yes. The 1986 Lake Nyos episode in Cameroon. Nearly hundred million cubic metres of carbon dioxide erupted, killing more than seventeen hundred people. The gas drifted quickly to the shores and killed all life within a twenty-five-kilometre radius,' Nick put away his tab and looked at his team. 'A similar occurrence in 1984 caused the deaths of thirty-seven people near Lake Monoun.'

'How much of these gases does Lake Kivu contain?' Arjun asked.

'Much more,' Nick replied. 'Some 55 billion cubic metres of methane and 265 billion cubic metres of carbon dioxide are estimated to be dissolved in the lake.'

'Whoa!' Natasha exclaimed.

'And this time we have a burning oil tanker,' Rasiq added. 'The heat and carbon dioxide it is generating combined with the already enormous quantity of gases in the lake make it a very dangerous, unstable and explosive situation.'

'Exactly what worries me,' Nick said.

'We must warn the government,' Vyom said.

'Where's this lake?' Halka rose from his comfortable perch, ready as always, for action.

'It lies on the border between Congo and Rwanda, in Africa. It's one of Africa's Great Lakes,' Nick replied.

When they tried to warn officials, however, their efforts were met with endless red tape and inaction.

'What do we do now? They don't seem to care. They're worse than our officials,' Natasha banged her fist on the table in frustration.

'We have to go there!' Halka said.

'Yup,' Rasiq agreed. 'We have a big team now. They'll manage the operations here for a couple of days.'

∽

As they made their travel arrangements, they continued their efforts to get in touch with the officials concerned. And when they were finally able to speak with someone, the official laughed them off.

'Is this some joke? We will manage the fire, of course! Why would you doubt that?' he said, nonchalantly. 'Nothing as fantastical as a lake bomb is happening here.'

'Not yet, sir,' Rasiq said. 'But this has precedence...'

'We'll deal with it if it happens.'

'But thousands of lives are in danger...' Rasiq tried to reason with the unreasonable person.

'I'm not going to create panic among people here just because someone calls to tell me there is a remote possibility of this kind. We shall control the fire and deal with anything else, if and when anything else happens.'

The phone went dead.

∽

'Don't you think we are carrying the precaution too far?' Vyom expressed his doubt as they were waiting for their visas.

'What's happened before can happen again. We can't leave it to chance,' Nick said. 'The officials in charge don't seem to care. For us it's merely a trip, but if we don't go, the citizens may be caught in a death trap.'

Rasiq nodded in agreement. 'Nick, can you reach out to some NGOs based there and see if they take the threat seriously? Maybe they can help when we get there.'

∽

A little less than thirty hours later they reached the lake and were confronted with the sight of the burning oil tanker. The fire was huge and had spread to the second of the eight tanks on the carrier.

'If that fire spreads to the other tanks and if they explode, then god help us all,' Vyom looked at the spectacle with fear.

A few NGOs who had been receptive to Nick's calls had sent personnel to meet the partners from DareDreamers at the lake.

'What's the progress?' Natasha asked an NGO representative.

'Our teams are speaking to the local community heads and explaining the peril their village is faced with. The word is spreading,' she explained.

'We've deployed volunteers to drive through the streets in jeeps and cars with loudspeakers instructing people to leave the area as soon as they can,' said another. 'But it isn't easy—there are villagers who are scoffing at the suggestion to evacuate. They think we are exaggerating the threat and in fact, are watching the burning tanker as if it's a source of entertainment.'

'We've deployed buses to ferry the villagers to safety,' said a third NGO representative. 'We've evacuated more than 20,000 people so far and there are more on their way to safe zones as we speak.'

Rasiq was impressed with their coordination.

Rasiq outlined a plan of action. 'With the evacuation underway, the next step is to plan for the people who have been relocated. First, we need to arrange for tents. These must be pitched beyond a twenty-five-kilometre radius of the lake, based on past experience. NGOs that are based closer to the city can take up the responsibility for organizing food.'

'And you should also arrange for tankers of fresh water. We don't want an epidemic breaking out due to lack of hygiene,' Vyom flagged his health concerns.

Once the NGOs agreed to collaborate and dispersed to coordinate the action plan, Rasiq approached the fire officials overseeing the firefighting operations.

'We can't run away and leave this fire unattended. We have to do our job,' the chief said.

'Please carry on with your jobs, but have enough oxygen cylinders and masks ready for all your men. Can you do that?' Rasiq had to shout over the noise.

'Of course,' the chief agreed.

∞

The fire got worse by the next morning as one after the other, the remaining fuel-carrying tanks exploded owing to the heat. A thick blanket of black smoke began to descend on the banks quickly. The cloud was so big, they could see it from where they were all camped.

By evening, it was on the news. Ninety-one people had died due to asphyxiation and thirty-five were in critical condition after a series of explosions had taken place, spreading from the tanker to the lake as the naturally occurring methane gases over the lake caught fire. Their worst fears had come true. The chain reaction created a large quantity of carbon monoxide and carbon dioxide.

The firefighters survived to fight the fires as they had oxygen cylinders and masks. They battled for more than sixteen hours before they were able to bring the fires under control. In the end, the poisonous mixture cut off the oxygen needed to sustain the fires and helped the firemen win their gruelling struggle. They emerged as heroes who had struggled nonstop, with little rest.

'You should also thank those guys from India. We would have been dead but for them. Their warning about what could happen, though it seemed ludicrous at that time, was backed by sound reasoning and logic. If only more people had followed their advice, they too would have survived,' the chief of the firefighting department stated in an interview on television.

As the DareDreamers prepared to leave, the survivors of the disaster flocked to bid them farewell. The team was overwhelmed by the love and affection the families showered upon them and the sentimental parting gifts they gave them.

'Come to my house whenever you visit Rwanda again.'

'You are our friend for life.'

'You saved me and my family and I cannot repay the debt we owe you.'

One after the other, people came and said these words to them. Some hugged, some kissed and some shook hands. Their emotions overwhelmed them.

∽

'Oye puttar, look! Your company is now world-famous!' Rasiq's father woke him one morning not long after they had returned. Rasiq opened one eye to see him waving a magazine.

'Let me sleep, pops,' he said. He turned his face away, it was too early to wake up. But his dad shook him till he opened his eyes.

'Look! Your team is on the cover of the *Time* magazine!' He continued to wave the magazine in the air like a magic wand.

Rasiq was now wide awake and he took the magazine from his father. It featured a story on the Lake Kivu rescue mission.

He flashed a V sign to his father and smiled.

'Maybe you should consider an international expansion now?'

Rasiq's eyes lit up with excitement. He leapt from the bed. They had pan-India operations already, but there was still a lot to explore—the paths that led to infinite possibilities.

He grabbed a juicy carrot from the breakfast table and ran outside the house where he fired up his jet pack to go meet his friends.

## Acknowledgements

We've often been asked which one of us wrote what parts in the book and how we write together, especially given the dynamics of a father-son relationship. For the second part of the question, all we have to say is that our relationship is enriched because of the time we spend exchanging ideas with each other. We frustrate each other through the stupid ideas (a surprisingly high majority) and encourage each other with the few good ones, a process that we cherish. For the first part of the question, it's only in the first draft that it's clear who wrote what. By the final draft, it's impossible to discern. Considering how long and arduous the journey is between the first and the final draft, we are too tired to tell the difference by the time we reach its end. And considering the difference in quality, we also try and avoid the question of who wrote what in the first draft. The goal, as is often the case in such things, shifts from taking the credit to avoiding the blame!

Given that context, we would like to acknowledge each other. It's not been easy but we loved every minute of it.

We would like to thank the readers of *The Quest of the Sparrows* for the love and encouragement they've shown us. Your support has nourished us through the process of writing *DareDreamers*.

We are grateful to Kamakshi, Rigveda, Aishwarya, Anushree and Yashika for reading the drafts of this work in various stages when it barely made any sense. Each of their contributions has helped in shaping *DareDreamers* into its final form.

We would be remiss to not mention the support from Rupa Publications. We can only imagine the patience required on their part to work with us!